The Chinese Sailor

The First Catrin Sayer Mystery

ALLAN JONES

ISBN: 978-0-9919072-8-1

Cover. The Menai Strait from Y Felinheli, North Wales at sunset
(author photograph).

THE CATRIN SAYER MYSTERIES

The Chinese Sailor
The Scottish Colourist
The Falmouth Model
The Carnforth Double
The Powys Deacon
The Stratford Hunter

CONTENTS

Prologue: St. Cybi's Church   1

PART 1: HONG KONG

1   St. Paul   5

2   Rebellious Offspring   16

3   Bad news   21

PART 2: ENGLAND & WALES

4   Brixton   30

5   The Offer   35

6   Bangor Mountain   41

7   The Cwmbran Kiln   49

8   The Komarov Sisters   53

9   Introductions   67

10   Welcome Week   76

11   Bangor Police Station   85

12   St. Paul's Cathedral   94

13   Scotland Yard   102

14 The Queens Larder   112

15 Catrin's Interview   121

16 The Middle Sister   131

17 The Rolex   139

18 Bangor Again   144

19 The Shep Kip Mei Street Bathhouse   152

20 Timings   165

21 The Reception at the Palais Des Nations 177

22 The University Sailing Club   188

23 PTSD   194

24 Dubai   210

25 London   221

26 The Chinese Link   233

27 The Invitation   245

28 The Confession   251

29 Where Angels Fear to Tread   260

30 The Baby Browning   267

31 Aberystwyth   281

32 The Earrings   285

33 Glanrafon Hill   292

34 The 'Ceinwen'   297

    Epilogue - China   304

    Notes   314

    About the author   316

PROLOGUE
ST. CYBI'S CHURCH

Tyrd, troedia donnau amser... Come, tread the tides of time.

Holyhead, Isle of Anglesey, Wales. The middle-aged couple approached Mavis as she stood by the archway leading to St. Cybi's Church. It was mid-May and the weather was warm and dry but the breeze was still a little cool off the sea at times.

"Is there an entrance fee, ma'am?" the man said very politely. He was American. Mavis found that sometimes tourists were either rude or incomprehensible, but she still smiled anyway.

"No, entrance to see the church is free. You can look around and take photographs. Welcome to St. Cybi's," she answered. "There are people inside who can tell you more about the church, too. It's very old."

"Could we ask you to take our photograph together, in the archway? This looks really old also."

He held out a small camera.

For a seventy-four year old, Mavis had kept up with the latest cameras and mobile phones, at least in the sense of pressing the right buttons, as it was a regular request she received when she volunteered to welcome 'cruisers' at the church. Her eyesight was holding up remarkably well for her age. Mavis took their photograph and passed the camera back. The man thanked her and they headed inside.

She had been standing for about half an hour by the ancient arched entrance leading to St. Cybi's; 'her church' as she thought of it. Soon she would go inside and have some tea, talk with her friends and Jack Hughes would spell her on the gate.

She liked to encourage the tourists to visit the church as it dated from 540 A.D. Quite a few visitors made donations when they did so, which always helped church funds.

She watched more tourists coming along the Celtic Gateway, the modern footbridge from the port. They were photographing everything in sight. Mavis didn't particularly like the bridge, popular as it was with others trying to restore the vitality of Holyhead. It was eye-catching, she would give it that. Its purpose was to link the port area with the town and bring in travellers and tourists. With its modern stainless steel structure, its swirls and turns and the Welsh phrases written into its stairways, Mavis thought it was gimmicky. To her, the 'tides of time' were better seen at St. Cybi's.

A couple of young women came along from the foot-bridge in jeans and T-shirts. She smiled at them but they were lost in their own discussion as they walked straight under the archway. The slogan on the T-shirt of the one having a larger bust was 'Look up! It's the head that's talking to you.' Mavis smiled. She knew her friend Irene inside will be muttering to herself all the time the girl was walking around. They saw some real sights at times, the clothes that tourists dress in.

As she had walked to the church this morning she had seen the big cruise ship, the *Manden Serenity*, tied up at the long pier in the harbour. It's like the others, she thought, sailing in from a different world. These great ships arrive silently in the pre-dawn hours and sail again by the evening, bringing all sorts of people here.

She watched the young Chinese man in gaudy, tight-fitting cycling gear and a helmet ride effortlessly along Victoria Road then stop to check his iPhone before turning back up the hill towards the Post Office. He was obviously from the boat, too. He had a small backpack and a long cardboard tube beside it, to which he had taped string to make a temporary carrying strap. Now he looks fit, she thought. There should be more like him. Too many of these tourists were overweight.

The contrast between the fit cyclist and many of the other passengers she saw that day stayed in her mind. Two nights later, when she saw the police request on the television, Mavis phoned in. They showed an image of the man and his bicycle and asked for anyone having seen him to come forward. A nice young police constable came round to her flat and took notes.

PART 1

CHINA AND HONG KONG:
JIAN LI'S STORY

1 ST. PAUL

The Celtic Gateway, Holyhead, Wales. Daniel Yeung stood on the pedestrian causeway, immaculately and formally dressed, looking out to sea. Yesterday evening there had been a vigil for Han at the old church he could see nearby. He had been overwhelmed at the number of people who came to pray, to offer support, a sea of faces and no names he could remember.

When he spoke he thanked them briefly and sat down again with his face turned towards the floor, his tears running down. At the rear he had seen two of the police officers who had talked to him earlier. Their eyes were on the crowd, not him.

Han had been missing nearly a week now and his ship was on the Atlantic, heading to New York. Out there, thought Daniel, that's where my son should be, not here, lost.

He wanted to go home already.

Nothing in his life had prepared him for this, not even the story of the upheaval and resettlement of his family from China when he was a boy and the misery he saw at

5

times on his mother's face at the separation from people back home.

~~

Near Tongzi, Guizhou Province, China, September, 1949. Shen Han Yeung watched the 'St. Paul' descend from the heavens. He and his wife, An Li, stood next to Old David and their British missionary, Pastor Harold Eckersley, transfixed. An Li was holding their baby, Daniel.

The group were from a Protestant church mission in the rural heart of China. The China Inland Mission since its establishment had lived up to its name and vision; to take Christianity into the interior of China. The Yeung family were second-generation Christians. Not being Roman Catholic, the most frequent reference to saints in their community these days was to the old war-surplus DC-3 aircraft named 'St. Paul', the transport workhorse of the Lutheran Church in China. It was about to land at the airstrip.

From the back they looked like any group of Chinese except for Eckersley's red hair in a braided queue, his unique identifier in this region; three men and a woman carrying a baby, standing together. They had left their village near Tongzi in a mule cart after dawn. It was now mid-morning and the landing lights of the aircraft were visible.

The 'St. Paul' was the first aircraft that Shen Yeung had seen from close up. In the past only David came with Pastor Eckersley to collect the bibles or other supplies shipped for the Mission and transported by the Lutherans. During the war, of course, he had seen aircraft high in the air, silent or buzzing like insects, but soon he would be close enough to touch one, perhaps. He watched, fascinated, as the aircraft landed smoothly and made its way noisily towards the ground staff waiting for it. As it came closer Daniel started to cry; the infant had never heard anything quite like it before.

Bishop Henry Ballard came from Pennsylvania and was a practical man. After landing and talking with his pilot, he quickly checking the logistics for unloading the supplies then waved to Harold Eckersley and walked over to him; a bishop dressed in fatigues meeting a missionary dressed like a peasant. Ballard would need to leave soon for the Mission Hospital in Zunyi.

He was now a bishop of the Lutheran Church, but Henry had first qualified as a medical doctor and he had nearly 15 years' field experience in war and peace in China. He knew that the staff at the hospital needed the help and supplies for the cholera outbreak as soon as possible. The British pastor may not be a Lutheran but he was a good man and a fellow missionary, so Ballard needed to hear him out.

Harold handed over to Henry the order written neatly in Chinese characters and Bishop Ballard read it quickly.

"No-one was injured though, Harold?" said Ballard.

"No, Henry, but Yeung stood with his tailor's scissors confronting the man until he backed down. In doing so, the soldier lost face. The commandant is in a dilemma and thinks the safest solution is for Yeung to relocate, at least for a while. He knows the soldier will bear a grudge and look for an opportunity to do... who knows what. Yeung has a wife and baby."

Four days ago a soldier of the local militia, drunk, had tried to pull away the young teenage daughter of Yeung's neighbour and he had confronted the man, making him let the girl go. Unfortunately several other soldiers had seen the issue and instead of helping the situation by taking their comrade away to sober up, they had started gossiping back at the barracks. Captain Zhu had then summoned Harold; he was concerned about what he was hearing.

"The Yeung family has been members of our mission since Ian and Deborah Wylie ran it," Harold Eckersley continued. "Zhu told me to get Shen Yeung out. It's a delicate time now with the tensions among the Nationalist soldiers. The Communists are almost on our doorstep. He passed me the order to shift the responsibility in case Yeung is killed, I fear."

Ballard understood. With the heavy fighting during the war against the Japanese and now the return of the conflict between the Nationalist forces and the Communist divisions, the soldiers were at breaking point. He made a fast decision.

"Harold, get them on the aircraft. It's going first to the Catholic Mission at Naning to pick up two nuns there and then it will be heading back to Hong Kong. The Yeung family can go to Hong Kong, at least for now. I will ask the pilot to sort it out on arrival with the China Inland Mission folks there; he can call ahead on the radio. They will have to be fast, though. The pilot wants to be away quickly; those storm clouds will be turning this airstrip into a muddy mess soon."

He paused then smiled, "Hong Kong, yes. I don't want to take them and their baby into a cholera epidemic and, after all, we can't leave them at Naning to fall into the clutches of the Catholics, can we?"

Shen Yeung listened to Pastor Eckersley and saw the

mixed emotions of fear and surprise on his wife's face, probably reflecting his own. They had thought that they would be going with Bishop Ballard to Zunyi. Now he would not only have the opportunity to touch The Saint, but to ride in it, too.

~~

When they landed in Hong Kong it was providence which prevented Shen Yeung, An Li and baby Daniel from being transferred to an internment camp. These camps were at bursting point with many others fleeing either the war on the mainland or the imminent fall of China to the communists. Providence came in the specific form of two feisty nuns and a DC-3 pilot who knew as much about customs and immigration processing as the officials meeting the 'St. Paul'.

On the flight down to Naning the fears and tensions of flying inevitably transferred to Daniel from his parents. The baby had cried constantly during the take-off and ascent. After their rapid leave-taking of Old David and Pastor Eckersley, the Yeung parents were in shock at their sudden change of circumstances.

The co-pilot had come back after the DC-3 reached its cruising altitude but he spoke no Mandarin. However he brought water and a smile. Slowly the family settled down and Shen became fascinated by the view outside, of clouds and the land below, of the constant motion of the propeller that he could see. Soon they started to descend. Daniel cried again and the couple prayed that they would land safely.

On the second flight now with two nuns aboard dressed in their strange attire Shen Yeung was lost again in the sights from the window. It was something of a surprise to him to turn and find his wife comfortably talking with one nun and Daniel fast asleep in the arms of the other. These Catholic women didn't seem as bad or as lost as Pastor Eckersley had sternly warned him about as he led them over to the St. Paul.

So several hours later, the China Inland Mission Director in Hong Kong, Philip Gavin, found two immigration officials and a Roman Catholic priest with his driver, all waiting outside the aircraft. The priest had come to collect the nuns but found them unwilling to move off the aircraft. He thought about ordering them to do so but he had met one of them previously, Sister Margaret, and knew of her struggle with humility. He had a feeling that either she would disobey him and face the consequences, or worse, she would obey him and he would face the consequences next time he visited the convent. So he waited.

Gavin talked to the immigration officials and then to the crew and passengers still on board. Everyone was expecting him to resolve the stand-off. It was all quite relaxed but no-one was budging. He sighed and went into the Operations Building.

Calls were made. More calls were made. In a surprisingly short time Shen had papers for his family he couldn't read which Gavin told him not to lose, ever. The officials stamped them. The nuns insisted on a last prayer with them before leaving the airfield, asking the priest to lead it. He spoke so fast even Gavin had trouble following the message.

The Mission Director then made a telephone call and took the Yeung family to the Apostolic Church of the Nazarene, an English-speaking church where members of the congregation welcomed them. Some of them knew

Pastor Eckersley and spoke Mandarin, so the family started to feel relieved. They had food and shelter and they could communicate. The first part of their ordeal, the journey, was over.

The Yeung family soon found itself in the hands of another Methodist church community in Kowloon, one that was Cantonese-speaking, the language of Hong Kong. Neither Shen nor An Li spoke the language but several members were fluent in Mandarin as well and helped them to learn.

Arriving only with Shen's tailor's tools, a bible and their clothes, they were heavily dependent on the aid provided by their new community, a generosity which so affected them they developed a commitment to the community there that was to stay with them lifelong.

It did not take long for Shen to find some piecework as a junior cutter in a shop making inexpensive clothing. An Li found part-time work through an English woman who came to the church recruiting maids for the wealthy English inhabitants of the island. Mabel Hoy and Gwen Ti, the two elderly ladies from the congregation who gave them their first home, enjoyed babysitting Daniel in An Li's absence. They were settling down, at least temporarily, wondering when they would return home.

~~

On a strange island with a new community and a new language, a thousand miles from their home, the Yeung family began to build a new life. Within a few months of their arrival, the doors of China closed. The Communist forces took complete control of mainland China and Bishop Ballard, the Lutherans, the China Inland Mission and other churches were forced out.

In mid-1950, not many months after their flight south, Zou Enlai, the new Foreign Minister of the People's Republic made the statement, 'While China is putting its house in order it is undesirable for guests to be present'. The new China was sealed off and it hit An Li particularly hard; they would never return home. They weren't guests being rejected, but as devout Christians not willing to become Communists, they were no longer welcome either, she was sure.

As they settled in Hong Kong finding their first small apartment, watching Daniel grow into a toddler and then a small boy, An Li had bouts of depression, sometimes severe. They were unpredictable in length and onset but between them she was a driving force for their betterment. Indeed, it was An Li that set Shen on the road to a good income and family wealth. However, when caught in their mesh she was reclusive, unable to work and, on occasion, unable to take care of Daniel.

It was in Spring 1953 during one of her good spells while cleaning in the home of a wealthy English lawyer that she listened to the man's wife complain. While An Li polished the furniture Mrs. Parr was on the telephone talking to a friend about Mr. Parr's irritability that morning. An Li's English had improved a lot, much more than Shen's, as she was determined that Daniel would grow up speaking English as well as Mandarin and Cantonese.

Mr. Parr suffered from incessant problems with his neck. As a lawyer having to dress formally for his profession he was plagued by soreness and irritation and constantly complained about the shirts he wore and whether or not too much starch had been used in their laundering.

An Li thought it through then went to speak to Mrs. Parr. He husband was a very fine tailor, she said, and it may be that Mr. Parr's shirts were not a good fit. Could he try to help?

Shen Yeung then found himself with his measuring tape on the following Friday morning in the dressing room adjacent to the master bedroom of the Parr home, while An Li waited patiently downstairs on a seat near the back door. When he came down he whispered to her.

"Two shirts, white cotton, within three days for a fitting," he said then smiled, "And I looked at his shirts and his neck and know what the problem is, I think."

The two shirts led to an order for ten more, and a little later a message to Shen to go to the premises of Coulter & Yarrow, a prestigious tailor's shop on Connaught Road that catered to wealthy clients. Apparently over a regular game of cards at his club with people they knew well, Mr. Parr had made comments on his clever wife finding a tailor who had made him new, comfortable shirts. He told Robin Coulter a satisfying witticism; at least, it was satisfying to Parr. "You may make my suits and win this game, Robin, but you've lost your shirts on this one."

In fact, the thought of Parr's braying about this shirt maker and the potential loss of business for Coulter & Yarrow if it spread quite disconcerted Robin, so much so that he deliberately lost the hand to Parr and stood him a drink afterwards while they chatted a little.

Shen sat opposite Robin in his office in the back of the shop, not sure how to proceed. His few phrases of English were to help him fit clothes, not negotiate work contracts. He felt more at ease when Robin started speaking passable Cantonese. Now he was in an English shop but in a Chinese negotiation.

After a while Robin signalled to Mr. Yarrow, who had just finished with a client, to join them. Yarrow's real name was Bernie Tessler, but at the outset they had to settle on a business name and the name Tessler didn't quite work, they both agreed. He had to sound English to the hilt. Coulter, the ex-Guard's officer, drummed up the business. Yarrow, the Jewish tailor with a name change, ran it efficiently.

"Mr. Yarrow, I have made Mr. Yeung our offer, fair as we know it is, and he has a counter-offer."

They had offered Shen a good rate to become a shirt-cutter and fitter at their firm.

Coulter continued, "He wants to make his own shirts but work with us; 'Yeung' shirts, to be hand-made by him alone. Mr. Yeung seems open to negotiation of terms, but not the manner of his doing business."

Yarrow's face stayed impassive. "Ask him how he will cope with the demand during busy times. Will he work with our juniors?"

Bernie spoke no Cantonese.

The discussion took place and Robin said very neutrally, "He says no. He won't work with other staff. The shirts will be his and known only as his and, if the orders are too many, he will have a backlog. And then he will raise his prices - and our profits."

Yarrow smiled. "He wants a brand, Robin. We under-stand that, don't we? I think Mr. Yeung and ourselves can do business, yes?"

Shen realised what was happening and thought that An Li had been right again. I was scared to do this, he thought, but it has worked out.

Some days later a small sign, 'Yeung hand-made, custom-tailored shirts sold here' went in the display window. Bernie had paid for the first box of Yeung labels for the shirts. They charged Shen at cost for the suit they insisted he wear, payable on reasonable terms. It was only fair. "At Coulter & Yarrow, Mr. Yeung, you must look the part, be the part," said Robin, and any suit that was not a Coulter & Yarrow suit simply would not do.

Coulter was thinking about his discussions at the club. Between Parr's happy neck and his own quiet words, the business for Yeung shirts would grow nicely, he thought.

2 REBELLIOUS OFFSPRING

Two decades later Shen was still at Coulter & Yarrow, having become an established fixture there, with a good business and a fine home of his own. He and An Li had been fortunate and had prospered but they had no more children; the doctor she visited linked it to her recurring depressions but no-one really knew why.

Shen had been astonished that morning when the man entered, standing just inside the shop entrance wearing a black mourning band on his arm, looking at him rather than Mr. Coulter. Enlai Lin was the owner of a large merchant shipping fleet and a number of related companies.

He was a powerful and wealthy businessman in Hong Kong but he was not a customer of Coulter & Yarrow. Shen Yeung knew by reputation Mr. Lin's personal tailor, a man who provided service exclusively for a select number of clients in their homes and offices.

Shen Yeung bowed deeply. "Mr. Lin, please accept our sincere condolences at the loss of your son."

Lin acknowledged the expression of sympathy and

said, "Mr. Yeung, Thank you. I have in fact just come from the hospital and have thanked your son Daniel in person for his bravery."

Three years earlier Shen and Daniel Yeung had the largest clash that they would have in their relationship over their entire lives together, father and son. Daniel had announced his application to join the Hong Kong Fire Services Department. His father had been gently hinting for some time about joining him in the tailoring business. An Li had told her husband that Daniel was trying to find a way to say no; Shen was being too persistent. Daniel needed to find his own way, she said repeatedly.

Their son's acceptance into the Fire Services Training School was the final straw. Shen had hoped that the heavy competition for places in the service would result in Daniel's non-acceptance. In contrast with An Li's happiness at Daniel's good news, his grudging compliment to his son on his success showed his true feelings on the matter, which then became a bone of contention between them until Daniel's injury three years later.

At the time of the injury Shen realised how wrong he had been. His son was well-liked by his colleagues, who were constantly at the hospital and helping Daniel's family as if it was their own. And a senior officer in the department spoke so highly of Daniel that Shen felt ashamed of his past behaviour.

A week ago, one of the young men Daniel Yeung had tried to rescue on a response to an emergency call was this man Lin's son. He didn't make it out alive and now his father stood before him. Shen didn't know what else to say. It was the ever-capable Robin Coulter, now the sole living partner of Coulter & Yarrow since Bernie's death, who invited Mr. Lin into his office to have tea with

Mr. Yeung. It was obvious to him at least that the man wanted to talk further.

Robin had left them alone and was now looking out at the Lin limousine with its chauffeur, partially blocking the street outside. He knew no policeman would move it on and whatever was going on in his office, it wasn't a bad image for their business at all. Whenever he glanced over he could see Lin talking and Yeung listening. He had some inkling what this was probably about; the news of the fire in which Daniel Yeung had been injured was the talk of his club for several days.

The fire had consumed an apartment on Pak Tai Road and the Fire Services Department had done very well to contain the blaze. That it was a party place for a group of young people was not known to most of their parents, it seemed. But the real news was that Simon Lin, the youngest son of the head of one of the largest shipping companies in Hong Kong and Shing Yau, the son of a Triad boss called Michael Yau, both died from smoke inhalation. Part of the club gossip was that a fireman called Yeung had his leg crushed when a beam fell down while he was trying to get the boys out.

One of the club members asked Robin if the Yeung who was injured was related to his shirt maker. Instinctively Robin said he did not know, but the feeling came over him that a tragedy had occurred in their closely-knit little group at Coulter & Yarrow.

"My son Simon was only eighteen," Enlai Lin said. "Rebellious, you understand; it's the age."

Shen nodded. And the environment, he thought, this mix of western culture with the traditional values. A rebellious son chooses to hang out with undesirable peers or become a fireman rather than a tailor.

"My business is big, as you know. And now I have a debt. Your son was badly hurt as a result."

"Daniel will recover and is alive," said Shen. "It is different, I think."

"Yes, but he has lost his livelihood. I have looked into it. He cannot continue to be an active fireman and he is still young. I asked him at the hospital what he would do and he said he was thinking of working with you, which is a blessing, no doubt, for a father?"

Shen nodded. "When my son told me I was saddened at the reason. I had come to realise that he was a good fireman, despite my reservations about him pursuing this career. But now I see a positive outcome of this sad event. He is talking about taking his disability pension and joining me in tailoring. He learned much about it as a young man and I don't think he has forgotten. With my wife now dead too, it may bring us closer."

An Li had died a year earlier. Mentally she had been in good health for a while despite the friction between her son and her husband. Once the cancer was diagnosed she was helped by many at their church and, with this support and her own religious strength, she seemed to keep her spirits up right through to the end.

Lin nodded. "I wondered. It is part of the reason I am here talking to you. One of my companies is putting some shops into a high rise office block in Causeway Bay. One of those could be a tailoring business, perhaps. If you will accept it, I would like it to be yours and your son's business."

Shen bowed and said, "Mr. Lin, I thank you for your kind offer. It is very well meant, I understand. But we must be realistic. I am settled here."

He opened his arms to indicate the premises.

"My son has much to learn if he comes into tailoring

and I specialize in shirt-making. He will learn with the other staff here. Your offer is very kind but ….”

He was at a loss what else to say.

Enlai Lin said, “Then we should, I think, talk about this business. Let us call in Mr. Coulter? He is now the sole partner here, I gather, and not so young.”

He looked intense, as if a business decision had just been made.

“Mr. Yeung, you must allow me to do this, please. It is very important to me.”

~~

Daniel Yeung showed considerable skill and sensitivity when he joined the firm of Coulter & Yarrow, but not only in the area of tailoring skills his father had discussed with Enlai Lin. Yes, he learned these quickly, but more importantly he showed the quality of decision-making that reminded Robin Coulter of his late partner. Whether these skills were honed through his prior training and experience in response to emergencies or were innate in the man was unclear to Robin, but Daniel had that intangible capability around business decision-making that Bernie Tessler had so ably demonstrated.

Within a few years Robin was handing over most of the operational business control to his junior partner who, young as he was, worked well with staff, suppliers and customers alike. The rift between father and son became a thing of the past; the shirt maker still had his exclusivity and niche, but he turned to his son for answers if it related to the business of Coulter & Yarrow.

3 BAD NEWS

Hong Kong, May. Daniel Yeung was at the shop talking with a regular customer from the law courts when his mobile phone rang. He took a glance; it was from his daughter Jian Li and so he answered. His family as a rule did not disturb him at work so it must be important.

"Dad, you need to come home, there is bad news."

It was four years since a similar opening sentence from his wife Eu-Meh had given him the news about his father, Shen. He had suffered a major stroke. Two weeks later he had died and he was now with the Lord. The feeling of foreboding hit him as he turned away from the customer and staff to talk with his daughter.

"Yes?" was all he could say.

"The police are here. Mom and I were just about to go out when they arrived. Han is missing from his ship."

"At sea?" said Daniel immediately. It was one of his fears since his son had chosen a maritime career working as a cruise ship navigation officer.

"No Dad, it's more complicated. He disappeared in a port called Holyhead two days ago. It is in Wales, part of the UK."

She pronounced the place as two words, Holy Head.

"The English police called our police. We are both very worried and Mom is in a real state, I can't stop her crying. You need to come home."

"I'll be there as soon as I can, Li, tell her. Please ask the policeman to wait." He closed the call and saw the entire shop was at a standstill, including the customer. Somehow they had picked up from his voice that it was bad news.

All he could say to those around him was, "I must go, sorry," and walked out. His permanent limp limited his pace as he headed towards the parking elevator, then he felt his balance start to go. He stood still, took a deep breath and walked out to the taxi stand instead.

How can my son disappear in a place called 'Holy' something was the inane thought that passed through his mind.

At home the policemen were still waiting. Daniel's arrival seemed to help Eu-Meh to calm down. At least she sat silently as the policeman explained again and answered Daniel's questions as best as they could. In reality, they had little information themselves and some of what they had heard could not be shared with the family anyway.

Han Yeung's ship, the *Manden Serenity*, had stopped in Holyhead, a smaller port on the west coast of the country, one of the policemen said. It was a normal port stop for passenger excursions. It was then sailing to Ireland and on across the Atlantic to New York.

Daniel saw that Li had her iPad open, looking at the map.

"That was on May 14, two days ago. Third Officer Yeung was not due to be on duty until just before the departure from the port. He used one of the bicycles that are reserved for crew use to go for a ride into town that morning. There was nothing unusual in that."

Daniel saw that the policeman who had said nothing so far was watching them carefully.

He let out a sigh and responded to the officer who was talking, "Yes, he had mentioned to us he enjoyed doing that in different places when he got the chance. The bikes are on a reservation system for crew and are quite popular, so he does not get the chance to do this too often."

The policeman continued, "He did not return to the ship before it had to leave. They were aware of his absence a little earlier than the normal security check before sailing, but he did not report when they called him over the ship's announcement system. They made an initial check and found he was still off the ship with the bicycle. They thought that something was wrong as Officer Yeung was regarded as a diligent employee, never late for duty, so a senior officer tried to contact his mobile phone. It rang but went to voicemail on two occasions.

"As it came closer to the departure time the port agent was informed and they informed the local police. By then a formal search of the crew and public areas of the ship had been conducted. The port police tried again to contact his mobile but by then it was not ringing at all. A further check confirmed it was no longer switched on.

"Eventually the ship left port, about two hours behind schedule."

Li said, "Han never switched off his mobile entirely, I think."

The officer waited, but she was lost in thought.

He then said, "When this sort of thing happens, there

are procedures in place that are followed by the local authorities, whether it's a passenger or crew member that does not return to a ship. The first check is for accidents, hospital admissions and so on followed by a local area search. The police sent cars over the routes around the port and town and then around the surrounding area looking for Officer Yeung or the bicycle. The following day, that was yesterday, a 'missing person' file was opened as your son by then was in the United Kingdom illegally. He had not completed immigration requirements; day visitors from cruise ships don't need to do so, generally.

"Mr. Yeung, they are putting out a missing person alert on television today which is why we came along now. You needed to hear this unfortunate news directly first."

Daniel had various questions, as did Li. but the police officer wasn't able to help them much. Li then asked for the contact information for the police officer in charge there, the one they should speak to. They had been anticipating this and had a sheet with details on the North Wales Police and also the key contact information for the Hong Kong Embassy.

The officer who had been silent so far then asked about their recent communications with Han and whether he had sent any emails, letters or parcels that had arrived in the last while. Li told him that he generally emailed his parents and he mainly used Facebook with her, but she had nothing from him in over a week. It wasn't unusual she said. Daniel told him that he had not had any emails this week and nothing had come in the mail.

After offering their condolences and reassuring the family that it was still early days for this missing person investigation and that they should keep their spirits up, the officers left.

Li said, "What do we do now, Dad?"

Daniel answered, "We call Reverend Kwan and ask him to come around. We need to pray for Han's safety and have others do so. He will contact the congregation to get help. I will make arrangements for your mother and me to go to Holyhead. It is better to be close by, I think. Probably we need to go to London first."

Li had been looking at the sheet of paper given to them by the police officer.

"Dad, we should contact the Hong Kong Embassy in London, I think; it is one of the contacts here. I think they should be able to help in some way."

He nodded, looking beaten.

The Methodist clergyman came straight over. In short order he organized a support group for them and helped Li in making contacts and arrangements. He seemed much more experienced with international matters.

By the following day they had contacted the police in Wales and made arrangements to travel, but Eu-Meh then decided to stay behind. She could not face the journey, the strangeness and wanted to be with her church family, to stay and pray for Han. For her it was in the hands of God now but for Daniel, he wanted just to be there, be close to the investigation.

Daniel could see that Jian Li was hoping she could now go with him but he took her on one side and explained why she could not. Her mother would need her more now and he wanted someone back home with whom he could communicate. They had to hope for the best but accept that it might be the worst possible news.

So Jian Li had the job of looking after her mother and being the communication conduit with her father. Neither he nor her mother was computer-literate, so she pre-preprogrammed his mobile phone to be able to ring her from the UK at home or on her own mobile.

After arrival, Daniel Yeung spent a week in Holyhead and visited also Colwyn Bay, where the police headquarters were located. Then he came home, worn out, saying he was of no use over there. When Eu-Meh, Jian Li and Reverend Kwan met him at the airport he looked thinner and tired. It seemed to Jian Li that her father had also aged in such a short time.

The police had been helpful and considerate, he told them, once they were home.

At Heathrow he had been met by a person from the Hong Kong London Embassy who accompanied him to Holyhead to make sure he was settled in the hotel; that he had a taxi service to take him around and so on, but the police drove him around a lot. They had even met them on their arrival by train in Holyhead - but they had no news.

"The following day, the investigating officer took me around. His name is pronounced Inspector David Powiss, but the card he gave me said Dafydd Powys; it's the Welsh language. Everything there seems to be in Welsh; I never knew that.

"I saw where the ship had been docked and some of the places around the town where Han had been sighted on his bicycle. They were still having people phoning in at the time to their television announcement.

"We went to see a search in progress of woodland nearby. Mr. Powys said that they were still searching anywhere he might have gone 'off-road' on his cycle ride and had a fall or something.

"Then the Embassy staff person had to return to London; he had been very helpful but had other commitments. He gave me a telephone number I could call twenty-four hours a day, but I never used it. I was also taken to the police headquarters on the mainland at Colwyn Bay where I talked with the detectives who asked lots of questions - to help with background, they said.

"Afterwards I went back to the hotel in Holyhead and waited. Some people from the local Methodist Church came along on the first day there; Reverend Kwan had contacted them and they were very supportive. We prayed a lot together and they took me to their church and fed me, but I was never hungry the whole time I was away, really. It was a small community but they were so good to me."

Li and her mother sat listening. He had told them all this on long phone calls during the week, relating his experiences. Li could sense her father needed to go through it again sequentially, face-to-face, to show the journey and the effort made.

"The third evening I was there they arranged with the people at the old stone church in Holyhead, St. Cybi's it is called, to have an inter-denominational vigil service in the evening. There was a big turn-out; it quite overwhelmed me, all these strangers praying for Han's safe return. I met an older lady there who had seen Han riding past the church. I stood with her outside for a moment after-wards; he had been that close only a few days earlier.

"But, apart from going to the church or walking, I found myself just waiting... lost. It was surprising how fast I wanted just to get home, to be with you both."

He looked on the verge of tears.

"There was nothing else I could do."

Reverend Kwan had been listening, silent, watching him. He said, "Daniel, we should pray again together now, for Han and for your family also."

Then, as a family, they waited for news, each trying to sort out how to adjust their lives while waiting for word about Han.

PART 2

ENGLAND & WALES:
THE SEARCH FOR HAN YEUNG

4 BRIXTON

Brixton, September. Anne had just closed the front door of her flat and entered the corridor when she heard the lift doors open and two police officers came out, turning along towards her. The older one, the man, was tall and heavy and his shoulder radio was chirping something. The female officer was young, blonde. As they passed her she smiled and said softly, 'Good morning' and Anne nodded, smiling back.

As she reached the lift, the doors had closed and it had just started to move up, so she pressed the button and waited.

'Typical', she thought.

Anne took a glance back down the corridor and saw the police officers stop outside her neighbours' flat. They hadn't been any noisier last night than usual, she thought. At least I can say I never made any complaint this time if she confronts me again.

Later, while talking with her friend Pat, she could recall the face of the tall policeman. The female PC had become quite unmemorable.

"Mrs. Chivers?"

Her partner Gary almost always knocked; he was big and intimidating. The middle-aged woman who answered looked hungover. They could smell stale beer emanating from the passage behind.

"Yeah, that's me. What d' you want?" Her voice was a little slurred.

Typical, thought Catrin. We come to tell a woman that her son has died of a drug overdose and she's drunk at eleven-thirty in the morning. It was like a chill memory from her past life.

"You have a son called Douglas, Mrs. Chivers?" Gary continued seriously.

The way to do it, he said, is to convey the news in the expression before you have to give it aloud.

"No, luv, I don't," she answered brightly. "You want the Chivers two floors higher, not sure of the number, though. In trouble is he, drugs, then?" she said. "She has a grandson on drugs, I hear."

The metabolized beer smell wafted out as she spoke.

"I can't abide drug addicts myself, you know," she added, sharing her virtuous opinion seeing as she wasn't in trouble herself this time.

"Thank you," said Gary in his monotone. "We won't disturb your busy day any further."

"Cheeky sod," she said to herself as she closed the door.

Ten minutes later, after a terse conversation with the despatcher about precise address identification, PC Gary Day and PC Catrin Sayer were higher up in the same building. As the flat door opened Catrin saw the array of potted plants on the hall table and the lace edge to the cloth beneath them.

"I'll do this one," she said quickly.

The face of the older woman who answered the door showed that she realised what it was about as she took in the two uniforms.

"It's about Douglas, isn't it? Is he back in hospital?" she asked, apprehensively.

Looking at her Catrin thought she may go down, some do. "Yes, Mrs. Chivers, it is about Douglas. Could we come in?"

Catrin reached quickly with her right arm to support Mrs. Chivers as the more awful truth sank in and she started to keel over. She helped the woman back inside and sat her down on a well-worn dining chair in the living room. This room smells of Pledge, not beer at least, thought Catrin.

A minute or so later Mrs. Chivers sobbed, "It's a blessing he is out of his suffering, that's what Reverend Wilson told me to think about, if this happened." She burst into a fresh bout of tears.

Catrin said, "I'll make some tea and Officer Day can call Reverend Wilson or a relative, perhaps? You've had quite a shock, Mrs. Chivers."

This is a crappy job at times, she thought.

'The Reverend' arrived about thirty minutes later, a woman nearer Catrin's own age of twenty-four, she thought. Catrin knew of her and had seen the priest once before during an incident at a homeless shelter.

In jeans and a sweatshirt she knocked and introduced herself as Joy Wilson. Then she walked straight over to the couch to sit next to her parishioner. She held her hand gently, put her other arm around her shoulders and talked to her softly, like a mother with a child. Catrin could see that the priest knew what to do better than she did.

Within a couple of minutes there was a further ring on the door bell and Gary admitted Detective Sergeant Cavanagh and a female forensic officer, a Scene of Crime officer, then he signalled to Catrin he was heading back to the car. It was getting crowded in the small flat.

Catrin quickly introduced Cavanagh and said quietly to both of them, "Constable Day and I will be going now but Sergeant Cavanagh will have some questions."

Cavanagh had asked the uniform team to break the news mainly to make it easier for him and the SOCO to conduct a search of the flat for drugs. He had just come from the house where the young man's body had been found, she knew, and would be broaching the subject of confirmatory identification of the deceased.

Reverend Wilson looked at the detective and said, "Will you check through for... anything?"

The grandmother just hung on to Joy Wilson, her eyes closed in prayer.

He nodded, knowing she understood.

"Yes, Reverend Wilson, the forensic officer will check, just to make sure there are no drugs on the premises. It's safer that way."

The great fantasy of drug addicts, the police officers knew, is that there will be a hidden stash left by a dead addict - and no-one has found it yet. Once Douglas Chivers death was made known they knew that the flat could be a target. Letting the word out that the Drug Squad had thoroughly checked the place may help protect the old lady a little but, there again, it may not.

As she left, Catrin thought Cavanagh would leave the SOCO to it and spend time sitting with Mrs. Chivers, carefully asking questions about her grandson's friends and his known movements. The heroin had been badly contaminated. It was the third death in the area in two weeks from the same source.

Gary was standing by the car having a smoke when she came out of the building. He had just acknowledged a call on his radio.

"You were switched off inside," he said. She nodded, switching her own personal radio back on.

"They want you," he said with emphasis, "to go over to Scotland Yard right now. I guess it's your interview."

Catrin looked surprised then said, "Damn, Gary. Haven't I even got the time to go back to my flat and change, clean up a bit?"

"You haven't got time for anything, Catrin. Anderson told me to drive you over as soon as possible and said you were to use the time in the car getting your head straight. You will have to use the 'Ladies' room at the Yard."

Inspector Anderson had approved and supported Catrin's application for a detective constable position at the Metropolitan Police Headquarters, but had also told her not to be disappointed if it came to nothing. The station at Brixton was a long way from New Scotland Yard and it wasn't an issue of geography, he had said.

"Anyway, I thought your interview was next week sometime," Gary said, as they drove along Dog Kennel Hill in the traffic.

"So did I."

Gary then stayed quiet. He could see Catrin was deep in thought.

5 THE OFFER

Catrin Sayer sat in the office area of the Art Crime Unit on the seventh floor of the Metropolitan Police Head-quarters, New Scotland Yard. She was feeling a little surprised and anxious. What struck her most was the relative silence. There were a few voices on phones but nowhere near the bustle of the two police stations that she had served in since joining 'The Met' three years ago.

Her interview for a position of Detective Constable with the unit had indeed been scheduled for next week. That had been confirmed, so she wasn't sure what to make of this sudden call. Either it was a quick and dirty dismissal or they were interested in her. She had no idea, one way or another.

At least it will be over, she said to herself.

Catrin had thought several times in the last few days how she would prepare for this interview; and now she had no time to do so. She was in a uniform with a mark on it from God knows where during the last shift, she had a tunic button loose and, to make things worse, she also had a faint bruise on her face that make-up couldn't completely hide. A little over an hour earlier she had been sitting with Mrs. Chivers giving her the news about her dead grandson. Hardly the right physical and mental preparation for a career interview, she felt.

Nearly two years in support of the drug squad felt like a long time and this new opportunity seemed such a different role. She wasn't feeling burn-out, she told herself, but she accepted that she was becoming inured to the misery that goes with her current job, particularly the early deaths of young people. She didn't feel good about that. Anderson had sent her on a training course on 'detachment' and also insisted she take a number of other courses that could open up other areas of police work as well.

She had not had any interactions with Douglas Chivers but he was well-known to the squad. In the past she had found herself at the scene of death of addicts that she had spoken to at some time or other, knew in a sense. Reverend Wilson's comment on addicts being out of their suffering resonated with her; too few seemed to find recovery or a way out, despite everything offered for treatment.

In general Catrin liked to look neat but she wasn't a fussy person; most women police constables serving in general duty roles had to deal with the real world and its grimier side at times. That made for practicality rather than style in everything from jewellery to hairstyles.

In her early teens she had been bothered by the fact she felt 'ordinary-looking' when there were some girls in her class that were stunning the boys. It was an art teacher who had been encouraging her to draw and paint that addressed that fear. Catrin had inadvertently revealed her insecurity during a discussion with him. He picked up on it, listened seriously and wasn't dismissive. He just asked her what beauty was and they talked about it. Half an hour later she was on the bus heading home with a lot to think about.

Catrin was 5'8" tall with dark blonde hair cut evenly above the collar. She worked out regularly, was fit and no-one would call her particularly thin or overweight. She had wished for a larger bust in her teens but was happy now with the proportions she had.

When she smiled her face became attractive but her expression was more usually on the serious side, which others interpreted wrongly as sad or worried at times. This was particularly noticeable when she became absorbed in a project, whether as a duty police officer or in her other passion, her work as a part-time artist.

Across the work area, in an office with a glass wall she could see Detective Chief Inspector Jane Worsley, the head of the unit, talking with a man dressed in a suit. She wasn't quite sure why but he didn't look 'police' to her, so she was not sure what he would be doing in an interview. It just made her feel more nervous and ill-prepared.

A middle-aged Asian woman in civilian clothes at a desk put down her phone and came over to her. She had introduced herself to Catrin as Aina Jinnah, the Art Crime Unit's Administration and File Officer when Catrin had reported on her arrival a couple of minutes ago.

"DCI Worsley will see you now," she said and led her over to the office.

Here goes, thought Catrin.

~~

Worsley got straight to the point.

"Constable Sayer, this is Professor Thomas Parry from Bangor University who is assisting our work on a case. Now I know you are expecting an interview with us but this isn't it."

She smiled. The young policewoman in front of her seemed tense as they had seated themselves at the small conference table. Worsley had quickly introduced herself and thanked her for the appearance at short notice.

Parry spoke softly in Welsh. "Good afternoon. How fluent is your spoken Welsh these days, Constable Sayer?"

Catrin responded in the same language. "Good afternoon, Professor. I am bilingual, so when I was talking last night with my mother on the phone it never crossed my mind I was using it."

He laughed and reverted to English. "Just checking; I was told that you spoke Welsh but I wanted to be sure. It could be useful."

Catrin had been born in Pontypridd, a town in South Wales. Her parents still lived in the same neat, terraced house there that she grew up in.

Worsley took the lead. "Catrin, your name came up and I called you in through coincidence, of all reasons. I was reviewing applications for our vacancy when this new issue arose and I thought you could possibly be a fit for what we need at present. I assure you that you will still get an interview for the detective constable vacancy in our unit whether or not our conversation today leads to anything. So relax a little, OK?"

Catrin smiled and nodded, not feeling relaxed at all. At least Anderson's concern that she would not even be on the radar was unmerited, she thought.

Worsley's accent was 'home counties'. Young for a chief inspector, she thought, taking in the good clothes, nice conservative jewellery. She was late-thirties, perhaps.

The Art Crime Unit seemed a world away from the front line grit and reality of her current work in Brixton.

"To the point; you are interested in working with us. We need to place an officer in a short-term undercover operation at very short notice indeed, someone who will fit in without a ripple in a Welsh university and with some semblance of art knowledge. Is this any interest to you?"

Catrin said immediately, "Yes. It's not much to go on, but yes, I am very interested, ma'am, as I am interested in working with this unit."

Worsley continued, "It will require between one and three weeks in place, we think, to see if it is productive. It won't be too exciting I should add, it may even be quite boring."

It sounded far more interesting to Catrin than many of the jobs she did at present.

"By the way, how did you get the bruise?" Worsley added, pointing at her face.

"It happened during an arrest two days ago, ma'am." She looked quickly at Parry. "I am currently assigned in support of drug squad activities in the Brixton area. We arrested a dealer."

"He hit you?" asked Parry.

"No." She tried to hide the smile. "The dealer was a woman. She pushed my partner so hard that his cap fell off and the peak hit my cheek. Gary - Constable Day - is quite tall."

Gary had been mortified; his face had been a picture as he held the little tornado trying to push him around. Catrin had handcuffed her.

She looked at Worsley. "I am due in court now for this arrest on the same morning as the interview. I heard it on the way over from Brixton and was going to let your office know, ma'am."

"Well, if you take on this assignment, you won't be at either."

No, thought Catrin, but I will be being assessed, which is not to be sneezed at.

"Officer Sayer," said Jane Worsley, "we want you to finish writing up a Ph.D."

6 BANGOR MOUNTAIN

Jian Li Yeung stopped briefly to take in the view and rest a little. She looked across from the path she was running along on the hill referred to locally as Bangor Mountain. She could see the Main Arts Building on the hill on the other side of town. Jian Li was studying law, not history or architecture, so the Arts Building appeared ancient, almost like a castle. She had been surprised to learn that it was purpose-built for the university in 1907.

As her breathing eased and she cooled a little, she took in more of the view. From her vantage point she could see how the many buildings of the university campus occupied much of the land on the western side of the main road through Bangor.

Li was nearly twenty-one years old and 5'6" tall, with long black hair currently tied back in a ponytail for her run. She was in good physical shape, although in the last minutes she had noticed the effects of her long hours of air travel and the change in regime. It had only been a few days but the run required greater effort than she expected.

Li had a round face, a 'water' face some called it, with

full cheeks. It was one feature she would gladly change for more oval, narrower features if she could. Her face could be incredibly expressive when she chose to show her emotions but like most other Asians, she could appear impassive and uncommunicative if she wished.

For a young Chinese woman she also had larger breasts and hips than average without being overweight; she had more western-style curves, as she thought of them, than a number of her friends.

I should be comfortable here, she thought whimsically; this too is a land of dragons. But it felt so strange at present. She had such mixed emotions; success at arrival on her first international trip outside South-East Asia, fear and uncertainty about what to do next about her brother Han and the challenge of her new course of study in a quite different environment. For the first time in her life she would not be surrounded by family and friends. She would have to make new friends here, she knew, and looked forward to that. It was something she had always found easy to do.

She also recognized her disorientation came from an eight-hour time difference, her first real experience of 'jet lag'. This was her third day away from Hong Kong and the periods of wakefulness and sleepiness at the wrong time seemed worse than ever, which was why she had decided that a run was better than napping in the hall of residence.

To move from Hong Kong to the coastal town of Bangor in North Wales was a culture shock. She had been warned that it might be so but had no experience to base it on. Now she was beginning to understand. Everything was different, from the feeling of the daylight to the smell of the air.

There were also things here that strangely reminded

her of home; the two languages, English and Welsh, for example. While she didn't speak the latter, the tonality differences walking along a street reminded her of English and Cantonese flowing over each other in the streets of Hong Kong. She also felt more familiar with the bustle of Bangor High Street and the shopping precinct than in the quiet streets of Upper Bangor, where she had first gone exploring after settling in.

Li wanted to visit the mountains of the nearby Snowdonia National Park soon. She had also looked at some of the materials provided to her in the Student Union where she had met one of the 'welcoming' students who sailed competitively. Li planned to join the university sailing club and get out on the water. Sailing here would be a different experience from the club she was a member of in Hong Kong.

Her room at the hall of residence seemed fine; nothing like home, of course, but a practical bedroom and a floor with a communal kitchen and meeting area. She had slept well in the bed for the first night and had left the window open. Li liked the air here, so much fresher than Hong Kong, but the noise of contractors starting up had woken her on her first morning and she sat up, disorientated about her location and surroundings.

According to her 'welcome emails', Li was meeting later today with someone from her faculty study area. They would show her around the college lecture areas, library and places the law students gathered and studied. And tomorrow a floor meeting was scheduled at the Hall of Residence she had moved into, Gwynant, part of a complex of residences near the main university site.

She didn't feel lonely though, yet. The frequent emails, texts and Facebook messages from friends at home, the initial success by her father in mastering Skype on the home computer and the chance to talk face-to-face that way with her parents all helped. He had look relieved to make the connection; her mother relieved with seeing her daughter in her new room.

Right now, her mind was on the additional issue she wanted to deal with soon after arrival - the need to contact the police here and talk about Han. It had seemed one of the various items on her 'to do' list when she started. Now, having dealt with a lot of that list, she found the thought of going to a police station and talking with detectives to be intimidating.

~~

DCI Worsley said to Catrin, "Your cover story at Bangor University is that you are finishing the write-up of your Ph.D., having completed the research work at Aberystwyth University - which you do know well as you did your undergraduate studies there."

"It's not perfect, I know, given the movement of people within universities and the chance you could run into someone who knows you, but it is only short-term cover. We plan to give you a room in the same hall of residence as a Chinese person of interest who arrived from Hong Kong this week. Your job is to get to know her, monitor her movements without visibly shadowing her and see if you can answer some of the questions we have about her coming here.

"First you will need some of the background. We will go through it in summary and then brief you in more detail tomorrow."

Worsley looked intently at Catrin. "This is a missing person enquiry possibly linked to stolen art, possibly not. Our unit's focus is art-related crime. That's why the Art

Crime Unit was set up, first and foremost. We assist in closing out criminal cases rather than focus on finding the stolen or forged art itself."

Catrin saw Worsley was checking if she had any insight there. She just nodded. From gossip in the Met she knew about the controversial decision to create the ACU a little under a year ago but felt it best to say nothing.

"A missing person investigation and an art smuggling operation seem to have come together in Holyhead on May 14. Han Yeung, a ship's officer, a Third Officer on the cruise ship the *Manden Serenity*, was off-duty and took a bike ride while the ship was in port. The passengers were out and about on their day tours. He never came back and has not been traced so far.

"He was seen leaving the quay on his bike with a long tube that could have carried a print or painting. Our good and much-loved colleagues, the Art & Antiques Unit, are interested in several paintings that they understand were being smuggled from Europe to New York on that trip. The paintings never turned up either. They were valued at around two million US dollars in total.

"We have no evidence to say whether Han Yeung was involved in the disappearance of the paintings or not, however the tube he was carrying is suspicious. The North Wales Police, the Heddlu Gogledd Cymru, are leading the missing person enquiry. How do you really say that, Tom?"

Parry patiently pronounced the Welsh name of North Wales Police Service for her.

"We have recently learned that his younger sister, Jian Li Yeung, has come all the way from Hong Kong to do an exchange year in law studies at Bangor. It wasn't planned in advance; it seems to have been a late arrangement between the City University of Hong Kong and Bangor University. So we want to fix it for you to be in the next room to her in the hall of residence called Gwynant."

Parry's expression at the constant mangling of the Welsh made both Worsley and Catrin laugh.

"More like 'Gwin-ant', ma'am," said Catrin.

Worsley turned serious again. "So you can see the sort of questions we have; is there something going on with her brother or family regarding this art; are they involved? Is she here simply to be around in case there is news of him, does she want to make a media issue of his disappearance or does she even plan to mount her own investigation?"

"Professor Parry is in the Faculty of Arts and has, for his sins, worked with A&A in the past on other cases. It is fortunate that Tom is at the university and also that he is very knowledgeable about these missing paintings, which are of Russian origin.

"He is going to be your resource contact there and will lie fluently about your Ph.D. work, how he is helping out your professor in Aberystwyth and so on, if asked. He will also fix up anything that the university needs to do to help us.

"Your local police liaison will be DI Dafydd Powys. He has led the investigation into Yeung's disappearance from the outset."

Worsley pronounced the Welsh name perfectly this time, Catrin noticed; she must have talked with the detective directly.

"Tomorrow morning you will come in here and read through the files and collect some materials to take with you. Detective Inspector Keith Marshall in my team will brief you on the case. Professor Parry will do likewise on the art itself."

Parry smiled, "There is quite an interesting story behind the paintings involved."

Worsley pressed on, not wanting digression at this point, "Dress as if you were a post-grad student, whatever that looks like these days, and before you leave home pack your suitcase, you will be leaving for Bangor at midday."

"Shall I bring my case here, ma'am?"

"No, a car will be collecting it later so let us know where to do that. It will come on here to take you and Tom back to Bangor. Well, it will take him all the way. You will be dropped off at Crewe or somewhere so that you arrive in Bangor like a lot of other students, pulling your luggage along the platform."

She paused and looked at Catrin.

"So you are on board?"

"Yes, ma'am. I am looking forward to it. Thank you."

Worsley said, "I will call DI Anderson and let him know. He thought you would jump at the chance. And thank you for helping us at such short notice."

She stood up and Catrin did likewise, absorbing that the meeting was at an end.

As she was leaving for the Tube back to Stockwell, where she shared the rental of a flat with two other police officers, she thought, 'and I was worried about whether I would be getting an interview.'

Catrin had rented a room in a flat in Stockwell when she started at Brixton Police Station; it was nearby. Currently she shared it with another female officer and one male, the newest renter just out of training college and starting his probationary period. The flat owner, a retired policeman himself, rented only to 'his own', as they would understand the routine and occasional nonroutine life of junior police officers. The three police officers got along, worked well together sharing the various household chores but didn't socialize much.

As she reached the Tube station she decided instead to call in on her friends Jean and Melanie, who lived in the Spitalfields area of London, before going home.

7 THE CWMBRAN KILN

The Cwmbran Kiln, a small boutique pottery and shop, was located in a building that was part of the Spitalfields Market complex. It was much of Catrin's other life outside her hours as a police officer and the everyday chores. She tried to organize her free time and work shifts to give at least a good clear two-day break about every two weeks to be there, for this was when she could concentrate most on her art. She did pottery decoration in the store.

It was a different Tube ride to get there than going back to her flat; the Circle line, the Northern line to Moorgate and a walk. If it was raining she would sometimes change to the Central Line to get a little closer to the Market on the Underground system or take a bus.

As a young person, Catrin, like most art students, had started with sketching, watercolours and oils. Along the way she got caught up for quite a while painting in acrylics and, on a project, had tried some pottery decoration in enamels. This led to the more ornate work that she now undertook with Jean Hughes at the Kiln.

Catrin walked in and Melanie, the co-owner and 'front sales' of the couple who owned the small business, gave her a smile. The only customer present was eyeing a vase prominently displayed in the front window. She glanced over and took in the police uniform then went back to re-examining the vase. Melanie and Catrin exchanged looks; it was a piece that Catrin had decorated, part of the 'high-end' individual pottery items that formed part of the shop inventory.

Melanie and Jean shared the glaze work and routine decoration for the majority of the pottery that Jean made; the dinner services, the tea and coffee sets and various other items that had become their staple sales line. Catrin did only the 'eye-catcher' intricate pieces that sold infrequently, but at higher prices. But sight of these in the window often brought people through the door.

She was happy to help and find a place to continue her interest in this aspect of art. Jean had been her friend from their childhood in Pontypridd and had chosen to study at Cardiff School of Art & Design when Catrin left for the University of Aberystwyth. There Jean had met Melanie; they had fallen for each other and, after their ordeal about 'coming out' to family and friends, had decided that on graduation they would set up a pottery business together.

It was Jean's dad who had put up the money to start the little enterprise and, after two years, it was holding its own. He and the two women had agreed on the name without realising the miscellany of mispronunciations the word 'Cwmbran' would generate in London, particularly from tourists. Melanie had partly solved the situation by a sign, a large decorated platter in the window; 'It's Welsh - COME-BRAN', which generated, in turn, questions about what it meant. Occasionally a customer would come in and start speaking Welsh to see if they were really from Wales or not and Jean would deal with it.

Catrin went back into the 'visible to customers' but separate work area of the pottery itself, with its work tables, potter's wheel and kilns. Jean, a large-framed woman with powerful arms and shoulders developed in part from the daily work with clay, was busy.

"Jeannie, I just popped in, I have to go away. Not sure for how long, so just wanted to check what you needed from me and say, whatever it is, I can't do it now or for a while." She smiled at Jean as her friend rolled her eyes.

"I've a couple of bisques ready for you - the bowl and water jug in the corner." she answered.

The bowl at its bisque-fired stage, plain and porous but hardened from its first firing in the kiln, was in a style Catrin regularly decorated for the shop. It was ready to be painted with the under-glaze decoration before Jean finished it.

Jean smiled. "But there's no rush, really, I still have a couple of your finished bowls waiting for shelf space." She looked down the store at the customer staring intently at Catrin's vase.

Catrin tended to develop a design and produce a number of pieces on that theme then something else would inspire her and a new design would emerge. The joy for her was that she never tried to duplicate; each one would build from the elements in its own way on that day. She received a commission whenever her items sold, a percentage of the sale price.

The largest work project that she had completed with Jean was a set of tableware for a nearby bistro restaurant in the Market. It had been a lot of work and they occasionally received orders for breakage replacements, although now Melanie had also been glazing a complimentary simple finish for items to allow the restaurant to 'mix and match'. It was a project that had brought home to Catrin she was not in the 'production line' business despite it being an important order in the early days of Jean and Melanie's venture.

"Where are you off to then, special duty at a conference or something?" Jean asked. Sometimes, she knew, police officers were assigned for crowd control or security work outside their area.

"Nothing like that," said Catrin. "I had a meeting this afternoon with the Art Crime Unit at Scotland Yard. I am doing something with them away from London."

Jean looked at her. "It's obviously not THE interview, right? You would have said. Well I won't ask more so that I don't have to sign the Official Secrets Act or something. Do you want some tea?"

Hopefully her vase would sell today, Catrin thought. Melanie called her over to meet the customer saying, "This is the artist who decorated the vase, Catrin Sayer. Catrin is also a police officer."

Catrin smiled. She was looking forward to spending an hour or so with her friends before heading back to the apartment to choose her clothes and pack.

8 THE KOMAROV SISTERS

The following day Professor Tom Parry was all business in the small meeting room at New Scotland Yard. They were in the Art Crime Unit area but DCI Worsley was nowhere to be seen. Others on the floor looked busy.

Have you read much about art theft?" he asked.

"Yes, as much as I could," said Catrin. "Well, all that I could find in books and on the internet since I thought about applying for the position here."

"Then you will know that a lot of art theft is opportunistic or for the purpose of illegal security use. There are relatively few sophisticated 'designer thefts'; stealing a particular work for a client interested in that item, despite the impression given in books and movies. Ironically, the Met thinks this case may actually be one of those.

"A lot are for illegal security use, as I said. You want to buy a load of cocaine but can only pay once you have made your own deals, so you offer a painting known to be worth a half a million dollars as security, that sort of thing. The artistic merit is irrelevant. It is the perceived market value that counts; the art becomes a sort of underground currency."

"Right," said Catrin. "I have read about that, too. I know that you teach a course unit on art theft at Bangor, Professor Parry."

"It's Tom. Most of the art recovery these days is by international groups with their own resources, or by police units like the Art & Antiques Unit upstairs here or their counterparts like the FBI Art Crime team. They are involved in recovering millions of dollars of stolen art. Investigators working for insurance companies, museum benefactors and wealthy families wanting stolen art back are also involved. I have worked with the Art and Antiques Unit as consultant over a number of years now on Eastern European art thefts."

He was settling into his stride, Catrin saw.

"This unit is new, still finding its fit, I guess."

He meant the ACU, Catrin understood.

"But Keith Marshall's work with the Shropshire Police on the theft of the Vernon Ward painting caught people's attention."

Other than Detective Inspector Keith Marshall was the person she would meet next and Vernon Ward was an English artist, she had no idea what Parry was talking about.

He continued. "So let's talk about the three paintings known collectively as the Komarov Sisters. We realise it is unlikely you will come across them but you need some background. If Yeung has an image on her computer, or you get to see a print in her room it is somewhat indicative of a connection, right? Are you familiar with any of the Russian Impressionists?"

Catrin said, "I am aware there was a sizeable Russian

Impressionist movement that developed from the French style, but to be honest, I can't say I recall anything."

"That's no problem. The artist was a Maxim Garin. He painted in a style we could say is similar to that of Matisse, more a neo-impressionist, really. He was born in Kamyshin, north of Volgograd and was from boyhood a friend of Antonin Komarov. Komarov became a doctor; actually he was quite a famous epidemiologist in Russia. They both lived in Volgograd for much of their lives.

"At some point Garin agreed to paint all three of Komarov's daughters each in celebration of their respective sixteenth birthdays, in the same summer room with its doors open looking out on the garden. Here, these are the prints I have for you; they are good quality ones, too."

He pointed in turn to each print. "This is Katarina Vasilisa Komarov, the eldest daughter, painted in 1931. Here is Elizaveta Tamara, painted in 1933, and last but not least is Svetlana Arina, the youngest, painted in 1935."

Catrin looked at each one while Parry spoke. She could see that the two older daughters were similar in features and dark-haired; the third, the youngest, was slimmer in body and face and with auburn hair. Each painting conveyed the sense of a young woman thrilled to be the centre of attention.

"The style is not Matisse, though, it is classic realism," said Catrin.

"Correct. It was the parent's request. The mother found Garin's paintings she had seen previously to be too avant-garde. That was a common reaction at the time in many countries to Impressionism, as you will know. To make everyone happy he offered to paint the girls in the classical style. As you can see, he was talented."

"Yes, I see that. Look, he has even captured very

nicely the changes in the growth of the apple tree behind over the years - and the shading in the blossom here is very effective; Elizaveta must have been born in the spring time. And the dappled light... it's quite beautifully done."

Parry said, "Yes, I know. I really like these paintings and Garin's work in general. Part of the commercial value of this set is that they are the only paintings by the artist in this style. The other reason is that Svetlana, the youngest, was a Night Witch."

Catrin's head shot up from the paintings to look at Parry, who was looking quizzical. "Any idea?" he asked.

Catrin thought hard. She had heard the term but where? Something in her second year at Aberystwyth, a history course module on... she couldn't think.

"Sorry, no, other than the thought of World War Two comes to mind, but I can't say why."

She could tell Parry was an academic. In her world these days there would be no guessing game around facts, they had enough of that with motives, culprits and timings of events. Facts were just put out there.

"Actually, that is good. Svetlana was a navigator in a Russian bomber, a woman's squadron in World War Two. The Russians during the war had no qualms about placing trained women soldiers into combat.

'The squadron Svetlana flew with used small old planes making night raids to harass the Nazis. They would get close, glide in quietly and drop their bombs before climbing out again. The Germans gave them the name Nachthexen, Night Witches as a result.

"Svetlana had actually had a few flying lessons before the war and wanted to be a pilot but apparently didn't make the grade, so she became a navigator. She was killed in 1943 in action. The planes were slow and if they were hit, they had no armour."

He stopped. Clearly the subject fascinated him, but he got back to the issue.

"So a lot of the two million dollar valuation for the three paintings is linked to hers as she was a recognized heroine from the war, particularly in Russia or among Russian émigrés. I have been told if the paintings ever went for auction the actual sale price could go significantly higher. They are still owned by the Komarov family which has no intention to sell. The family gave them on permanent loan to the Volgograd Museum of Fine Arts early in the 1950s and the paintings were displayed there until they were stolen.

"The news of the theft in January led to Katarina's youngest son, who is now quite old, having a mild stroke, I gather. 'The Sisters' are still highly valued by the family. The theft was a professional job is all I know. That's it for the paintings. Any questions before you see DI Marshall?"

Catrin thought. "Just one, Professor Parry; they are oil on canvas and about eighty years old. If they were kept in a tube rather than stored flat, as DCI Worsley mentioned yesterday, what damage is likely?"

"Hard to say really, it's a horrible thought, but like you it has concerned me. It could be substantial depending on the quality of the canvas used, its aging and maintenance. At least it could make a lot of work for a restorer. But the witness in Holyhead who saw Yeung with a tube insisted that it was around six to eight inches in diameter. She was an older lady, so who knows. The larger the diameter, the easier it would be on the material, of course. The truth is I don't know."

Catrin nodded. Some seniors she had met would fly through the police cadet training unit on observation;

they were eagle-eyed and missed nothing. Others, well... it would be questionable.

Parry was calling an extension number. He spoke briefly. "DI Marshall is coming. And Catrin, if you succeed in your interview and want a job here, I suspect that he is person you will be working with directly."

The tall man looked to be in his forties and was slim and fit, Catrin thought. He had a receding hairline, short, cropped dark hair and was clean-shaven. His suit looked good quality material and he was clearly a careful dresser, military smart.

Catrin, aware of the need to appear a student, had worn black casual pants, a casual shirt and was wearing trainers. She had brought a rain jacket and had a winter liner for it in her suitcase. She suddenly felt distinctly underdressed.

Marshall introduced himself and placed a Mac laptop and Samsung mobile phone on the table.

"The laptop is secure," he said, firing it up, "and here is the access password."

After a moment he opened a file on the machine and said, "Here also is your draft thesis, resource files, backups and heaven knows what else validating your studies, courtesy of Tom.

"You won't have access to secure police files online on this laptop but this folder here - he pointed - has a lot of the case file material in it for you to read up on."

Catrin nodded, eyeing the worn but functional unit.

Marshall continued. "And this is your new work mobile. Secure also. All key contacts are in here, including DCI Worsley and myself.

"Finally, you will need money. This is a float of £500. Please sign the sheet behind the envelope after checking it and give it to Aina before you leave. Remember to keep any credit or debit card receipts for reimbursement. Now, let's talk about the Yeung case."

He looked at Tom Parry, who got up.

"Catrin, I will see you at noon here to meet the driver," Parry said as he left the room.

When he had gone Marshall said, "Let's get some coffee before we get into this."

"A&A, and now also our unit, are working with Interpol and others agencies investigating an organisation involved in both art theft and international smuggling. They are moving stolen art, principally paintings we think, around the world with particular ease, it seems."

They were back in the meeting room. Marshall had gone straight into the file, no preambular 'get to know you' stuff, Catrin noted. Perhaps he was busy and needed to get through this and back to something else.

"The Swiss first approached us about it; they have a person in mind they think is a leader or the leader of this group. How they know they won't reveal at present.

"Collectively we, the big global 'we', that is, have a theory that some of the international movement of this art is not by air, but on cruise ships. Ships belonging to one particular company called the Manden Line are the focus for us, to be specific. We have checked on their ships and their crew and gone as far as placing our own people on board on a cruise posing as art-loving passengers. You can imagine the comments that drew for the officer who went with his wife."

Catrin smiled. That would be an assignment, she thought.

"We have also had Customs authorities do apparent routine audits of their art gallery inventories but have learned nothing new. Nearly all cruise ships sell art. It is a good income generator and many cruisers buy art on board so it was an obvious area to focus on. But the franchise that holds auctions on the Manden line is, as far as we can tell at present, uninvolved in smuggling activities.

"We would by now have spotted anything hidden in their collections. Ship art sales are fairly well-defined areas. Normally they have some eye-catching originals, say a Picasso or a Renoir sketch or two, but most of their items are contemporary artists that either the franchise or the art world say are collectible investments. Many are limited print runs, perhaps selling for several thousand dollars or so a print, so nowhere in the league of Garin originals, for sure. But there are enough art lovers on board these ships to make a stolen work like a Garin stand out like a sore thumb if it was seen.

"Finally, the auction house doesn't ship art out with the customers to take with them as Han Yeung may have done. They reframe and package the items in their central facilities or send another print from the same run and ship them by courier to the home of the purchaser. The last thing they want is any damage to the artwork and a dispute with a client that gets a bad reputation for the cruise line or themselves.

"The bottom line is we still don't know how the works are being transported on these ships."

Catrin had placed Marshall's accent as Northern England from the vowels, but it was not an obvious local accent. He must have moved around, she thought, before coming to the Met. Her own accent had a characteristic Welsh lilt that people picked up immediately.

"Five months ago we heard about the movement of

some stolen art to New York, the three paintings that Professor Parry has told you about. The Swiss put an agent on board the *Manden Serenity* as a crew member this time, a woman. The ship's routing was first from Le Havre to Dover. Then it went to Holyhead, Dublin, Ponta Delgado in the Azores and afterwards straight to New York. Each of the intermediate stops was a day visit for tourism. The FBI team were ready there to take over in New York on arrival.

"The Art & Antiques Unit had the responsibility to keep tabs on anything happening in the UK ports. Nothing unusual was noticed in the Dover stopover. However in Holyhead all hell let loose. Yeung and his bike disappeared which brought this case into the ACU assignment area.

"Apart from the natural commotion among passengers and crew about his disappearance, nothing later turned up regarding the paintings in New York. They still have not surfaced. In fact, the only item of note about the trip after Holyhead was that the hotel manager on board, a German national, had apparently unleashed a reprimand to a staff member. She reported him saying it was an unfair and inappropriate overreaction to the loss of a shipping tube from his office. It then came out the two were having a relationship. While onboard relationships are not in themselves an issue, the man's failure to deal appropriately with the situation was. And as a senior manager he was held to a higher standard. He left the ship in New York."

Catrin said, "Was this tube big enough to contain a painting, sir?"

"From a witness statement who saw Han on shore, I think so. Our agent on the ship never got to see any tubes, even though she searched the office before arrival in New York.

"The A&A officer assigned in Holyhead was looking for art-sized items coming off. He saw nothing suspicious and may have been engaged checking the cargo changeovers when Yeung disembarked. In any event, he did not see him. There are some questions being asked now as to why there was only one officer on watch but from A&A's perspective the art was destined for New York; they expected nothing to happen in Holyhead.

"Nothing has turned up in the investigation by the North Wales Police into Yeung's disappearance. Either he was involved in this operation and, for some reason, made a break for it - or he ran into foul play. But he left the ship on a bike, with just his cycling gear, his mobile phone, watch and wallet, we believe. He had his ship ID card and driving license but his passport was still on board in his room safe.

"Jane Worsley and I think he ran into trouble but we don't have any factual basis for saying it.

"The sister, Jian Li Yeung, arrived at Heathrow on the Tuesday and headed up directly to Bangor. International students arrive at the university a week earlier than the main arrivals to let them settle in before Welcome Week.

"You know about Welcome Week no doubt, with its opening events and the booze parties?"

"Yes sir, my own was not that long ago," Catrin smiled.

"So we want to get you in place as soon as possible."

Catrin nodded and asked, "Do we know of any links between these two Chinese people and any art theft activity that Interpol is following, sir?

"No," said Marshall, "but Asia is a market for European art, and it has been a growing market for stolen art for some time. With the changes in China and its growing business elite, European art is in high demand. If we had something more specific it would be easier."

'What about the Swiss officer in place at the time?" asked Catrin, "Did she see anything of note in Holyhead?"

Marshall shook his head.

"Ironically she was in quarantine with two other staff who shared her quarters; a suspected Norwalk virus outbreak. It turned out that the sick woman had something non-contagious but the Swiss officer didn't even get a sighting of Holyhead, never mind hear anything useful about the disappearance of Yeung. She did, however, pick up the news about the hotel manager which was useful. The best information on sighting Han onshore came from a local woman, a senior called Mavis somebody."

"And this hotel manager issue?"

"We looked into it and were quite keen to pursue it further. It is possible that he is linked into this but there is nothing we can prove or tie in at present. He never left the ship other than to deal with items in the quay area, I gather; what I don't know. Also he left New York almost immediately afterwards, flying to Dubai and taking a job on a luxury yacht belonging to someone in oil. Being a German national and out of our hands there is not much we can do about it and, speaking frankly, the German police are up to their eyes in bigger art issues than this at present."

He stood up. "More files, more reading, I am afraid. They are all on the laptop."

He looked at his watch. "We'll go down to the cafeteria at around 11.30 and I'll deal with any questions arising. Then around noon you are off to Bangor. So... welcome aboard."

Catrin said, "I have one question now, sir. You waited for Professor Parry to depart before briefing me. What should I discuss or not discuss with him while there, if he is a consultant to us and to A&A?"

"That's a good question. I'd not thought of it actually and I should have. Consultants sign secrecy agreements containing some Official Secrets Act provisions but it is still a 'need to know' basis. DCI Worsley is quite strict on this so I would say anything about the paintings, or about your cover, discuss freely. Anything about the crime links or any progress, if we make any, is within this team and your link person in the North Wales Police in Bangor, DI Powys."

~~

On the drive up to North Wales in the unmarked car Catrin found herself reading files and occasionally in discussion with the driver, Janine, a PC from Traffic Division.

Parry, it turned out, was lost in papers and reading on his laptop for a lot of the time. She sensed from the discussion that away from the subject of art he was the sort of academic not interested in small talk. Early on the journey he had talked a little more about the three paintings and Garin's work in general and it became clear that regular visits to Eastern Europe were part of his life.

She had briefly looked up Thomas Parry on Google and the Bangor University web site the previous evening. His name had been known to her from the preparative work she did on art crime for her interview; that is where she had come across his art theft and fraud course at Bangor. He was Welsh, had a Fine Arts degree from Cambridge and a Ph.D. from the University of London.

He then moved to do a post-doctoral fellowship at the University of Latvia at Riga before his appointment at Bangor University, where he had first been an assistant lecturer. He made full professor about eight years ago.

Parry suddenly asked her about her studies for her own degree, nodding when she mentioned some of the courses she had taken at the University of Aberystwyth and the people there. He asked her if she had sailed as a student; it turned out he was a yachtsman and had a boat he kept on the Menai Strait.

He then switched the conversation to Jian Li Yeung, asking if there was anything he could do to assist her. Mindful of Inspector Marshall's instruction she closed that down quickly, saying that she first needed to assess the situation on the ground and changed the subject back to him.

"You studied in Riga I saw, Professor, how did you like it?"

"My mother was Latvian, my father Welsh, so I learned both national languages as a boy, as well as English. Latvian came back pretty quickly while I was there but it was rusty and I was never fluent. But Riga provided a great base for me to start to see some of the Eastern European paintings that most people from the West never get to see. I travelled a lot on train passes."

He stopped and then said, "Sorry, I must get back to my preparations for some lectures I am developing for this term."

Catrin talked a little more with Janine but it was soon time for her to be dropped off. They had finally chosen Rhyl rather than Crewe after checking their own travel timing with the rail system. Twenty minutes after being dropped off, a thirty-five minute train ride would get her into Bangor.

She was about to become a student again.

9 INTRODUCTIONS

Steve was just cleaning up the brushes and putting the drop cloths into his van when his mobile phone rang. He looked at the number and answered.

"I have just heard," she said without preamble, "that the man's sister is now in Bangor."

"Not the dad again, then?"

"No. She is here for the duration though, it seems. She is staying in Gwynant as a student. Apparently she is studying here."

"Why?"

"I have no idea. Unless she just wants to be around in case of any news. She is his sister. Who knows?"

"So what do we do?"

"Relax, Steve, we are doing nothing. Besides, I hear that the police are watching her, so we don't want to get anywhere near this one. Just keep calm. It will all go away."

~~

Catrin found a neatly-written 'sticky' note on her room door.

'Reminder! There will be a floor meeting for arriving students in the Common Room at 5.00 p.m. Please come and don't bring in visitors at that time. Gwyn Powell, Floor Warden.'

Last night on arrival she had unpacked, found somewhere to eat then made herself tea in the deserted kitchen on her floor in Gwynant. She had not run into Jian Li Yeung.

One student had passed through the kitchen and introduced himself as Gwyn Roberts. He spoke English until he found that Catrin was Welsh then switched. "There will be a student floor 'get-together' tomorrow for the early arrivals; a number of others are arriving now."

She had realized how tired she was from the events of the day and the sudden change in her life. It took no time at all to get to sleep.

She saw the same notice on some other doors on her corridor. The adjacent room assigned to Jian Li Yeung had one but still had its door closed.

Catrin had just returned from the Registrar's office, where the manager took her away from the main area that dealt with students to a room where he went through a package of documents. They had prepared a number of items, including a student identity card and a list of the security staff telephone numbers. He said that only a few people in Administration, the Vice-Chancellor's office and Professor Parry knew of her role inside the university. If anything occurred out of the ordinary where she needed university help the people on the list should be the points of contacts.

Catrin had then spent some time orienting herself in the area.

When she entered the common room/kitchen area just before 5.00 p.m., there were four people in the room. A large, somewhat overweight man in his mid-to-late twenties came up and introduced himself as Gwyn Powell, the Floor Warden, and asked if she spoke Welsh, which they then used for the remainder of their brief discussion.

"You were at Aberystwyth, I see," he said, looking at a list he had printed out.

"Just finishing, yes, with Professor Llewellyn and now writing up my thesis."

"Good luck with that. I am in my second year doing a post-doc in biochemistry here. I remember writing up my thesis too; it consumed my life. Glad it's done with. Anyway, there is coffee and tea that I made and we have some beer and wine, so help yourself and take a seat."

"Thanks."

As she got herself some coffee Catrin looked at the others. Yeung was already seated and holding a mug with tea, the string of the teabag hanging over the side. There was an empty seat next to her. Good, thought Catrin.

"Catrin Sayer, hi," she said, sitting down and holding out her hand.

"Jian Li Yeung, from Hong Kong, still getting over jet lag, but call me Li," she responded sleepily, shaking Catrin's hand briefly, "I am just waking up from a nap." She had pronounced her name 'Lee'.

"I'm in room 47," said Catrin.

"Then we are neighbours," responded Li. "It is very nice to meet you."

A woman in her forties or fifties, Andrea, then introduced herself to both of them as Gwyn said, "Let's get started." Now eight people had gathered.

"Hi everyone, I have met all of you now but just for the record, I am Gwyn Powell, the Floor Warden. It's my job to bring peace, order and good government to Floor 4 and this is my second year doing this. Last year was no problem so hopefully this will be the same."

He held up another sheet from his folder. "In your residence contract there are rules of behaviour, so please follow them. I will be doing the same job with the remaining students coming in next week, Welcome Week. They are all undergraduates who chose this 'quiet floor' so... we'll see."

He gave a dramatic sigh. "My main job though is to welcome you and say I am here if you have questions and problems. I am a post-doctoral fellow in biochemistry and did my undergraduate work here, my Ph.D. in London and then I came back. I think I know my way around and should be able to help. So please, it is not a token gesture, come see me if you have any questions or concerns. We are a community here, a good one I think.

"But let's go round the room for some brief introductions. You are all either international students, mature students or graduate students who have arrived early, the last week of the calm before the storm."

He nodded at the older woman and said, "Name, what you are doing here and perhaps one or two items about you, to begin, please."

"I'm Andrea Teller, from Wolverhampton," she said, 'I am obviously a 'mature student' but don't feel one, to be honest. I am just starting an undergraduate course in history and I spent the past 22 years working in hospital administration. So I may be older, but I am in a new, strange world, too. Glad to meet you all."

An African student started to ask a question to Andrea and Gwyn cut him off, "Introductions, first - then we can talk," he smiled. He worked his way apparently at random around the group.

He is good at this, thought Catrin; people are going to talk after the opener, not head back to their rooms.

When the finger pointed at her she said, "Catrin Sayer, hi everyone. I am finishing writing up my Ph.D. thesis here but actually I did my postgraduate studies at Aberystwyth. I studied Fine Arts and Art History there. My Ph.D. subject is 'Influences on nineteenth century Welsh Painters', particularly one called Thomas Jones, but I won't bore you to death with that, at least not now."

"I am here writing up because my professor fixed it for me, really. My grandmother lives in Llanrwst, about 20 miles from here and she is terminally ill. We were very close and… it's much closer here, for me to visit. I think that's personal enough for now."

This was the story Parry and Worsley had concocted. They wanted to cover any absences on police work by Catrin that may arise. Also, Parry said coldly, "Chinese young people are very close to their older relatives in general, so it may give a point of contact with Yeung."

Gwyn Powell pointed his finger sideways at Gwyn Roberts. Wide awake now Catrin saw he was small but quite handsome; she must have been really tired last night.

Powell said "And who, please, are you?"

"My name is also Gwyn as he well knows," he smiled. "Gwyn Roberts. Hi. I sing with this character at the folk club and we are good friends."

Then in mock solemnity, he added, "He is Big Gwyn; I am Little Gwyn; that's what everyone called us last year, just so you don't mix us up."

People laughed at the expressions on their respective faces. A pair of comics, thought Catrin.

"I am starting my master's degree in electrical engineering. I did my undergrad here and I like the place. Other than sing and study, I come from Betws-y-Coed, not too far away. My family and my fiancée are there, so I generally go home at weekends."

Have to watch that, Catrin thought. Betws-y-Coed is less than ten miles from Llanrwst, the location of my fictional grandma.

Finally it was Li's turn. She suddenly sounded formal. "Hello everyone, my name is Jian Li Yeung. Please just call me Li. I am studying law, the third year course. I am from Hong Kong, just arrived. I ..." she stopped.

"And something personal," Gwyn said. He had had to press the African student, Macharia, on the point also.

Li thought, and then smiled, "I will be joining the university sailing club, I hope, to advance my training. I learned to sail in Hong Kong but here it will be a new experience."

"Thank you, Li, thank you all. I could see some had questions of others and I think the ice is broken. So let's just mingle and chat."

Catrin started asking Li about sailing; it seemed a good start.

~~

The following day Detective Inspector Dafydd Powys picked Catrin up at the bus-stop at the bottom of Glanrafon Hill. "Constable Sayer, I take it?" he said in Welsh.

"Yes sir."

"Well, when it is just us, I am Dafydd, you are Catrin, OK?"

Catrin understood; recognize rank and authority in the

presence of others.

"We are heading up to Llanrwst to get you familiar with your supposed grandmother's territory and build your background. And it will give us a chance to talk about the case."

Catrin looked at DI Powys. He was in his late-forties, she thought, and looked a little overweight. But he certainly looked a Welshman. He was driving expertly up Llandegai Road to join the main A5 road heading into Snowdonia.

"Thank God you are mixed in with the university crowd on this one," he said. "If it was local, people would be asking if you were taught by their Aunt Mary in primary school."

Catrin laughed. "The closest shave so far is a student on the same floor who comes from Betws-y-Coed."

Dafydd said, "Afterwards I am going to drive you over to Holyhead to see a couple of the routes that Han Yeung possibly took after leaving the ship. And show you some of the nice parts of Wales, Catrin. Do you have any of those in the south?"

Catrin laughed again, "Dafydd, is this going to be a North-South rivalry? We haven't even talked about rugby yet!"

She looked at her watch. Ten minutes and this inspector had put an apprehensive constable completely at ease. Good going.

They discussed the two aspects of their common work; the investigation into Yeung's disappearance and the ACU interest in the possible link to the missing paintings.

"What I don't see," said Powys, "is why Yeung would give up everything for some pictures. Even given an assessment value of two million dollars for the three paintings and the top one worth about eight hundred thousand, I gather, they would be worth much less in the hot art market. Still a lot of money, I know, but hardly worth giving up a life and career for, I would think.

"His father came for a week, you know. He said while he was here that his son loved the job on the *Manden Serenity* and was proud to be a qualified ship's officer. It doesn't tie in, somehow, for me."

Catrin nodded. She was trying to remain open-minded without any evidence one way or another but intuitively she was coming to same viewpoint as expressed by DI Marshall; the man had run into trouble but what and why, they had to find out.

Three-quarters of an hour later as they entered the town of Llanrwst Dafydd stated talking about its history, the people there, the tourism growth. "This is the road your grandma lives on," he said, "just be vague about the number if you have to talk about it."

Catrin was absorbing it all.

"You know it quite well, then?" she said.

"I know all these places around here a little. Been a policeman in this part of the world for twenty years so can't help but do so. I once arrested a man from a small village close by here, just up this road. He killed a drinking mate in a fight on the way back from the pub. Both were out of their minds, people said. We went to his house and he was sitting there in a stupor. He had no memory of it. The shock on his face when we got through to him that his friend was dead.

"Who killed him?" he said.

"According to witnesses, you did, Hugh," I told him. "He just fell apart."

'Yes," said Catrin. "They are hard to deal with."

"You too?" asked Dafydd.

"Two and a half years in Brixton and Lambeth. Yes, we have incidents like that, not necessarily homicide but grievous bodily harm and assault, a lot. Now it's the drugs more than the booze that does it."

10 WELCOME WEEK

It was when she was Skyping home to family and friends that Li felt the enormity of the decision she had made. Before she left for England she had carefully shown her father the Skype tool on the home desktop. The relief and nervousness on his face while adjusting settings after she connected the first couple of times showed his discomfort with the technology and revealed, despite her mother's smiles, her anxiety in having her remaining child so far away. Not just anywhere away but in the same part of the world that her other child had disappeared a little over four months ago.

It had been the hardest part in making the decision. "I know Jian Li must return to her studies," she said, "but does it have to be 'There'. Why not here or Australia or..."

Anywhere other than Europe, she meant; anywhere other than moving to the part of the world where Han had disappeared.

Her father, however, saw the importance of Li's decision. After all, he had spent over a week in the area unable to help but part of him not wanting to leave in case some news came.

"So you will go to see the policeman I met, Li," said her father anxiously. "It would be useful to make the contact."

"It took me a day or two after arrival just to begin to feel that I could move around with a clear head, Dad, so I did not want to call the police until I felt up to it. And it is so different, as you say, so even now I am still adjusting. But I telephoned his office and he called me back. He has the local simcard number that I gave you, too. He will see me this week; we have an appointment."

"Good," said her father, glancing sideways at her mother. "Perhaps he will have some news."

Li said nothing in response. Inspector Powys had not hinted at anything on the brief phone call.

"Let me tell you about my new study course and where I will go for lectures. And about the students on the same floor of the residence I am living in."

~~

The small group of first year students emerging from the Harp Inn on Bangor High Street were boisterous but were not visibly drunk or in any way misbehaving, Li thought. She saw one with the 'pub guide' list printed as part of the Welcome Week materials.

She had participated herself in the opening events of the university week and had emerged with a bag printed with the University logo, an array of print materials, several guidebooks and many invitations to join university clubs and societies. The only booths she had lingered over were the Chinese Society and the Sailing Club, both of which she joined.

It was the expressions on the two local women outside the neighbouring church hall as the students passed by that resonated with Li, a mix of expectation and irritation. They were speaking Welsh so she had no idea what they were saying but she could read the message on their faces; the students are back, it is going to be noisy and disruptive, but at least they spend money here.

Li walked down the High Street through the shopping area, seeing the Debenhams and Marks & Spencer stores across the road. Coming out of Debenhams carrying a backpack and a shopping bag was Catrin Sayer, the woman in the next room at Gwynant. She had spoken to her a few times since the session with the floor warden and she seemed friendly, but Li knew she must be working very hard. Li wasn't sure if she should ask about her grandmother, not wanting to be impolite, but equally feeling unsure of the social customs here.

She had seen a poster from Aberystwyth on her wall as she passed Catrin's room - it looked a nice place. In their introduction as floor mates she had said she had only just come up from there, was in the process of finishing her thesis and getting it submitted. Li felt that Catrin was even more transient than herself, with her own one-year exchange course arrangements.

Li waved at her and Catrin crossed over.

"Hi Li, how are you? Finding your way around OK?"

"Yes, thank you." She hesitated. "It is different, but I am settling in. I want to buy an electric kettle and some other items."

"Well, do you need a hand in choosing them? I was just heading back to Gwynant but I am in no rush. I could help."

"No, please, I do not wish to delay you, but thank you," Li said immediately, "I know you are busy writing and I am not sure what I want yet."

She smiled again and entered the store.

Catrin had worked out the intercept to meet up with Li and had hoped for more. There was a limit on how often she could bump into her. As she walked back up Penrallt Road she wondered if the quick selection of a Ph.D. student identity had been sound; Parry should have realized the gulf between undergraduates and postgraduate students coupled with the polite reserve of Chinese people for strangers would make a 'good opening' a little difficult. Hopefully some communication bridge would be built soon. Catrin was even thinking about joining the sailing club.

Apart from the meeting with DI Dafydd Powys, Catrin had immersed herself into being around the hall of residence, walking to the library and other places where it would be likely that Jian Li Yeung would come across her, rather than Catrin be seen to be following her. She had got into conversation with Li but Catrin was sensitive to the need not to overdo that, either, it had to develop naturally.

She had met with Professor Parry once, at his home in Upper Bangor, mentioning to Gwyn Roberts she was visiting the professor who had arranged things with Professor Llewellyn from Aberystwyth, all part of building her cover. Parry lived with his sister, also a professor at the university. She was away on sabbatical in California currently, it turned out. Catrin thought it was politic to accept his invitation, given his consulting role with the Met, but it was not useful, despite Parry's repeated offer to help in whatever way he could.

She saw several paintings, good ones, that he had collected over the years and his knowledge of the painters involved and his passion for Eastern European art was evident. His sister was an oceanographer; her photographs on display in the home contrasted with his but the atmosphere of two academics sharing a house came through very clearly.

It was one of the new students called Thomas who unwittingly broke the ice between Catrin and Li. He came into the kitchen early the following evening with two other students saying, "Who is for the pub? We are thinking of a little preparatory, let me repeat that, preparatory imbibing before we go to see people in Reichel." He smiled, looking expectant. Reichel was another student residence.

"I will go just for one drink at the pub, Tom." replied Macharia, the African student.

"Thank you but no, I won't go," said Li.

It must have been Catrin's expression as much as what she said that set Thomas off. "I don't drink Tom, but thanks anyway."

"Well, you don't have to booze it up, you can come along and have a drink though, be sociable, Catrin."

"I don't drink alcohol at all. And I don't hang around people getting drunk either," Catrin said, deliberately putting a distinct hardness into her tone.

The atmosphere became uncomfortable instantly. Tom said, "Okay, okay," and he and his small group left. Others left for their rooms.

Catrin looked at Li, who was the only one left. "Sorry. I was a bit hard there, but I don't drink because my mother is an alcoholic. She is recovered now but I have seen the bad side of it and… it is hard for me to be around people getting drunk. I found that at Aberystwyth too. I don't want to take the risk of getting drunk myself, that's all, ending up like my mother was."

She wasn't sure how the confidence she had shared would be received by Yeung, but she needed to break through somehow and she actually felt good saying something truthful to her for a change.

She added, "I like meals in pubs and don't mind others having a drink... so if you want to go explore some time, I would be happy to go with you."

She got up, starting to head for her room and was hoping for a response when Li said, "So can we go now - for a coffee or tea instead?"

In the café bar in Upper Bangor they talked for a while about why Catrin had chosen art history at school, about her family and then, in a lull, Li said, "You know, I have only been here a week. It's so different and lonely, to be honest. I have my friends at home that I Skype with but it's not the same now, even with them. Talking to them makes me realise how far away from home I am."

Catrin nodded sympathetically. "I think it is the same for many of us, Li, whether we come from far away like you or a hundred miles away like me. We have to make new friends.

"But you are Chinese, so inscrutable, true to type, right? Remember when I asked why you would come all the way here from Hong Kong, the answer was 'to continue to study law'. Not 'I want to go sailing off the Welsh coast' or 'see Snowdonia' which now I know about. If I can borrow a car from my relatives, I can take you into Snowdonia, at least."

Li laughed and then said, "I am glad we came tonight. I was concerned about bothering you because of your family situation and the worry with your grandmother. It seemed intrusive."

Catrin thought 'Worsley and Parry and their great ideas'. Instead she talked a little around the fictional grandmother and the way the family was dealing with the stress of it all.

When she stopped talking, Li said, "I understand some of the stress. There is another reason I came to Bangor." She paused. "My older brother disappeared around here four months ago. Yes, I need to continue my studies but this area has been haunting me since my dad came back home from Holyhead, from trying to find him. So I chose to do an international study year here."

Catrin asked, "So are you trying to find him instead, then?"

'I don't know," said Li, "I truly don't know yet what I am doing here other than to be close by in case something new comes up about Han. I have no idea where he is, or where he could be, whether he is alive or dead."

Her eyes were moist. Catrin felt it was not simulated. Li doesn't know where Han is, she concluded. She would email Worsley later.

Li gave Catrin an accurate summary of the information that she already had from her files and talked more about Han; she filled in a lot more about the man than was in the file.

"He was really enjoying it, working on the *Serenity*; both the work and the places he visited. I would get emails, some really funny ones about the antics of the passengers. They could be crazy at times. And he wrote to me about the people he was working with and sent photos of places he visited. You know; all the stuff that he wouldn't share with my parents. They are quite religious and a little... conventional."

"The ship had several bikes for crew use in port and

he would book one to go on rides, to get exercise and a have break from the ship. The ship had stopped for a day at Holyhead before heading to Dublin. Off he went for a ride. Crew members saw him set off but he never came back. He did not respond to calls on his mobile and hasn't been seen since. The ship sailed two hours late after searching for him on board and informing the authorities.

"My dad came over a couple of days later, after the police contacted us and he stayed a week before realising he could do nothing but wait. The police put out an alert for Han and searched the area, but nothing came from the efforts. Then Dad came home and we all just waited - and kept waiting. That was four months ago."

She paused.

"Tomorrow morning I go to the police station to meet the detective leading the case. I have some information I want to show him and hope when we are face-to-face he can also tell me more about what is happening."

Catrin remained looking interested and concerned as the news of new information was floated. Careful she thought. Don't ask.

Instead she said, "I hope it is helpful, for your sake and your parents. Are you OK going to the police station, do you know where it is?"

"Frankly I am a little nervous. I have never been to one before even in Hong Kong and... this is a different country, too. It's been on my mind."

"Would you like me to come with you? I could wait in the reception while you were in with the detective, if you want. We could walk back together, it might help."

Catrin thought she would get the response 'I don't want to trouble you' again.

Li said, "Would you? I think I could sleep better if you

did." She sounded quite relieved.

"I'd be delighted," said Catrin.

11 BANGOR POLICE STATION

Bangor Police Station stands on Ffyor Gwynedd, a low stone building on a road on the other side of the A5 main road from the University. Li and Catrin had walked down the hill to it together mainly in silence.

While Catrin had been elated to have made the breakthrough she also constantly had to remind herself it was her job to mislead this woman who, she was increasingly convinced, had no ulterior motive in coming here other than to try to find her brother.

Catrin stood back a little after Li had asked at the reception for Inspector Powys, who came along immediately and introduced himself to her.

He invited Li into a meeting room he had reserved and almost as an afterthought said, "Miss Yeung, you can bring your friend with you if you want or she can wait here, as you wish."

Earlier that morning he had listened to Catrin's summary of their discussion and had told her of the way he would approach it.

"If she leaves you outside, I will fill you in later,

perhaps in a call with DCI Worsley."

Li looked at Catrin and nodded. Catrin smiled at her and followed the two of them, trying to look uneasy in a working police station. It actually felt more normal than her life over the past week.

Powys began with a quick summary of the current situation by describing the early efforts to find Han Yeung, most of which he had already covered with her father.

"The only new factual items I can share are that we received an on-board investigation report by the ship security chief and then another report from the New York Harbour Police, who also went on board when it arrived in port. Nothing stood out from these reports to help our enquiries, Miss Yeung."

He was looking through attachments as he spoke.

"We also have a possessions list for your brother, details of his on-board list of purchases and his credit card statements, mobile phone call lists and so on. The only odd thing is that Han bought a print at the art gallery on-board the day before he went cycling. It was in his purchase record but the print wasn't found in his possessions. Neither was his wallet, ship security card, his cycling gear or his watch. Everything else seemed to be there."

He looked at Li as he spoke.

"We placed a trace on the mobile phone, even though it is an overseas number. If it is used, we will be notified. Nothing has been reported yet.

"We have made enquires in the area at hotels, at hospitals and with the Chinese communities in a number of towns in North Wales. There is no trace of your brother other than the early sightings of him as he cycled away. As you know, we conducted a number of searches of the roads and areas around Holyhead during the week your father was here.

"Nor have any other police services around the country given us any indication of his whereabouts, although he is on a national database now.",

Li nodded. She had told Catrin that one of the security staff had seen Han put his key card back in his wallet after they swiped it through the reader to record his exit from the ship. He then put his wallet in his backpack, so she knew he had that with him.

Catrin thought Jian Li was holding up, but was also not that far from tears. Li reached into her bag. "I found this photo, Inspector Powys. It was a bookmark in one of the technical manuals in his belongings returned from the ship."

Catrin looked closer at the photo as Li passed it over to Dafydd. It was a young Chinese man around the same age as Yeung dressed in business casual clothes. He was standing near a stone or sculpture, she saw. She recognized the location; it was in the grounds of the St. Paul's Cathedral in London, but she said nothing.

Dafydd took it, looked at it and read the back. "It says 'Taking a break, regards, Paul', nothing else. Is this a friend of Han's, perhaps from the ship, do you know?"

Li shook her head.

"He is not a person I know. At least not someone I know from Han's contacts in Hong Kong or anyone he emailed me about, but who knows? He had been working for more than a year away from home and he would have made new friends. I thought it might help the investigation, you know, someone perhaps he knew in the UK."

Catrin saw that Dafydd Powys wasn't too energized by

the new piece of information. She looked a little closer again at the capstan-type stone. "A Paul at St. Paul's," she said, "It's the monument to the people of London during World War II, at St. Paul's Cathedral in London."

"You know it?" asked Li. Dafydd just looked at her.

Catrin wasn't sure now whether she should have stimulated the discussion or just reported to Dafydd afterwards, but she had taken the plunge. Part of her role was to build a working relationship with this woman, she told herself. She had worked out her improvisation.

"I was in a school group that went to London when I was fourteen and we visited St. Paul's Cathedral. I have a picture of a bunch of us standing around one side of this monument. Our teacher wouldn't let us sit on it for the photo although other tourists had done so. It wasn't respectful, she said."

In fact, she had twice been on crowd duty at St. Paul's during her time in London and had seen the monument then.

"We will look into this, Miss Yeung," said Dafydd. "Thank you." He kept his voice even, but it was clear from Li's face she had hoped for more energy in his response.

"The other thing is Han's watch," said Li, "It is a Rolex."

"Yes," responded Dafydd without looking at the notes, "a Rolex with a plain steel case and strap, I recall. I said to your father we would also look out for it but Rolexes, while very expensive, are not too uncommon actually. If it was more unique, or had distinguishing marks ..."

Li was reading her own notes. "Yes, Inspector Powys, it is a Rolex. As to distinguishing marks, it is a Rolex Oyster DateJust Calibre 1570 with a light brown face and stainless steel band. It is a vintage watch, perhaps from around 1956, and its serial number is 252479."

She popped her head up and saw David's intense stare. "My dad likes old, good watches and bought this for Han when he graduated from the Academy. It doesn't look fancy, but is worth about $3000 and should be pretty unique around here. If it turns up, that is. I can identify it, if it is found. I was there when Dad gave it to Han. I found the box for it in Han's room at home."

Powys had been noting down the details.

"Well, Miss Yeung, thank you for the information. We now have the serial number so, if it turns up, we will ask you to come in and make a statement about its ownership."

Catrin thought Li was looking a little anxious. "The watch and the photo are all that I can find that is new, I think. I was hoping for more, perhaps, from the police."

Dafydd looked at her and then at Catrin and his voice softened. "Well Li, we are still pursuing enquiries. It is an active investigation, I can assure you. We can't really go into all the steps at present but it is not on the back burner. I assure you that if any news of your brother turns up, no matter how small an item, I will contact you straight away. I do understand how stressful it is for you and your family."

He could see the frustration building in her. "Tell me, was Han particularly interested in art, do you know?"

Li's face showed puzzlement, "Not that I know. Why do you ask?"

Catrin saw Dafydd appearing to review the file although she knew the question was scripted, agreed with Worsley. Asking it revealed their interest in the painting.

"It is just that one witness statement said Han appeared to be carrying a large tube when he rode away, that's all." He looked up at Li. "We thought he might have used the tube to send the print that he bought on the ship or something else he obtained to someone he knew, perhaps."

Li's face gave nothing away, Catrin thought.

She said, "He might have, I suppose. But I am not aware of any specific interest he had in art. And we haven't received anything in the mail that is in a tube, as you describe."

She paused. "I will ask my parents again in case something arrived after I left, but I think they would have told me already and... even surface mail, in four months it would be in Hong Kong by now. They would tell me of anything concerning Han."

"I am sure you're right," said Dafydd.

Catrin was sure that a tube of artwork hadn't arrived in Hong Kong by mail or courier addressed to anyone in the Yeung household. DI Marshall had said it was being monitored.

Dafydd escorted the two women to the reception area and promised to keep in touch with Li.

"Thank you for coming in, Miss Yeung," he said formally and headed back to his office.

The student at the enquiry desk apparently engrossed in a filling in a 'lost or stolen' report about his laptop looked up quickly, seeing a Chinese woman with another person finishing with a detective. 'Now I know where I have heard the name Yeung recently', he thought.

Students take seriously the loss of a laptop, which is why Francis Lloyd was there, but to him following a story lead was also important. He folded the form, put it in his pocket and headed out the door behind them.

~~

As Catrin and Li walked towards the door of Gwynant, they were suddenly approached by another student.

"Miss Yeung?" he asked.

"Yes," said Li.

"I am Francis Lloyd, in Media Studies, but I also write for the Student Union web site as well. I saw you in the police station just now and heard you name. Are you by any chance related to the missing cruise ship officer, Han Yeung?"

"Let's keep walking, Li," said Catrin. The bloody cheek, she thought, he wasn't even proper Press.

But Li stopped. "Yes," she said, "I am. He is my brother." Her face looked confused, unsure what to do.

"Great," said Francis, "So I take it you are here looking for him, right? Is there any news? Are the police doing anything useful, do you think?"

Before Li could answer Catrin said, "Look, she is here to study, just like you, and if you want an interview with my friend do the decent thing and ask her in advance!" She took Li's arm and led her into the building.

"I should have seen that, Catrin," said Li. "Perhaps I should talk to him; perhaps it will help."

"Think about it first, Li, and then decide."

Over my dead body Catrin thought. As soon as she could get to her room she would phone Tom Parry and get Francis Lloyd straightened out. But she called Worsley first.

On hearing the update Worsley said, "It may not be a bad thing for the news to get out. It seems Yeung is not involved in anything other than finding her brother, from what you say. See what she decides on and whether the media student gets back to her, but keep your distance on it, Sayer. You are not there to manage things for Jian Li Yeung.

"But it was a good call on the St. Paul's thing. I think you did the right thing – Dafydd and I talked about it. She may talk more about it with you."

~~

Later that evening, Li knocked on Catrin's door carrying her laptop.

"Can you tell me how to get to the monument in the photo when I get to St. Paul's Cathedral?" she asked.

"Are you thinking of going there, then?" asked Catrin, surprised. Then she added, "It may be nothing, you know, and it's a long way. Whoever Paul is he may have just visited that one time."

Li sat in the easy chair as Catrin returned to her desk. "I can go on Saturday. And perhaps it may not be futile; look."

Catrin leaned forward and looked. The image was a large magnification of the man's shirt front and pocket. It showed a pen bearing a logo, just in focus, of what was obviously St. Paul's Cathedral.

"I had scanned in the photo I gave to the detective and enlarged it. The note on the back said 'taking a break' so perhaps he does work there? I checked the St. Paul's Cathedral web site and then its gift shop on-line. The shop does not sell such pens but, like other gift shops I have been to, such small items are often sold only in the store and are not mentioned on-line. If so, he may use the pen at work.

"I think it should be checked out but I don't think the Welsh police would be interested in doing that."

Catrin could see the resolve in Li's eyes.

"I have asked my dad to let Jenny, she's my friend from City University, search Han's laptop for any more pictures of this man. She is very good with computers and told me she would do it if my parent's agreed. Jenny will let me know what she finds. I didn't see anything when I looked through it myself before I left."

Catrin said nothing. It never occurred that the computer the missing man had on board with him was not with one of the police authorities involved.

12 ST. PAUL'S CATHEDRAL

The teleconference the following morning between Worsley, Powys and Catrin did not begin well.

"They let his laptop go back to the family?" said Jane Worsley. "I don't believe it."

"Apparently so," said Dafydd. "It was released by Manden Security to New York Harbour Police on arrival there and then sent back to Hong Kong two months ago. Our file record has a NYHP entry saying 'nothing of interest related to the investigation was found'. We didn't question that at the time."

Catrin was wondering why Dafydd Powys' team had not picked this up previously and requested access. There were too many cooks at the pot, she concluded, with the various jurisdictions dealing with this cruise ship issue.

Worsley said, "So what now?"

Catrin jumped in. "Well, it is Thursday, ma'am. Saturday she wants to go herself. Unless you want others to do a search today or tomorrow at St. Paul's for this man 'Paul', I can go with her."

"And how will you work that?"

"I told her I had some discount vouchers for rail travel that were due to expire and that I know the way in London on the Tube. I could see she didn't want to bother me, saying that she thought I went to see my grandmother at weekends ... but I could see she liked the idea, too. All I have to do is press it home."

Worsley said, "Dafydd, it is sounding to me from the reports from Catrin and your recent interview that Jian Li Yeung is not involved in this theft issue, she is just looking for her brother. It may be too early to be sure but that is the way it is looking to me right now."

"Agreed, ma'am," replied Dafydd.

"Let's work it on Saturday. I will get Aina to do a quick check on employees listed to be working at St. Paul's Cathedral and email you if she discovers a Chinese person called Paul. If we do and find any flags we'll go ahead and pull him in. I don't want this Yeung girl in harm's way at all. If not, let's keep the cover intact.

"Catrin, if this is a wild goose chase use the time to build the relationship with Yeung and we will give your undercover role a little while longer. Even if she is in the clear she may provide more information that could help in some way. But if the trip gives access to either this man Paul, to Han Yeung himself or to the paintings, call it in and we'll take them in. I'll talk with Keith so he or I will be available on Saturday, perhaps we both can be. Any questions?"

"I need some vouchers or a discount card for the train... or something, ma'am. I have the student image to protect, particularly if this is, as you say, a wild goose chase."

Worsley smiled. "Dafydd, send a PC round to Bangor station and sort it out, will you?"

Powys said, "It's all done on-line now but we will fix

it. Forging discount travel cards is just up our street. We even arrested one of Catrin's fellow students for the same thing a few years ago. He had quite a little business going."

~~

Catrin was up early on Friday getting her breakfast in the kitchen when Gwyn Powell came in.

"Catrin, have you seen the Union web site this morning?"

"No. Why?"

"It has a report by a student saying Li is related to a man who went missing in Holyhead and she is working with the police to help find him. That's why she is here. You are her friend now, it seems, so I thought I would mention it to you as well as to her."

Catrin just stared. "We'd better go and talk to Li."

Li and Catrin read the article together on her laptop.

'Bangor student linked to the mystery of the disappearing cruise ship officer. I was in the police station dealing with another crime, the theft of my laptop, when I spotted a fellow student Jian Li Yeung, Third Year Law, finishing a meeting with detectives.

'Remember back to the end of last term, if you were here? An officer on a cruise ship went missing in Holyhead. He rode off on his bike but no trace of him has been found. His name is Yeung too. I posed the question to Jian Li whether she was related to him and was here to pursue the disappearance of this man. She confirmed Han Yeung is her brother but she declined to be interviewed at present.

"Hopefully more will be revealed in due course and the brother and sister will be reunited.

Francis Lloyd, Media Studies.'

As they read the article an email popped up on Li's computer, copied to her and others on their floor. Gwyn Roberts had written to Francis Lloyd, saying that if Francis was found in Gwynant other than by invitation he would be ejected with all appropriate speed; it was a residential property and was not public access for reporters.

"He could get into trouble for that if Francis complains," said Li, sounding like a lawyer, "if it is interpreted as a threat. That is also against the rules."

"I don't think Gwyn cares, Li," said Catrin.

Li had left a note prominently displayed in the kitchen that she would like to talk with the floor at 5.00 p.m. if people were available. Some, but not all, came along. She was intense and nervous when Gwyn Powell said, "I think this is all, Li."

"I am sorry I did not mention this issue of my brother before it appeared on the Student Union web site. But I am here to study, you need to know that. I was going to stay in Hong Kong but when my brother Han went missing and Dad came back after a week, he said how hard it was to deal with things here, with the worry of Han's disappearance, the jet lag and everything being so foreign for him... you know what I mean?

"I miss my brother, so I thought I would study here for a year as an international student, to be available if something turns up about Han. I will then finish my course at home in Hong Kong, close to my parents. At least I will have studied abroad.

"I am not here under false pretences, which the article could infer. Thank you."

She stopped.

Several people started to speak at once and quiet Andrea cut across them all.

"Li, you just need to know we are here for you, not to question you. You have a lot on your plate besides your studies, it seems, so if we can help, let any of us know. OK?"

She walked over and gave her a hug then Catrin heard her whisper, "I am praying for you and Han."

It's strange how fast a floor bonds together, thought Catrin, remembering her first year at Aberystwyth. Somehow she wasn't feeling so good herself about her role at present.

~~

The ride to London on Saturday was uneventful. It was direct, without changing trains. Li and Catrin talked a little about the places they were going through. Li worked on her iPad for much of the way and Catrin typed away on her Mac, catching up with friends or fiddling with the draft thesis. Li had printed out some copies of the photograph of Paul, the close-up of the pen and she also had photos of Han.

From Euston Station Catrin led Li to the Tube starting on the Northern Line, heading down to the Tottenham Court Road station and then east on the Central Line to St. Paul's Tube Station. As they came out of the exit Catrin could see the tension building in Li.

"Remember Li, he could just live or work around here, not at the cathedral at all. He may have just bought or been given the pen, so don't build your hopes up too much. But we can find out, I hope."

They walked down Payner Alley towards the cathedral

and Li just stopped and stared. Her first time seeing St. Paul's, Catrin realized, recalling her own first visit. She just waited.

"It's big," said Li, awed, "If we do not find this Paul, then I am still glad I came. It is beautiful. Where shall we go to ask?"

They began in the cathedral gardens, looking for staff. Then they went into the cathedral itself looking for anyone Chinese in the main dome area, without success. Catrin said, "Let's go back around to the gift shop entrance. They will definitely have shop staff working there we can ask. If not we will go inside and find a member of the clergy to help us."

Cho was working on opening new inventory in the storeroom of the Gift Shop when Jimmy popped his head in. "Paul, you lucky man, there are two young ladies here to see you at the desk."

"Jim, I am doing some re-stocking. I know it's busy so I will…."

"No they want you. One has a photo of you. They must know you or something."

Cho came out into the shop; it was busy. It was like this every day with the cathedral being a constant visitor attraction. Two women, one Chinese the other a blonde European, were looking at him.

The Chinese woman spoke to him in Cantonese, "Are you Paul?" she said, holding up the photo.

"Yes," Cho responded in the same language, "I am called Paul here but my name is Cho Zhou; and you are Jian Li, I have seen your photo. Do you have any news of Han?"

He saw the expressions on both women's faces and said in English, "We must speak English, my Cantonese does not have a good accent, I know."

He said to Catrin, "I am Cho Zhou, but I use the name Paul as Cho sounds so like Joe here and I don't want to be called Joe."

I don't care what you want to be called, thought Catrin, we have found you.

Li was looking like she didn't know where to begin so Catrin asked, "How do you know Han, her brother?"

"He is my friend," he said and in doing so, in the tone in his voice and his expression, it became clear to Catrin that this man was perhaps more than Han's friend. Cho had the voice and mannerisms of some other gay men she had met, the sort parodied or ridiculed at times.

She looked at Li and saw that she was absorbing it too and it looked as she had only just realised that her brother may be gay.

"We need to talk to you," said Catrin.

"Yes, but I am working now unfortunately, so perhaps at my break or can we meet after my shift is finished?"

Li suddenly said, with emotion, "We have come all the way from Bangor!"

Cho looked lost.

Catrin said, "Who is the manager?"

Cho pointed at Jim, the man they had first approached with the photo.

"Leave it to me," said Catrin.

She went over to the manager and talked a few moments as Cho asked Li, "Have you heard from Han yet?"

"No, I hoped to find you from this picture and ask you that. We have heard nothing for four months," she said. Then she added, "I don't know who you are. How do you know my brother?"

"We met on shore, I was a guest on the ship and Han

was out shopping in the same place I was." He paused, uncertain how to go on.

Catrin came back. "We can talk in the store room." She was closing a call on her mobile phone, Li noticed.

Cho led them in the room and they just stood there.

Catrin asked, "Do you know where Han Yeung is?"

Cho shook his head.

Then she asked, "Tell me, did Han send you a poster or a painting in a tube?"

"Yes, he did, a Magritte print. How did you know?"

"Where is it and where is the tube it came in?"

Li was looking at Catrin, wondering where all this was coming from.

Cho looked at Catrin also and said, "Why do you want to know? I want to know where Han is and what has happened?"

Catrin said, "I am a police officer. Please answer my question." She had taken out her warrant card and was holding it for Cho to see. He looked surprised.

"It's in my room, at home. The Magritte print is on the wall. The tube is under the bed as I haven't found a use for it yet. My niece wanted to make something from it but I said no."

Li's face showed her surprise too.

Catrin turned to Li and said, "Li, I am a Metropolitan Police officer working with Inspector Powys but I am also involved in a search for missing art works that may be linked to Han's disappearance. So we are going to wait here and I am going to ask you two not to talk to each other at this time. Police cars are on their way here. We are all heading over to Scotland Yard."

She looked at Li trying to quell the feeling of betrayal of trust she felt; the feeling she saw so clearly reflected on the Chinese woman's face.

13 SCOTLAND YARD

On arrival at the Yard Catrin had watched Jian Li Yeung and Cho Zhou being taken to separate rooms as she was met by DI Marshall.

"Let's go to Jane's office. She is in, too and we want to debrief you before we talk to either of them. But I just need to speak to Zhou briefly first."

He disappeared for a few minutes while Catrin waited. When he reappeared he called a uniform officer over, giving some instructions. "Mr. Zhou has agreed to let us collect the print and tube from his room at his parent's home so we don't need a warrant; which is a good sign regarding him, I think, but we will see. We are sending a patrol car and a SOCO over now."

The Scene of Crime Officer would deal with the retrieval of the print and the tube it was sent in.

"After debrief, DCI Worsley will see Yeung; we will interview Zhou." Marshall said.

Back in the ACU area Marshall asked Catrin for her room key and student ID and questioned whether any of her belongings were elsewhere in Bangor; in a sports locker, perhaps? She shook her head, suddenly realizing that her role in Bangor was over. With it, she then realised, so was her role with the Art Crime Unit.

"A female PC from Dafydd's unit will pack up your things, they will be couriered here this evening."

He looked at her carefully. "This is what undercover work is like. It's hard."

"Yes. I am beginning to see that, sir."

Marshall said, "Catrin, in a sense, you have been thrown off the deep end. You were placed undercover without any opportunity to settle into the team you're working with here. And you were in your role for well over a week, continuously. Your emotions are probably on a rollercoaster ride. Am I right?"

"Yes", said Catrin, suddenly glad that he understood so clearly. "You have -."

"Oh yes, I know exactly how it feels, believe me."

He suddenly got very businesslike. "Let's go in and see DCI Worsley before we interview Zhou."

~~

Cho was looking worried as the two police officers entered. They had kept him quite a while. He had been given tea and water and had been escorted when he went to the bathroom but, other than the police inspector's request, he had been left alone in this interview room for well over an hour.

They identified themselves for the record and Catrin observed Keith Marshall take Cho Zhou through a series of questions about his relationship with Han Yeung, how they met and how often, covering events up to the point of the receipt of the tube in the mail.

Cho was openly gay. He and a friend had taken a

cruise on the *Manden Serenity* and had a bad argument one evening. On a walk by himself in the port the following day he had recognized Han, whom he had noticed on the ship in his fine uniform. Han was in casual clothes, shopping. That is how it began.

"He shouldn't have mixed with me, Han being a member of staff, me being a passenger, but I approached him and started talking, then offered him a coffee. We hit it off. I really liked him and so we arranged to meet next time his ship was in Dover. That is when we became lovers."

He looked at the two officers, gauging their openness - and got nowhere.

"It wasn't his first time but he was not experienced. He fell for me and I loved his company but…."

He stopped.

"It didn't work?" said Keith, reading Cho's expression.

"We met in London, then in Barcelona. I once went to meet him on a stopover in Jersey, but all these were just one or two days. He wanted desperately to find a way for us to be together more, but he knew his career choice wouldn't allow it, particularly as he couldn't come out in the open about us. He was very scared of that, of his parents finding out."

Catrin thought of Jean and how hard she struggled until she told people she was gay, when to Catrin and other friends it was obvious. She was happy that Jean and Melanie made it through that.

Cho continued, "All junior officers with the Manden Line get nine months on ship duty, three months off on leave. When Han had his long leave he returned to Hong Kong for almost all of it. It was too expensive and too difficult for me to go there. His parents are very Christian, old school, you know. So I missed him and realized not only that it wouldn't work, but I would need to be the one to force the breakup."

"We met only twice after he came back from leave, the last time before he went to Paris to start this last trip."

"So you didn't go to Holyhead?"

"No, we had finished by then; it was over. There is a note from him with the Magritte; I stuck it on the back. You can see when you get it. It is even dated, telling you when it was sent."

Keith Marshall then asked about Cho's interest in art. In a matter of moments the interview became a discussion of styles, artists, galleries that she would have found in any bar or common room in an art college or university. DI Marshall knew his stuff, she realized, and she saw why Han, who had no interest in art himself, would consider a Magritte a suitable parting gift; Cho loved Surrealism in particular and the art scene in London was his passion.

Marshall then brought the interview right back to point by opening a folder.

"Do you know this man?"

He led Cho through a series of photographs of men and women carefully watching and listening to his negative response to each query. Catrin had no idea who they were.

"And why didn't you come forward when he went missing?"

Cho said, "I only found out about it when I went on the internet later. I hadn't got an email back from him to my very polite 'thank you' email for the print. We kept our emails quite 'neutral', you see. I did a search on where the Serenity was then and the article came up."

Keith said, "We have already checked your alibi and it appears you weren't away from London at the time he disappeared. But you have lied to the police once in this case, haven't you? That could become a problem for you, you know."

Cho looked upset.

Keith went on. "Your mobile phone was in the list of contacts on Han Yeung's mobile; we have just checked back. A detective contacted you in early August in a routine follow-up once we had Mr. Yeung's phone records. The file just says you knew him through a mutual friend who worked for the Manden line and occasionally you would talk to him, give him advice on places to buy things or how to get around, but that you didn't know him very well."

"I didn't want the detective to know about us, that was all. I am sorry."

"And you say he didn't come to see you after Holyhead. So I don't see why you didn't come forward to the police when you knew he had gone missing, frankly."

Cho looked steadily at Catrin, "How long did it take for you to spot I was gay?"

"And you?" he said, looking at Keith. "How quickly would it have become obvious to her parents, if they got to know about me? Just look at how his sister reacted."

"It was respect for his wishes. And I don't know anything about his disappearance to help anyway. So why should I become visible on this and perhaps hurt his family?" He was getting emotional, angry.

Then it was over. Cho Zhou was asked to wait and Keith noted for the record that the interview was terminated and nodded to Catrin that they should leave the interview room.

"What do you think?" he asked.

"I have to say my answer is based on both the

interview and the time spent with Jian Li Yeung. Both Zhou and Yeung are uninvolved with the theft, I think, as is Han Yeung. He simply picked up a packing tube that I think contains a painting, somehow, and sent it to his friend. It was the wrong tube, for all involved, really. I think somehow the disappearance was spotted quickly and the criminals got on to Han by some means or other – I don't know how, given that probably the only person involved was on the ship in Holyhead, the person who was hiding the paintings."

"Sayer, I agree with you, almost. We'll let Cho go. We have the tube now and I will tell him we will return the print.

"And we will be sending Jian Li Yeung back to Bangor. She's got a lot to assimilate, her brother being gay and in a relationship. On top of that she will now realise that we suspected he might be involved in an art theft - and that we were trying to establish if she was involved, too. I think it is only fair to her that we clear away that cloud. I know Jane is trying to do that right now."

He took out his mobile and made a call. Catrin realised he was talking to Worsley and probably that she was still with Li. He turned his back and walked away a few steps after a moment and she heard that he and Worsley were sorting out a difference of opinion. He closed the phone and came back.

"The thing I don't agree with you on in your analysis is that the only person 'in the know' in Holyhead was the courier on board. He or she may have had other works than the Komarov paintings to deliver and perhaps Holyhead was also a collection point. It is a minor port, quiet, low key and members of this ring could have come into Holyhead for that purpose from anywhere. Han may have walked – no cycled – straight into trouble with criminals who were already there to pick up another stolen work.

"And you are to go back to Worsley's office and collect Yeung, see her to the train, have a meal, whatever. I think you need closure with her and you won't get that by a formal goodbye in an office in Scotland Yard."

So that's what he had been arguing over. Keith Marshall started to go up in her estimation. His analysis of the situation was further along than hers and he clearly wasn't simply a 'Yes, ma'am' for Worsley.

"Catrin, you will report back here on Monday morning and complete a report on the time in Bangor. DCI Worsley has cleared it with Ian Anderson. You did well these last few days and she is bringing your interview for the position here into next week."

"That's great!" said Catrin. She suddenly realised that her efforts in Bangor had been recognized and she would still be working with the ACU at least into next week.

Marshall continued, "It will depend on Superintendent Taylor's calendar. He insists on sitting in on the interview and, I shouldn't tell you this, but he vetoed an earlier applicant before Worsley brought you in. He's no push-over."

"I can't believe a superintendent is taking so much interest in the appointment of a DC." said Catrin.

"Catrin, the Art Crime Unit is his baby – it is a small team, but it reports directly to him and …."

He stopped.

"Look, when you finish with Yeung, give me a call. Let's meet for a drink… but off-duty and totally off the record, got me? I think you need to know more background. And perhaps I need to tell you how to prepare for Taylor. So give me call."

"Yes, sir," she said. Then she headed for the stairs and

took a deep breath before facing up to Jian Li Yeung. She needed to move on, she knew.

~~

"It's a lot to absorb, Catrin," Li said, "You being a police officer, Han being gay and having a lover and this painting business."

They were in the food court at Euston Railway Station, eating. Li had about forty minutes before her train. Apparently Worsley had insisted that they send her back First Class. Her fare would have included a dinner on board if it was a weekday but not on a Saturday, so she was eating now. Catrin was drinking tea and picking listlessly at a small salad. She suspected that she would be eating with Keith Marshall in a while and didn't want to arrive already full.

"What is the worst aspect, I think for me, is the news that Han was not involved in this art thing," Li mused. "That may seem strange but perhaps if he had been he would be hidden somewhere, hiding from you. But now I know there was a crime involved I am sure he is dead. He got caught up in this by accident."

Catrin just looked. She knew she couldn't tell Li more than Worsley had chosen to share and she had nothing to rebut about her analysis.

"We are still investigating his disappearance, Li."

Li had been in Jane Worsley's office talking intently to her, Catrin saw, as she returned from the interview with Cho Zhou and knocked on the door. Li's back was to the glass partition. Catrin had wondered when she would get to talk with her alone.

One of the first things that happened when Catrin

entered was the DCI's comment to Li.

"Constable Sayer was doing her job, Li. If you feel deceived by her, remember that. We had to pursue all lines of enquiry, as I have explained, and we are trying our best to find your brother."

Li had stood up and had taken the high ground, "Thank you Chief Inspector Worsley, you have been very clear and I am glad I now know more about the investigation. At least I am now not under suspicion, I hear, even if we are no closer to finding out more about my brother's disappearance. And I am glad you now think he wasn't involved in this art smuggling either."

Worsley had turned to Catrin. "DC Sayer, please assist Jian Li in getting out of here and back to the train. You probably want to talk." Her face showed that she wasn't too happy about that aspect.

In the station Li was sipping her tea as she finished her meal. "What was more important, can I ask, the stolen paintings or my brother?"

Her tone was neutral now and had been since Worsley's office, not unfriendly or resentful but not now having the trust or any sense of friendship. There was a distance between them. Catrin felt it would be a loss for Li; she was already feeling it herself.

"Other officers in the Met were already working on the theft of the paintings before Han disappeared. That is when the Art Crime Unit got involved. The primary focus for us is to find Han or find out what happened to him. And you know that is what I want to do, just like you."

Li said, "But they are linked."

Catrin saw she was thinking of something.

"Can I tell the Gwyn's and the others?"

"Yes; about me. And that my presence was part of the

investigation into Han's disappearance, but I wouldn't mention the art issues," said Catrin. "And tell them I enjoyed their company and wish them well and that I was doing my job… and I really liked the way the floor was becoming so friendly."

Catrin had choked up delivering the sentence and wiped her eyes, then she searched for a tissue and blew her nose. Thank God Keith Marshall wasn't here, she thought.

Li smiled. Something had clearly sorted itself out in her mind.

"I'll tell Little Gwyn that you will arrest him for issuing dark threats to Francis Lloyd."

They both laughed, the tension lifting a little.

Later, as Catrin walked Li towards the train platform entrance Li said, "I guess this is it? We can't really stay in touch, can we?"

Catrin smiled ruefully, "It's probably for the best, at least, under the present circumstances. But I won't forget you and, who knows? I have your email and…"

"Probably a lot more information about me than you could tell me," Li said. She shook hands with Catrin politely then headed down the platform.

Catrin stood for a moment, lost in thought. Then, snapping out of it, she took out her phone and rang Keith Marshall's number.

14 THE QUEENS LARDER

Detective Inspector Keith Marshall was still in his suit when he came into the pub 'The Queens Larder' just south of Euston Road at 7.00 p.m. that Saturday evening. It was obvious he had come straight from the office and he still looked fresh.

Living half-way across London and not having any opportunity to change after seeing Li off, Catrin was still in her student clothes. She looked worn out. Keith bought a pint of beer and a large club soda with lime for Catrin. They decided to eat.

"It's been a long day, sir," she said. "It's hard to think I was in Bangor this morning."

Keith smiled. "We won't be long, then you can head home, but I wanted to fill you in on the Art Crime Unit. Frankly we need another body working with us. Jane Worsley and I are up to our eyes in casework and I think you would be a good fit from what I see. If I am asked, I will say that, but really I have little input in this, right?"

"Ok," said Catrin, "And thanks."

"So there are three things I want to go through; the

De Marr affair, which gave rise to our unit; why Jack Taylor is so close to our action when he has much bigger serious crime teams to manage and my advice, for what it is worth, on how you may want to prepare for the interview."

"I've read a bit about the De Marr matter," said Catrin.

"The media got part of it right. This time the outrage was appropriate," said Keith.

He took a long pull on his beer. "Peter De Marr is a crooked art dealer. The Art & Antiques Unit arrested him for his role in handling and selling a stolen painting that came from a robbery in Lincolnshire. He is still in prison in Chelmsford but will be free on parole in less than a year - as light a sentence as you could ask for under the circumstances, given he has prior record."

He paused. "Peter De Marr is also the person who set up the burglary for the painting, one of several that were stolen that night. He provided the thief, Ian Grant, with the firearm and he was instrumental in a number of earlier similar robberies. He went down only for the single painting this time, a wrist slap."

The burglary had been front page news. The Templeton couple who were robbed had the tragic coincidence of losing a son and having a daughter crippled within the same week. Templeton was a retired army officer. Their son Andrew was with the Royal Anglians, his father's old regiment.

The son had been killed in a roadside bomb incident in Iraq around the same time as their daughter Sarah, a nurse, had come home from her night shift early with a migraine. She arrived around 3.30 a.m. and disturbed Grant in the act of stealing some of her parent's paintings. She screamed, he panicked and shot her. The parents were at the hospital waiting to hear the outcome of her surgery when the news of their son came in.

The media, the public and various Members of Parliament called for a whole life sentence for Grant; the incident and the trial received a lot of media coverage. He got fifteen years, Catrin recalled.

Marshall continued, "The reason that Ian Grant stayed quiet about the source of the firearm, other than saying he had never used one before and 'it went off in his hand' or some such crap, was the deal A&A struck with De Marr and, we think, a lot of money changing hands from De Marr to Grant. You know Detective Chief Inspector Neville Coltrane?"

"Of him," said Catrin, "he is the head of the Art & Antiques Unit."

"Coltrane knew that De Marr had a lot more to tell on stolen art they were interested in. We had grounds to believe that De Marr was in much deeper in the Templeton case but, to be fair, not quite how much. Coltrane wanted information on other paintings and was prepared to reach a deal with De Marr and his lawyer."

"You were in A&A then, sir?" asked Catrin.

"I was there for four years; a detective sergeant." He went on. "Freeman, he was my DI, and I both thought that DCI Coltrane arranged the deal with De Marr prematurely. We objected because we thought he should go down as an accessory to attempted murder, as we were sure De Marr set the robbery up, but at the time we had no evidence. We didn't know then that he supplied the weapon. Our concerns were overridden, the deal was struck. When the full story came out the Prosecutions Service had to stick to the deal although by then it stuck in their craw too.

"Freeman took early retirement in disgust and I

applied to get out, to transfer to Serious Crimes Command. The media had got a hold of the involvement of De Marr in planning the robbery but not the gun aspect. If that had surfaced it would have become a major issue for the Met.

"Then Superintendent Taylor called me telling me to 'hold steady' and he passed back my transfer request form. He asked me to wait a while. He planned to do something about this, he said. So I waited and... here I am."

Catrin said, "So that's why Taylor formed the Art Crime Unit within his control in the Serious Crimes area, outside Specialist Crime Command."

Their meal was arriving. Keith moved his beer and napkin out of the way and said, "Yes, with the ACU in place now A&A can't cut deals of the sort they did with De Marr. As soon as some other element to the crime than theft or forgery appears we get a look at it and, if it is serious enough, we follow it up.

"But how Taylor set up the ACU will show why he treats it like his first born - and why he is so careful about who is in it."

~~

The meeting of senior staff to make a decision on the proposal was now folklore in inner circles. 'Jack Taylor had lost it and would get roasted' was the general opinion circulating in the days before it was to be discussed at the Structural Review Committee's quarterly meeting.

Assistant Commissioner Sandra Hunt had the invidious job of chairing the Structural Review Committee for a three-year term, with its membership of two Commanders and four Chief Superintendents. Small in number but a powerful decision body in the Met, it did the main 'high level' work of balancing and rebalancing resources, approving new operating units and canning old ones.

At the quarterly meetings, Divisions and Units affected by each agenda item had their champions or executioners brought in as the agenda item came up. Any unit getting new staff or approval were delighted, but they forgot about it over time; the people in any unit losing resources or getting closed down remembered it until it became enshrined; and they remembered who had made the decision. For the senior staff involved on the committee, they knew they would win temporary friends and permanent enemies within their own ranks; it went with the role.

Specialist units were particularly vulnerable as their champion moved on or retired. So in times of tightening budgets they held tight and flew beneath the radar if they could. Jack Taylor's proposal for a new specialist unit apparently overlapping the work of another 'prima donna', Art & Antiques, was seen as exploitation of the De Marr debacle or idiocy, depending on your viewpoint. But obviously, everyone knew, it wasn't going to fly.

Superintendent Taylor had an earlier item to speak to on the agenda, on the planned rearrangements in West End Serious Crime Units, so he had been invited to stay at the table afterwards. Finding Jack Taylor seated already was no surprise to DCI Neville Coltrane when he was brought in for Agenda Item 7, 'New proposals, Part (ii), Art Crime Unit within Serious Crime Command'.

They went through the discussion very civilly. Coltrane was convinced it would be an item of half an hour or less and then it would slide into obscurity. 'Marks for innovative thinking, but…' would do nicely, he hoped.

Taylor went through his proposal in a matter-of-fact manner. He wanted to establish a small unit headed by a Detective Inspector, with a Detective Sergeant and a Detective Constable with different ages and experience profiles. The team's role would be to fill the gap between the investigative paths that the A&A followed and those pursued by the regional crime squads. It would focus on catching criminals linked to art crimes, not the recovery of art itself. Like the A&A, it would liaise nationally.

"Too many art-related crime leads are being dropped if they diverge from the art itself," Taylor said, avoiding looking at Coltrane. "The A&A mandate is to recover stolen art and put the thieves or forgers away, not deal with these peripheral issues. If a regional unit doesn't pick up this element of the case, or if it covers several jurisdictions or police services each with their own priority lists, it can easily slip away."

What was needed, he said, was a small team with a national oversight that could work at one end with A&A and, at the other, work effectively with the regional units without tramping on their turf. And it would report to him in the Serious Crime Command.

Matheson, Chief Superintendent of the Specialist Crimes Command in which the A&A had their home, had asked Coltrane to present the objections to the proposal, which he did with the eloquence he was noted for.

DCI Coltrane said he was sympathetic to the reason behind the proposal, but resources were always limited and trade-offs had to be made in every area of policing. Superintendent Taylor's proposal would cause confusion, incur extra cost and would bring 'non-specialist' officers into a highly specialized area of investigation. People would be falling over each other, reducing effectiveness not increasing it.

Jack Taylor watched Coltrane's delivery impassively. It was impressive, articulate, far more so than his own, he knew. Neville Coltrane's brother, Richard, was a senior staffer in Christie's Auction House, thought Taylor, and the wealthy Coltrane family own more art than half the dealers in London. Taylor thought that Neville looked as if he was running an auction himself, waiting to bang the gavel and declare that the item didn't meet its reserve bid; then send it back to its owner and into obscurity.

Assistant Commissioner Hunt called for clarifications prior to the wrap up. If there were going to be missiles thrown and voiced raised it would be then, Coltrane thought. Strangely enough, the Q&A went smoothly. Coltrane checked his watch; he may be able to make the reception at the Tate after all.

Hunt spoke after a brief conferral with her four committee members.

"We understand, of course, the proposals and the very solid reasons why it should or should not proceed. If it was just about jurisdiction and cost-efficiency you know what the decision would be; it would go nowhere. However, our committee sat through a conference call two days ago with our counterparts in other police services to update each other on organizational changes and proposals. Good national coordination, as per our mandate, right?"

She continued. "Bill Telford, the Lincolnshire Police Assistant Chief Constable, commented on this proposal when we mentioned it. He was with his Chief Constable when they met with Mr. Templeton after the media release that De Barr was also complicit. The Chief Constable was told by Templeton that he had served our country with distinction, his son had just died for it and his daughter's life, health and demand for full justice for those responsible, were, in his words, 'worth less than the price of an oil painting'. Templeton questioned the values and ethics of the Metropolitan Police Service.

"The media had certainly said the same thing more colourfully, of course. Bill Telford thought Jack's proposal was right on the money to address this problem head on."

Coltrane couldn't believe he was hearing this criticism so openly, so explicitly. He glanced at Matheson and saw on his face that he knew this was on the script; he was just weathering his way through it.

Hunt paused, looking around the room. "The members of the Committee do not take lightly this issue of the public perspective around the ethical behaviour of the Metropolitan Police. So we are going to agree to Superintendent Taylor's proposal. The new unit, the Art Crime Unit, will have three years before major review, with annual budget decisions on scale."

She then focused on Coltrane. "With one revision; the head of the unit will be a DCI not a DI. We approve an appropriate budget amendment to adjust for the ranks needed to make it cohesive.

"I think that completes item 7(ii), now let's move on to …"

DCI Coltrane kept his face as impassive as he could as he and Taylor stood up to leave. It had been a *fait accompli* all along, just not the one that he and everyone else in his area thought would happen. The last message made it clear; this bloody new unit would be head-to-head with him in terms of rank.

He looked at Jack Taylor and then remembered that Jack and Bill Telford were from the same place,

Yorkshire, from the same academy graduating class even, he recalled. They had the same northerner's resentment of the south, deep down, Coltrane felt. Taylor had fixed it with Bill - and God knows what had been traded behind the scenes between the Met and the Lincolnshire Constabulary on this one.

~~

"So," Keith finished, "we are constantly in the lime-light to see if we duplicate A&A's work or if we tread on any regional toes. Jack wants this little team to succeed and despite having much bigger serious crime operations under his command, he keeps his eye on Jane, Aina and me."

The plates had been cleared away. He looked at his watch.

"Now some quick suggestions for your interview if it is going to be anything like mine. Then use some of that expense money and take a taxi home; you look like you will fall asleep if you take the Tube."

15 CATRIN'S INTERVIEW

The interview had been scheduled for Tuesday first thing in Superintendent Taylor's office. There were just the three of them; Taylor, Worsley and Catrin.

Despite being tired on Saturday, Catrin had not slept well after the meeting with DI Marshall. Part of it was the sense of loss and disappointment associated with the deception of Jian Li Yeung, which all the logic of her police role couldn't counter. Part of it was nervousness about this interview now she knew the political sensitivities around the appointments to the Art Crime Unit.

Catrin kept thinking about the issue of friendships and acquaintances. She had good friends in Jean and Melanie and some from university who lived elsewhere now. She had a lot of acquaintances she got on very well with too. Friendships are less logical than acquaintances, she thought, less based on mutual interests or time spent together doing things; they are more about the chemistry between people. Intuitively she felt that she had lost the opportunity to make a good friend in Jian Li.

She got together with Jean and Melanie on Sunday afternoon and told them why she was out of sorts. By mid-afternoon she had talked herself into telephoning Inspector Anderson first thing on Monday and telling him she wasn't ready to leave her job in Brixton. By supper time Jean and Melanie had talked her into just going through with the interview and seeing where the chips fell.

"Just give it your best shot," said Melanie.

~~

"So you could talk knowledgeably about, say, Modigliani and Monet and discuss differences and so on?" asked Superintendent Taylor.

"Yes sir, I can do that," said Catrin, trying to show enthusiasm for the question. This was the third question on her art knowledge since they had moved through her education and her police career to date. She had hoped they would focus more on her police work at Brixton in support of the Drug Squad than they had.

The aspect of her work experience that Taylor had concentrated on most was her decision after a firearms training course; not that Catrin had undergone training but that she had not wanted to continue in this direction.

In the UK most police officers were not equipped routinely with firearms, but of the more than six thousand who were, around half were with the Metropolitan Police. It clearly had not been because of the ACU vacancy; her decision to withdraw from the later stages of training had occurred much earlier.

"I see in your assessment for firearms rating that your psychological suitability and weapons capability were high. It says you could have progressed much further, into SCO19 perhaps, yet you chose not to do this, why?" he asked.

SCO19 was the current acronym for the armed response units in the Met. Catrin had expected the question.

"I volunteered for the firearms course at the end of my cadet training. This is my career, sir, and by the time it came up, I was gaining experience in the narcotics area. I was part of two incidents in which SCO19 responded, took over the incident scene and resolved the situation without any use of their firearms. I admired their discipline and teamwork. I discussed it with Inspector Anderson and several others and they suggested I consider the preliminary two-week training on weapons familiarisation and use.

"It was there that it really hit home that it was not for me, at least at present. I realised I would miss the case work in a tactical response unit like SCO19."

He nodded, seemed happy with the answer, she thought; she hoped.

Taylor said, "Yes, it's not just technical capability, I understand. But you are still young. Don't rule it out completely for the future, it is a valuable role."

They had then moved on to the motivation for joining the ACU. Plain-clothes work was a re-assignment to a different work area, not a promotion in the world of UK policing. That had led into art knowledge and Taylor's new tone of questioning.

Keith had warned her. Taylor will lead you along. He is a policeman who wants to catch criminals. He will want to know if you can fit into the field, hold your own with A&A staff but be on his wavelength.

"So I see you paint, yourself," he said, appearing to

study her file.

I had better not smile, she thought, given the thought of coating herself in body paint. "Yes sir, I now decorate ceramics mainly, but I have experience as a watercolourist and with other media."

"But do you do proper painting, oil on canvas and the like, so if we wanted to place you undercover in a museum or an art college looking for criminal elements, you could fit in."

"Yes sir. I can paint in oils," she said. Worsley's glance seemed to indicate, 'careful with the tone' but Catrin had been stung at little by his dismissive tone and simplistic approach to art.

Worsley said, "DC Sayer seemed to fit in well last week in the Bangor case, I think."

He looked unimpressed. "Describe for me a painting you like; describe it first then tell me about it and the artist."

Catrin thought a moment. "I can think of several, sir, but will pick one. It is oil on board, not canvas. The landscape could be seen as hills or water depending on your first perception and your re-evaluation. It seems like it is rolling towards you, engulfing people. Some people are in the foreground, arms raised in supplication, horror or despair. It's by a British artist, Dorothie Field."

She went on to talk about the technical aspects of the painting in greater depth then stopped, not sure where Taylor was going.

Taylor said nothing at first, then, "Can't say I know it, or of her. What's the title?"

"It's called 'Aberfan', sir. It's at the National Museum of Coal Mining."

In Wakefield, she left unsaid, where you come from.

It was a painting about a mining village not far from

her home in South Wales, one which lost 144 people, mainly schoolchildren, when the coal slag waste that had built up outside the mine slipped down the valley and buried the school and other buildings.

"And, other than you come from Wales, why do you like it?" said Taylor, absorbing it, his voice softening a little.

"Well, it moves me, sir, and there is a story behind it I know well, coming from near there. Nearly every work of art has some story behind it and I think for those that come on to our radar we need to know about it during our investigations. Not all of them I realise, but for those works where, if we know why someone values it or would want to steal it for more than just money, it can lead to an arrest.

"Sometimes it is not just the money trail, whether with art or anything else. We need to understand the motive as fully as possible to help us catch the criminal."

Keith had said, if he looks you straight in the eye look back at him, not down or at Worsley. He was looking hard at her now so, uncomfortable as it was for her with this gruff senior officer, she stared right back.

~~

Later Worsley called her into her own office. It had been only half an hour since Catrin had come out of the interview and returned to the ACU floor with a coffee. She was exhausted. Worsley had come down fifteen minutes ago. It seemed like an age.

"Congratulations; you begin here on Thursday, Detective Constable Sayer, which gives you the remainder of today and all Wednesday to clear up and say your goodbyes to Brixton - and to get enough clothes to come to work in without needing a uniform. Your promotion will be processed tomorrow. I have just called Ian Anderson and he sends his congratulations."

Catrin just beamed.

Worsley continued, "You did well with Superintendent Taylor. He has a habit in interviews of appearing vague on some questions and then hitting hard. The Dorothie Field did the trick; he said that showed you have spirit. Thank God you didn't pick a popular Monet or something similar to talk about."

'Thank Keith' for the heads up, thought Catrin.

"Did you know Taylor comes from Wakefield?"

"Yes ma'am, but in any event the accent was Yorkshire and at that moment I thought of Yorkshire mine towns having a common bond with mining towns in Wales. I guess subconsciously that may have made me think of the painting, and it is one I like."

Worsley hesitated then said. "Actually, what he said was, 'you show balls and know your art, so you'll do'. That's Jack Taylor."

"Well, I am -"

"Catrin, if you utter a comment referring to testicles, I will have you assigned to traffic duty at Wandsworth Bridge in rush hour. I get enough of that in this place. Let's go and talk with Keith Marshall before you have a day and half reprieve. He is your new boss now."

She smiled, "Welcome to the team."

~~

Catrin eventually went back to her newly-assigned desk to get her things and head off home.

The last time someone had made the comment about her 'having balls' was during her probationary period at

Shepherd's Bush Police Station. Word about new probationers got around the regulars and somehow her interest in art had surfaced, generating some interesting questions and discussions with others in the station. But it also produced a comment one day from Sergeant Terry Hallam in the cafeteria. He would be happy to pose nude for her sometime, he said, the implication being clear.

Hallam was a good enough cop, she thought, but she had seen already in his interactions with others that sensitivity training had missed him completely or had slid by his Teflon surface. He was sexist and crass at times.

She had made a response in the cafeteria that she would have to bear it in mind or something like that. The second time he made the innuendo was in the presence of two other male officers. She said nothing, just looked at him and then walked off. She had seen one of the others wince slightly as Hallam spoke but had said nothing. She had to deal with this herself, she knew, but wasn't sure how.

It was at the shift briefing several days later that the final item from the duty inspector, given in the same matter-of-fact voice, was the need for some assignment change for the following week, Monday through Wednesday, to cover for Sergeant Hallam and Constable Sayer.

Apparently Sergeant Hallam had volunteered to pose for Constable Sayer, who most people would know painted as a hobby. They would be in Chelsea Art College each morning as Sergeant Hallam, he smiled at him, would be posing nude for a life class for second year students. Constable Sayer would paint him there and her painting would be donated to the Senior Staff Dinner & Dance silent auction. This year it was raising money for the Muscular Dystrophy fund drive.

"I am sure people will be happy to adjust shift coverage," he said straight-faced, "It's for a good cause."

There were a few smiles and ripples of laughter.

"Nice one," said Hallam, laughing. Then he saw the envelope being passed over to him. Inspector Kennedy said, "Terry, there is a letter and a college release form that you have to sign."

After the briefing Hallam came up to Catrin, his face impassive. "So this is really set up, right?"

Catrin was a little apprehensive now. She had been indecisive on whether to just go to him directly or do it the way she had. Her worry on making a direct approach was that she would get more of the same suggestions that had annoyed her in the first place. So she had gone the whole hog, hardball.

She said, "It can go ahead or be cancelled, sergeant. The college is waiting for confirmation or cancellation. I said I would give it today."

He nodded. "I deserve it, I guess. Sorry I touched a nerve there."

That's the wrong thing to be sorry for, she thought, but said nothing.

"Well, you have balls, Catrin," said Hallam. "And it is for a good cause, so I will do it."

It was Millie Sanderson, whose retirement date had been announced at the beginning of the briefing, who quipped back. She had loitered a little, not sure how Terry Hallam would handle it and felt protective of the new PC.

"And twenty odd students at Chelsea and then all the women at the station will be seeing if you have them too, Terry. At least you are going ahead with it, good for you."

The painting when it was brought into the station was admired by a lot more people, largely without the blather of sexual innuendo which had given rise to it. To Terry's relief, although he tried to hide it, his genitals were not a feature. The class instructor had posed him.

Catrin had chosen a position to paint him in three-quarter profile from the right side. He was seated with his right leg raised slightly, left leg extended. He had a facial expression she had caught during the initial layout sketching; muscular, tense, brooding. By the second session he had relaxed visibly with the students and staff and was at ease. Terry had seen a number of their paintings during development. He actually liked Catrin's work and could see she was a skilled artist.

From then on he gave her no more problem and they got along much better.

Inspector Ian Anderson had heard about the issue and seen its resolution. He liked the way Sayer had handled it and he called her in for a brief chat. Near the completion of her probationary period he made a transfer request for her into the uniformed support group for the Drug Squad, to be based at the Brixton station.

At the Senior Staff Dinner & Dance, Superintendent Halliday had seen his partner head out after the main course before the speeches, dessert and coffee. A final bid at the silent auction before it closes, he thought, not a bathroom trip.

So to find that she had won the painting was no big surprise for him. At £540, he saw later, she had bid £60 above the last bid, in a sequence that was going up in £20 increments. Either she really likes this or the extra glass of Chablis during the reception had loosened her credit card, he thought.

She was an accountant by profession and had an interest in art, particularly from an investment value. In fact, two of their best overseas holidays over the years had been paid for largely by the profits from buying and selling paintings. He wondered where she would want this hung, if it wasn't going to be re-sold soon. He wasn't too happy about sticking a portrait of Hallam on his walls.

16 THE MIDDLE SISTER

On the train back to Bangor Jian Li had changed trains at Chester. She had plenty of time on the journey to think and was considering calling Mr. Lin.

She had only once spoken alone to this powerful friend of her father. He and his wife had attended Han's graduation ceremony to give him and her parents their congratulations. She was never sure when or how often her father met or talked with him, but her mother said they went regularly to the same bathhouse, it had become a weekly institution. Being that Mr. Lin was a generation older than her father and very wealthy, while she knew the story of the initial contact between the two men, she was a little surprised that they stayed in touch.

Mr. Lin had called her on her mobile phone the day before her departure from Hong Kong. It was only afterwards she wondered how he had obtained her number.

"Jian Li, this is Enlai Lin. I hear that you will be going to the UK to study, but also hopefully to be there if the police find any news of Han."

"Yes, Mr. Lin; that is so. I am doing one of my under-graduate years there with some courses that perhaps will help me later when I specialize in maritime law."

"Well, LinTan Shipping will always want good legal staff in our corporate headquarters, so when you qualify, you must please contact me. However, it is your current situation that I am calling about. If you need help at all, particularly in the matter of your brother, please let me know. I have a UK free number for you to call. Do you have a pen there?"

"Well, yes thank you, but - ."

He had interrupted her to give her the number, asked her to read it back, and then emphasized that if she needed any help at any time, she should call it. His final comment had been to encourage her to study hard and also call her parents frequently.

A nice man, she had thought, but a strange call. Now on Chester station waiting for the connecting train, she wondered about calling that number. Clearly the police were no further forward on locating Han other than to rule him (and her also) out of a criminal activity.

In the end she decided to hold off. She needed to get into her studies and get some normal student life under her belt. At least the investigation into Han's disappearance was active.

She also resolved to say nothing about Han and Cho to her parents. They had enough grief to deal with. She was still wrestling with the news that her brother had experienced a gay relationship, as she knew of two girls at home that he had dated while training to be a ship's officer. Neither relationship appeared to get very serious, but in her world brothers and sisters didn't talk about sexuality so she never knew what went on between them.

She was not judgmental about her brother and she had

no hang-ups about sexual orientation. For her parents it would be a different matter, more pain to bear. She just felt that it had been a lost opportunity to understand him better.

In Gwynant on Sunday morning she sat around with some of her floormates giving them a synopsis of her strange Saturday, but referring to Cho only as a friend of Han's called Paul.

Several of them had seen the female police officer and a university administration staff member go into Catrin's room late on Saturday, leave with her belongings and close the door. When they left a cleaner was sent in to prepare the room for a new occupant.

Andrea said, "I was worried that she was ill or worse, in London."

"So Catrin is a policewoman, not a student," said Thomas, shaking his head. "I am sorry about that as she seemed nice."

"She is nice," said Andrea.

Li said, "Catrin had a job to do, but she is gone now. I wonder who will get her room now?"

"Perhaps Francis Lloyd?" said Gwyn Roberts.

They howled their dissent at his joke. Li felt good to be back.

~~

"It's Elizaveta Tamara Komarov, the middle sister," said Bertie Wells, the forensic technician who had opened the tube.

Worsley, Keith and Catrin were in his lab looking at both the painting and the high quality prints he had prepared for their use.

"The casing, the tube, is exceeding complex and is more interesting to me than the painting, although I wouldn't tell Gloria that."

Catrin looked at Keith who leaned in slightly and said cryptically in her ear. "Wife; she is a conservator at V&A."

Bertie went on. "The painting has been laminated between two sheets of specialized plastic with a paper outer coating. The plastic is quite clean and inert and slightly cushioned. We think it was then vacuum-pressed around some sort of cylinder to form the tube. The temperature it was kept at during the rolling stage would be critical, we think. Then the outer layers of paper and the end pieces were added to mask the 'sandwich' and make it seem like an ordinary tube. When we X-rayed it on arrival it looked very similar to a regular tube at first glance, so this is a clever way of beating routine Customs surveillance.

"I have already talked with the gallery in Volgograd where the theft occurred. Their conservator sent us images of the work from files in the museum. We in turn sent him files of our images. We are both amazed at the minimal additional surface cracking. The painting is in very good shape, all things considered. Whoever did this is a specialist and is very, very good."

Worsley nodded. "What can you say about the equipment to do this?"

Bertie said, "It's probably a stationary set-up. Perhaps it is moveable by van but not easily mobile, I would think. This couldn't be taken to each theft location, for example."

Worsley nodded. "So there is probably a processing centre. The sequence would be first the theft, then move the painting to the tubing unit and move on to...

wherever."

"How about opening the tube?" asked Catrin.

"I'm glad you asked," said Bertie. "It's as easy as pie, if you know how. We didn't, but I worked it out. There is no need for any special equipment on arrival. Any good art shop could do it, although I hate to think of that.

"You know, we see more damage from time to time in stolen paintings cased in standard museum packing and moved by amateurs than we have seen here."

It was Thursday, Catrin's first day formally as a member of the Art Crime Unit. They had come over to see the painting after Worsley had confirmed that she would work directly with Keith and would start out on a different case. "But you should see what you helped to save first."

Worsley and Bertie Wells were off that evening to Switzerland, to 'coordinate' yet again with the Swiss, now the packaging technique had been discovered.

As they were finishing the visit another man with sandy hair came into the lab. He was in his late thirties. He was another elegant dresser like Keith, wearing glasses and looked to be a man who had expensive tastes. Catrin heard his voice before she saw him.

"Jane, I came to see the Komarov. Hello Keith, Bertie."

Worsley said, "Hello Neville. DCI Coltrane, meet DC Catrin Sayers. She joined our unit today."

Coltrane shook Catrin's hand and said very pleasantly, "DC Sayer, welcome to the world of art crime. Where were you before?"

"Brixton, sir, thank you, it is good to be on the ACU team."

Coltrane looked at her and said, "It's not a big team

but you have just made it bigger. What do you think of the painting?"

He looked at it closely. Catrin had been absorbed in it when Coltrane had entered. She wondered if he was testing her out.

"I really like it, sir."

"Anything in particular?" he continued.

Now she knew.

She said slowly, "The brushwork, the chiaroscuro inside the room here bringing out the vase on the table, the light spectrum from the garden, all are done very well. The other technical elements are excellent, but it is not those which make it for me. It is the way Garin has brought them together to surround a young woman loving her sixteenth birthday, being the centre of attention. It's alive and vibrant but the technique to do that is controlled, carefully constructed. The print we have is good but it is nothing compared to the original. I would love to see the paintings of her sisters."

Coltrane was nodding as she spoke.

He said, "Yes indeed; again, welcome aboard." He moved over to Bertie, asking him a question about a painting that was being examined for the Art & Antiques Unit. Once he had his answer, he left the room.

Worsley looked at Keith Marshall. "He didn't say anything, not a damn thing, Keith."

Marshall just smiled.

Catrin said, "He did leave rather abruptly ma'am, yes."

Bertie Wells said, "DC Sayer, what DCI Worsley means is he didn't say anything in response to your comments on the painting. He is noted for giving an exposé - some would say more a lecture - about any painting to anyone who expresses an opinion that differs with his own. And he is very knowledgeable; I have to give him that."

Keith Marshall said, "Catrin, I think you just passed the Coltrane test."

~~

Catrin mentally said goodbye to the Komarov Sisters and started reading up the file on a theft from a gallery in Chichester of a small sculpture by a local artist. It was held in high esteem and the ACU had been called in after a knife attack in Coventry several days ago on a person rumoured to be the thief.

Over the next two weeks she was mainly in the office, settling in, doing a lot of computer and phone work. It was a change from being shift-based. Now she had a regular working day and weekends off. She caught up on a number of things she had been putting off, including some pottery decoration for the Kiln.

Catrin decided also to move, to look for somewhere between her work at the Yard and her time in Spitalfields, if the right place became available. She eventually decided on the Spitalfields area and she started looking around and asking Jean and Melanie to ask people; she needed to share a place with someone. She would love a little place of her own but on a junior police officer's salary with London prices she had no choice but to share.

She also went shopping for more clothes suitable for work, looking for bargains on quality items. The dress standard at Scotland Yard was pretty high, she noted, so she wanted to fit in and look good. Intuitively she knew that promotion would be linked to looking and fitting the role as well as the core capability to do it.

The 'normal' work of the Art Crime Unit was now

unfolding for her. Keith Marshall had taken her with him for a meeting in Coventry with the West Midlands Police and to the totally unproductive interview with the suspect thief at the hospital. The treatment for the knife wound to his chest had led to further tests. The man had much bigger medical problems; he was terminally ill. Keith was hoping this would break open the attempted murder case if he was granted immunity for the theft, but he remained tight-lipped and uncooperative.

On the Saturday night a week after she returned from Bangor, Catrin went to a party with a fellow police officer, Sonya, from the Brixton station, one which was not 'company only'. A lot of police officers socialized together; it was easier in a lot of ways. But she and Sonya had shared early on that they wanted a broader social life and had gone to parties and events together from time to time.

The guy she met seemed nice enough to begin with; good looking, about her age, he worked at Heathrow Airport. They got on well but then she saw how fast he was putting back the beer and his voice started to get an edge to it. Perhaps he is nervous, there again perhaps not, she thought. It was the third time he suggested that she should have 'something stronger' that made her move on.

At least he hadn't done the great 'Oh' when she answered his question about what she did. She always came straight out with it, 'I work for the Met; I'm a police officer.' Sometimes just those words made them ease away or talk of nothing but police work or television melodramas.

In the end she said goodbye to her friend who had hit it off with another guy and left the party early.

17 THE ROLEX

It was nearly two weeks after her return from London when DI Dafydd Powys called Jian Li, leaving a voicemail. She had just finished a lecture and had picked up his message before heading into a team assignment with two of her classmates. She called him straight back.

"Miss Yeung, we don't have any news of your brother. Let me begin with that. But we have a watch which may be his. In fact, given the movement number you provided, we believe it to be his but would appreciate it if you could identify it. Can you come by?"

"Well, I am just preparing some class work, an appeal of a conviction. It's a team exercise, but I can miss it and come right over."

"You don't have to miss much of anything. I will drive over there and collect you, then take you back if you can break away for half an hour. Let me know where you are."

Thirty minutes later Li was in the passenger seat of Dafydd's car in tears as they returned from the police station to the college. Yes, it was Han's watch, she was sure. And suddenly as they set off in the car the overwhelming loss of Han hit her again. Dafydd wished he had brought a female PC with him.

Her classmates were getting on with the project assignment, covering for her. By now, given Francis Lloyd's article, most people who knew Li were also aware of the mystery surrounding her brother.

"Can you tell me how the police got the watch?" she asked.

"In general, Li, yes I can. With the information you gave us last month we put out an alert for it. An officer was called to an incident - an accident - at a pub in Bangor the night before last and he noticed a watch with a light brown face on a bystander. He looked a little closer and saw it was a Rolex, so he called it in."

"Is this man involved in Han's disappearance?"

"We don't know for sure but don't think so. In fact, we interviewed him pretty hard yesterday and understand he bought the watch in the same pub some weeks earlier from a man. If he knows the person he is not saying, but he wasn't involved in Han's disappearance on May 14. He has a solid alibi for that time.

"He and the seller argued a price of about £20 pounds for the watch. He was pleased he got it down from £25; they had both thought it was a fake Rolex. We have charged him with possession of stolen goods and are keeping an eye on him."

Li felt her anger building.

"You let him go?"

"We have no basis for holding him. He has bail on a charge of receiving stolen goods. The bail conditions will keep him here but in any case he doesn't even have a valid passport, so he can't go far."

"But he may know the person who kidnapped or took

Han. He may have been involved later on," she said.

Li's voice was now showing her anger and frustration.

"As I say, we are keeping an eye on him."

He couldn't tell her, Dafydd thought, that they have the man under twenty-four hour surveillance and his mobile phone was now being monitored.

Li suddenly became very controlled. "Thank you, Inspector Powys, for keeping me informed and for all your efforts. If you need more from me... but I should get back to my class."

She got out of the vehicle and headed back into the Arts Building.

As Dafydd drew away and she went back to work with her team she decided that tomorrow morning Hong Kong time she would call the number Mr. Lin had given her.

~~

Trevor Gerard walked up to the bar, choosing a space between the couple lost in conversation and the person ahead of him currently placing an order.

He looked at the mirror shelf behind the bar reflecting the liquor bottles and said softly "Bail, for handling stolen goods. But I said nothing."

"Keep it that way, Trev."

"I will if you see me right, Steve. Solicitors aren't cheap."

The man next to him said nothing.

"By the way, the watch was real, they told me. It belonged to that Chinese sailor that went missing. They said I was in real shit," Trevor continued.

He then raised his voice, "Pint of bitter and a vodka and orange, please."

The barman had just delivered a pint to the man next to him and had looked at Trevor for his order.

As Steve turned to go back to his table, Trevor said, "The watch is worth about two or three thousand dollars, it's vintage, and has a serial number, they said. I said nothing."

"Sorry, mate, what did you say?" said the barman, "It's the noise in here."

"Nothing, sorry; I was just talking to myself, lost in thought."

Steve called his sister thinking through what he had just learned. It frightened him. He and Trevor were close and Steve knew that his friend would keep his mouth shut. You don't grass on a mate you served with, were under fire with; it was a given.

Her first comment was, "Christ, Steve, you kept the watch! What a bloody stupid thing to do."

"I thought it was a fake; nice for the weekend, for going out on Saturday night in my good clothes. This watch I am wearing has paint splashes; it's crap."

He was looking at his everyday wristwatch.

She said, "Well the other is not crap and is fully traceable. Damn. If it has your fingerprints they will be after you."

"I haven't been in trouble with the law."

"But you have been in the army, so you are on file."

Steve said angrily, "I don't know how this all came up now. I thought it had died away."

"I told you that his sister was here, studying and 'helping with enquiries'. She is probably badgering the police for action."

"So what do we do?"

"Nothing, I told you. We wait it out. Trevor bought a

watch from someone he doesn't know. That's it, right?"

18 BANGOR AGAIN

In the morning meeting on Friday with Keith and Catrin, Jane Worsley updated them on the telephone call she had received from Dafydd Powys the previous afternoon.

"I have agreed that you both should work up there with his team for the next week; Powys says that they are stretched on a number of cases and he could use the help. I think this watch seems a good possible lead. Take a car up.

"What I really want, though, is for you to go back over the entire file they have. We have access to the on-line reports, I know, but a fresh eye going through it all may find something. Do the analysis; leave the routine surveillance and follow up to the locals, as much as possible.

"Catrin, make sure you touch base with Jian Li Yeung. Dafydd said that his discussion with her during the identification of the watch wasn't too good. He had caught her working on her studies and she took it hard, particularly when she knew this man Trevor Gerard was out on bail. She doesn't have a name, obviously, but she knows that someone locally obtained Han's watch from another person.

"And it's pouring up there, has been all week and the forecast is the same next week. Just so you know. Enjoy the weekend before you go."

"Yes ma'am, I'll take my umbrella." She hid her smile at the thought of seeing Jian Li again.

~~

On the Monday morning Keith asked Catrin to drive. Until the M1 motorway they talked a little about the file as thoughts came to each of them. Then, after a brief lull, Keith said "I bought one of your pieces on Saturday."

"My pottery?" said Catrin. "Well, you must have gone to the Cwmbran Kiln in the morning then, I was there all afternoon. But I didn't think that was your sort of thing."

In the last two weeks they had talked a couple of times about art. Keith's interests and extensive knowledge were firmly rooted in 17th and 18th century masters.

Jean had sent Catrin an email last night. There had been a flurry of activity on her work; two vases had sold and the water bowl and jug she had finished was now set aside for a customer, on hold for several days while they decided. She finished with the cryptic comment that, 'Hopefully, Catrin, you can find a day or two to come into the pottery soon...'

Fat chance of that, thought Catrin.

Marshall said, "I was curious and, once I saw it, I liked your work, to be honest. And it wasn't just idle interest either. I bought a bud vase for my sister, Elizabeth. She has a small gallery called, of all things, 'Liz's Place' off Fulham Road and sells work by contemporary British artists. I think you and your potter could sell some pieces there. Liz is of the same mind once she saw it, so I will give you her card if you are interested."

"Well, thank you, sir. I have only sold my work through Melanie and Jean so far, but it sounds very interesting."

"Liz says you could get a significantly higher price in a gallery environment if you are careful about maintaining an original output. You and - Jean is it? - could work out your split of the sale after commission. Think about it. My sister has a real eye for what can sell."

"Anyway," he added, "I heard from Jane about Jack's art questions during the interview."

He heard her snort with amusement.

"I think you could probably do a pretty picture or two undercover in an art college. Hard call but, probably you would be OK."

She laughed out loud. "Don't remind me! I would probably end up painting a Modigliani nude on a Monet backdrop for hanging in Superintendent Taylor's office."

Interspersed with work discussion, the topic of art got them to the A51 turn-off from the M6 and almost by common understanding the discussion came back fully to the case in hand. Catrin knew she would not be having any time to paint either canvas or pottery in the days ahead.

In Bangor they checked in at the Eryl Môr Hotel over-looking the Menai Strait and then went straight over to the police station.

"Not much free space, unfortunately, but we have fitted you in together in here," said Dafydd, showing them a newly-cleared office, "unless Keith requires a separate office, that is."

"No, it will be fine," said Marshall, "we can camp out."

They were then taken on a tour of the station to meet key staff. The Divisional Superintendent, a man called Morgan, was visiting from the regional headquarters in Colwyn Bay. He recalled Keith.

"Never occurred to me you would be that Marshall," he said. "We did advanced weapons training together, my second refresher and you, your first time, I recall, right?"

"Yes," said Keith, "Correct, sir."

"You knew your way around firearms, I recall. You still AFO?" he asked.

Keith said, "Not currently. Not in this role."

'Authorised to carry a firearm', thought Catrin, something she had started but not completed.

Then she saw the two men look at each other and knew without any basis whatsoever that both had used weapons in the line of duty. She also knew intuitively she would have to leave it to her boss to tell her more if he chose to, in his own good time. Art was open terrain for discussion; she felt firearms were not.

The following day after still further introductions Catrin started a review of all witness statements.

"I want a new timeline, in detail," said DI Marshall, unabashed.

Dafydd Powys was listening and she knew that he or his team would already have undertaken this exercise. But they all knew that rework was not criticism; it was a fresh eye trying to find something new.

Powys was taking Marshall on a familiarisation tour and to see the surveillance exercise on Trevor Gerard.

Keith said, "Sometime, also take a break and touch base with Yeung."

Catrin nodded. She settled into the desk work and easy interchanges with other staff once the two detective inspectors had left, slipping naturally into Welsh and in doing so deflating the 'Scotland Yard' visitor image. Two PCs had a bet that Dafydd's 'tour' would try to include a visit to his sailing boat in Y Felineli, a coastal village about five miles away.

"I don't think Inspector Marshall is dressed for any sailing," said Catrin, smiling.

'Won't put Dafydd off,' said one. "Marjorie, his wife, is always complaining about how he treats his own clothes because of his visits to the Ceinwen," he said. "It won't even occur to Dafydd that his guest is in a handmade suit."

The other one said, "Remember the shoes?"

She said to Catrin, "DI Powys hates shopping but Marjorie dragged him out one Saturday for shoes. She made him buy two pairs, as he would wear old ones until the soles fell off. Within a week he scuffs up one really badly at a farm on an enquiry.

"Didn't have time to put his wellies on, he told Marjorie. The following week he gets a varnish splash right on the toe of one shoe in the other pair. 'Just touching up, passing the Ceinwen,' was his excuse that time."

Catrin smiled to herself. This was a small station, one where everyone knew everyone else and their wives and kids. Colwyn Bay, as the regional centre, would be more like her own experience; a larger facility where you knew only some of the people really well.

She got back to her work. She had already called Li and arranged to go to Gwynant later in the afternoon.

The morning went quickly. Catrin did a sequencing of

all sightings of Han. Then she pulled out the file of all the people that had been interviewed but had not seen Han and worked through those statements, also noting the locations. Quite a number of the interviews were with the fleet of coach drivers servicing the cruise ship that day and the regular bus drivers servicing Anglesey.

It was clear from what they now knew that Han Yeung had ridden along Victoria Road in Holyhead and then turned back to go to the Caer Gybi Post Office near the church. That was where he had posted the tube. Both were close to the quay where the *Manden Serenity* had tied up.

The analysis then worked on the basis that he went on a bike ride along Kingsland Road, a secondary road also known as the B4545, riding further into Anglesey. There had been a firm sighting as he passed the MacDonald's restaurant, where the B4545 separated from the expressway.

Han had set out at 9.15 a.m. from the ship and was last seen at near Trearddur Bay at 10.40 a.m. The assumption was that he had continued further into Holy Island, the isthmus on the west side of Anglesey. She saw that after sending the parcel he had kept up a good speed, so he was getting his exercise. It was then she thought of the report she had read previously; that Han was supposed to be on duty for the departure. He would need to cool off, shower and change and grab a meal, thinking of her own regime if she exercised before duty.

She had the thought, 'but which duty?'. She did not recall any mention in the files of Yeung's role on his return to the ship, only that he was missing and it had been noticed because he was not at his duty station. The timing was prior to the security report of persons on board that occurs before every departure.

She looked through the files to see how many times Han had been on duty during departure and in what role. The files showed nothing. It was starting to bother her, but she wasn't sure why. She phoned Aina and asked her to get what she could on Han's duty role that day from Manden directly sent to her. The cruise company had been excellent in their responses to date so she felt it should not take long.

An idea was growing that perhaps some of the sightings were wrong. Not every statement mentioned the direction Han was travelling; some had only the direction the observer was driving. These would need to be re-interviewed, if her idea was correct.

~ ~

Li was both happy and nervous about seeing Catrin again, once she got the call. The news that she and a colleague were back in Bangor assigned to assist the enquiry was good to hear. Perhaps this would help.

She had spoken with Mr. Lin and had brought him up to date. His comments were helpful but she had felt the great geographic distance between them. Li had asked whether someone in Hong Kong could ask the UK police to be more active. Perhaps this was the outcome.

"Please be patient, Jian Li," he said. "It is very sad to hear that the police thought Han could be involved in a criminal enterprise at all or that they thought you may be linked. It shows how little they know about his disappearance, I think."

He paused. "I think Han may have inadvertently become the victim in this criminal matter, or even in another crime at Holyhead."

"That is my conclusion, Mr. Lin, but I have not said

anything to my parents."

The presumably expensive telephone call she received went quiet for some seconds. She wondered if the line had been lost then, "Jian Li, I will look into this, but please do not mention it to anyone. I have many contacts, and you never know. Also please do not let your studies suffer. I know it must be hard, but you must do well, for yourself of course, but also for your parents."

"Thank you, Mr. Lin, I am studying hard and doing well in my class and, I have settled here more now. I have some friends and it is an area with much beauty."

"Enjoy it, Jian Li. We will talk again."

And then, as before, the line just closed. It was good of Enlai Lin to offer to help. A word from a man as important as him to the British Embassy may send a signal back to the UK that helps, she thought at the time.

19 THE SHEP KIP MEI STREET
BATHHOUSE

Enlai Lin had put the phone down after his talk with
Jian Li and somehow the image of his dead son Simon
came to mind. It was always the same image, from 1973.

Enlai was in his study at home at the time and had
started singing softly for some reason, a favorite song
from years ago. In his youth he had a good voice but in
recent years he had not sung at all. In fact he had hardly
been home, with late hours at the office and frequent
business trips. While his wife and two older sons saw this
as 'duty' and were respectful of it, Simon was resentful of
his absence. That had been part of the difficulty between
them. And now he had no idea what Simon did with his
days and evenings.

Nearly eight months earlier two police officers had
brought Simon home and explained he had been caught
with others during a domestic break-in of an empty house
where someone was trying to start a party. There were
drugs and alcohol involved. The Inspector, recognizing it
was Enlai Lin's son, had spirited Simon away with some

others so that charges were laid against two other young men, the ringleaders. What should have been a lesson and a lucky escape in fact increased the gap between father and son, as if the Lin family standing had interfered with the right for Simon to live his life on the same basis as his friends.

But on this day, the day of the memory, Simon had heard his father singing to himself and had started accompanying him on his guitar from the other room. Then he walked into his father's study and on the last verse father and son had harmonized and their joint voices caused Mrs. Lin and Shen-li, the cook, to come along and applaud at the end.

Simon had said, "Dad, you should sing more often."

Enlai had started to say something and stopped, not wanting to ruin the moment. He had smiled and simply nodded his agreement to his son.

Two weeks later he was burying him.

~~

Over the years Lin had watched the development of Daniel Yeung and the success of Coulter & Yarrow. Robin Coulter had been very responsive to his offer and had been, Lin felt, very fair in his negotiation; he had a lot of respect for the older Englishman. Daniel had come on board at the tailor's shop and picked up the ropes quickly without interfering with the existing staff.

Enlai Lin met in public with Daniel from time to time with his father, Shen. He had sent gifts on the birth of Han and later Jian Li. Years later he had attended their school graduations. It seemed to others an incidental and infrequent contact.

However, for years they had met weekly in private

with Michael Yau at the Shep Kip Mei Street Bathhouse in Kowloon. Enlai had started going there at the invitation of Yau and later, when they found that Daniel Yeung was attending the same bathhouse to ease his leg pains, they invited him to the private room they used each week.

Several years later Daniel had confided in the men how he felt that first day he had been invited to join them.

It had been a fellow fireman, still a friend, he told them, who recommended it. He found the experience there had helped his shoulder pain so why not give it a try? Yeung went with him and found, surprisingly, the dull ache in his leg did ease more effectively than when he took a hot bath at home. He wasn't sure why.

At each visit he paid the bath fee until one day he was told by the person he took to be the owner that there would not be a charge.

"Is it a holiday I don't know about?" joked Daniel.

"No, you will never be charged here again; you are our honoured guest now."

He was directed into a different room to find a large private bath with much more sumptuous surroundings.

"I was shocked when I saw you both. I felt quite intimidated," he said.

Sitting in the bath already was Enlai Lin and washing himself in preparation for entry was Michael Yau.

"Welcome," Enlai Lin had said.

Daniel had bowed slightly and mumbled that he did not know that they came here.

"We have been coming here weekly for years, since shortly after our sons died," said Lin, "and we heard that you had started using the bathhouse, so we thought it was time for you to join us. We timed our visit this week to fit with your booking."

"I don't want to intrude," said Daniel "if you have things to discuss…"

"Join us once. Give it a try."

"Were you intimidated by the big businessman or the notorious Triad boss?" asked Michael.

"By both of you and the fact you were together."

"I could see that," said Enlai Lin.

When Daniel had settled in the water, Lin explained. "We don't discuss business at all. Our worlds are different. And we don't want to talk about suits and shirts, either, with you. We just talk as men about our lives, our families, our children, those with us and the ones who aren't. That's all; an hour in a week to be just human beings."

He swirled his arms in the water.

"We got off to a bad start, Michael and I. When my son Simon and Mr. Yau's son, Shing, died in the fire I assumed Simon had fallen into Triad business and I blamed Mr. Yau."

He glanced over.

"So I went to see him, threaten him in fact, in my anger and grief. It was probably not the wisest move in the world, to threaten a Triad boss. But it did get us talking."

Yau nodded. "When he threatened me I decided not to hack him apart with my meat cleaver, the one I never possessed. It was not the wisest move, I thought, to kill off a big shipping tycoon."

"I just told him that our Triad would not employ a pair of kids like our sons and what they had actually been up to. I had looked into it, petty stuff, break-ins to hold 'rave parties' or whatever they called them then. And I had just found out who was to blame for the fire and had dealt with them."

Daniels eyes widened. The name Yau was known to him. Triad territory and infighting was the sort of thing firemen sometimes talked about waiting for calls.

"You ..." He was about to say 'killed' but stopped short. He thought he had better leave; he was still shocked to find Mr. Lin in the presence of this man until Yau laughed.

"No, I just invited them to go and confess to the authorities, something they seemed to find an attractive idea. It was in the news at the time that they confessed, did you not hear?"

Daniel shook his head; he had wanted nothing to do with that incident after the hospital and his recovery but he then recalled he had heard that the culprits had been caught.

"Perhaps they had repentance in mind, who knows? You are a Christian, right?" said Yau.

"Yes, I am," said Daniel.

"So repentance is good for the soul, right?"

"If truly meant, yes, it is ..."

"It was the fact we all got talking so easily that settled me and brought me back," he said to the two men, years later, "And my leg. Driving home it was the best it had been in years and I couldn't explain it. Still can't, but my leg is much better after our weekly get-together."

"It's the aura from being in close proximity to great men, Daniel," said Michael Yau.

Enlai Lin splashed Yau like a kid.

At that first meeting, within a few minutes for some strange reason, Daniel had found himself talking openly with these two men. At one point, something to do with the way that the conversation had turned, he mentioned how he had never really apologised to his father for his own behaviour during their 'falling out' period, as he thought of it and it was now too late - he wished that he had. Mr. Lin told him how Shen Yeung had confided how proud he was of his son and how wrong he felt he had been to oppose Daniel's choice of career as a fireman.

Somehow the intimidating backgrounds and the very different positions of power that each of these men represented disappeared for Daniel during that conversation. As he drove back home he found that he was looking forward to the next visit to the bathhouse on Shep Kip Mei Street.

It was Enlai's attendance with Mrs. Lin at Shen Yeung's funeral which brought home the strength of relationship he now had with Daniel, seeing him afresh as the head of the Yeung family.

After the disappearance of Han and Daniel's return from the UK Enlai Lin had met separately with him, to offer his sympathies and best wishes for good news. Daniel later mentioned in the bathhouse that Jian Li had decided to study in Bangor to be close in case of news of Han. It was on his way home that Enlai thought to make contact with Jian Li to offer assistance, including setting up an 800 number direct to his personal assistant Mrs. Cheong for Li's ease of contact.

~~

This new development of stolen art and the mistake regarding Han Yeung disturbed Enlai Lin but he had no intention of putting pressure on the UK authorities, as Jian Li had suggested.

Mrs. Cheong knocked and entered to tell him his next appointment was in fifteen minutes and, as usual, she passed across a leather folder with the briefing notes for it.

"Mildred, please rearrange my schedule so that this afternoon at 4.30 I will go to the bathhouse, in addition to my regular timing. Ensure Mr. Yau knows. Also, please get me Anthony Chan or find his whereabouts and ask him to call. Make it before this appointment, if possible."

Mildred Cheong knew the arrangement of the additional bathhouse visit in Kowloon would throw into play a series of actions; from the re-scheduling of his chauffeur to a rearrangement of a number of appointments of clients for a particular room at the bathhouse. A simple command and a number of people would suddenly become very busy. Existing clients would be called individually, told an array of reasons and apologies why their own appointment was to be cancelled, re-scheduled or simply moved to another, less sumptuous bathroom.

Specifically requesting the owner to know about it was a code she had long understood. He was a member of a Triad and Mr. Lin wanted to talk with him sooner rather than later. Neither Mrs. Cheong nor Mr. Lin's security team were happy about their boss going to this location regularly but he would accept no suggestions, subtle or otherwise. To his chauffeur, who had to wait outside for him in a parking spot always held available by two men until he got there, he just said, "This is Mr. Yau's territory and we are safe here."

The call back to Lin from Anthony Chan did not take long. Chan was an inspector in the Hong Kong Police Force and happened also to be married to a niece of the shipping magnate. Jane Worsley would have been incredulous but this was Asia, not the United Kingdom. By his meeting at the bathhouse Enlai Lin expected to know everything that the Hong Kong police knew from Interpol and others about an art smuggling racket involving three Russian paintings that had disappeared in the UK in May.

He stood and walked from his desk towards the senior executive from a Middle East island state as Mrs. Cheong was showing him and his assistant in. They were to finalize some of the new business developments for LinTan Shipping. Lin's mind was already on more familiar business.

~~

Catrin had called Li from her mobile as she walked towards the entrance to Gwynant. "You will need to let me in. I don't have a key anymore."

She waited until Li came down, watching a decorator loading his van. There is always on-going maintenance, she thought, as she recalled her brief time in residence here.

As she and Li walked through the kitchen to get some tea the first person she saw was Gwyn Roberts carrying his guitar along to Big Gwyn's room. He saluted. "Constable Sayer, I presume," he said.

"Detective Constable Sayer to you, please," she beamed.

"Gwyn, Catrin's been promoted. Did you put in a good word for her or something?" he yelled.

Big Gwyn popped his head out. "Hi, Catrin; welcome back. You idiot, get in here," he added to his namesake.

Inside her room, Li said, "When I got your call I was very happy."

"I wasn't sure how you would feel, Li. First, I want to apologise again for deceiving you for so long. It was my job but I feel also that our friendship grew quickly and..."

Li just smiled and said, "Catrin, everything is OK."

As they talked and caught up, they could hear softly in the background the songs that 'The Gwyns' were practicing. It was folk group night, Catrin suddenly recalled. She had gone with some others including Li that first week but had no chance to talk to Li then. They called their duo 'Cytgord', the Welsh for harmony, but everyone just seemed to call them 'The Gwyns' and clearly they were a well-liked fixture there.

"Welsh people would cough phlegm in four-part harmony, if they had to," said Li, suddenly. "They sing so beautifully, so naturally. We Chinese know more about coughing phlegm."

Catrin laughed, "Well, you are certainly learning about us Welsh; we like our singing."

"So..." said Li slowly, "what do you have to tell me about the case; anything?"

"Well, I actually came because I think Dafydd - Detective Inspector Powys - felt badly about the last discussion he had with you, that he could not tell you more and you were so upset."

She looked serious.

Li took a deep breath. "Yes I was," said Li, "still am, frankly, but not with you or Inspector Powys, honestly."

"Catrin, we Hong Kong Chinese have to understand both races, Europeans and our own Chinese; we have had to do so for a long time. Europeans will not easily understand Chinese in legal matters or anything else really. British people consider the Chinese justice system they read about to be at minimum, what is the word, peremptory, or perhaps just a forgone conclusion, a farce."

"But underpinning it is the principle that if the guilty confess and seek forgiveness, the punishment will be less; if not it will be severe. And that is not a facet of the People's Republic and communism; it is embedded in centuries of practice in China.

"Chinese people see that European law is interminably drawn out and favours the rights of criminals, not the rights of victims. Remember, I am studying law and now I am a victim, as are my parents, so I know how that feels. I am well aware that I cannot know all that the police know, but it is now five months since Han disappeared and, other than the complication of this art investigation, we still know nothing."

She paused, looking at Catrin.

"Except that a man had Han's watch and you cannot get him to tell the truth about how he got it, I think."

She stopped, realizing her answer had turned into a speech, but one she was glad to have made visible to her new friend. At least it was clear. She wondered how she would react.

Catrin looked at her and waited a few seconds. "How well did you know Han's actual job on the *Manden Serenity*?"

"Well, he talked about it in his emails but I can't say I understand his role well."

Catrin said, "Well, if you want to help rather than wait, can you get those emails and others he might have sent that I could read?"

"The ones I received from him are here, on my laptop and," she pulled a thumb drive from the desk drawer, "all emails off his laptop to anyone are here. I asked my dad to let my friend Jenny copy them. He and mom would have been lost to do it. She sent them over to me."

She paused and looked at Catrin. "I thought you had them all before the laptop was released."

Catrin said, "Let's go through them together, it could help… but it will be a long evening perhaps."

"Then let's eat first and make a start at least. You can always take the thumb drive; I have it backed up."

~~

If Catrin Sayer had visited Hong Kong around this time she could have walked along the busy streets in Kowloon totally unaware of the world she was in. She would have no idea what was behind the street level shops selling everything under the sun. Unless she went into these buildings she would not have known whether they contained thriving little businesses or residential apartments. And without an expert from the Hong Kong Police to guide her she would have had no understanding of the power structure and divisions in this society.

In the 1950s, with the new regime in mainland China eliminating the societal structure which supported secret societies like the Triads, their migration to Hong Kong swelled. It was estimated that there were over 300,000 Triad members in many different groups there at the time. Police action and territorial in-fighting whittled down that number over the decades, but it was an ever-present underground structure.

Even if Catrin had been able to locate the bathhouse on Shep Kip Mei Street she would have no knowledge of the world of its owner, Michael Yau, the 'White Paper Fan' or administrator of a Triad known as 'Folding Square', which these days focused almost exclusively on commercial espionage.

"I take it this is just us?" said Michael Yau.

Enlai Lin settled himself in the bath and without preamble recounted what he had learned first from Jian Li Yeung and later from Anthony Chan.

Yau took it in and thought about it a little. "What do you want, Enlai?"

"I want Daniel and his family to have closure, Michael, to know what has happened to Han and, if it is what I think, for them to locate the boy's body and bury or rebury him properly, if possible. To do that we have to reach the people who were dealing with these paintings, I think. It is highly likely that they were involved somehow. The young man didn't simply disappear."

Yau nodded. They had both seen the changes in Daniel Yeung as the three men met here each week. Both had travelled the path of losing a son but each was acutely aware that in their sorrow they had a son to bury, a funeral rite to help the grieving process.

"And I want whoever killed Han in prison. And any others involved in his disappearance in prison too. Not killed, put in prison, legally."

Yau thought about it further.

"Not 'we' Enlai; 'me'. Let's be honest, this is my world these people operate in, not yours. I will deal with it, but on your terms. They will go to the authorities and confess."

"I can provide funds," said Lin.

"Daniel tried to save my son also, Enlai. No money changes hands and there has never been a business obligation between us; it is still best that way. Each of us has more money than we can ever need. I know someone who can do this job well."

20 TIMINGS

At the briefing session the following morning they went through the updates, with DI Powys leading the morning meeting.

Yesterday evening Catrin had called Keith as she and Li went to eat. She could hear the wind blowing, picked up by his phone.

"We are in Y Felinheli, dropping by Dafydd's boat," said Keith.

From his careful tone she knew that Dafydd must be close by. He actually pronounced the village name quite well, she thought. She told him briefly the findings of her timeline review and he agreed that she should bring it forward in the morning.

By the time she finished with Li it was late, but she felt that she was on solid ground.

There was nothing new from the surveillance team on Gerard. An officer reported that the only finger prints identified on the Rolex belonged to Trevor Gerard.

Dafydd nodded at Catrin who had been reading

through an email she had printed out before they gathered in the conference room.

"Well, sir, I have been through the witness statements and also spent some time trying to understand Han's movements.

"First point, he held the rank of a Third Officer, we know. He was trained to be a member of the navigation team, the command team of the ship. I looked into the sort of duties he was assigned and found that one of these was to pilot the ship at times.

"Controlling the movement of a cruise ship is more like piloting an airliner these days, everything is computer controlled from a complex panel. On five occasions in the last year he has drawn the assignment of a port departure. Normally one of the senior officers has this responsibility working with the harbour pilot, but they assign the duty at times to junior officers for training and experience; with supervision, of course.

"It is very precise work with a departure plan that has to be followed, so is quite a coup for a junior deck officer. This email I received from Manden confirms that Han Yeung was scheduled to pilot the *Serenity* out of Holyhead harbour as part of his duty watch.

"I think he would want to be well prepared for his duty. He would need to be back from his ride in time to clean up, eat, prepare himself one final time with the course details, the harbour plan and procedures. He wasn't going to be back just in time for the ship's departure; he was returning much earlier."

She stood up.

"Can I, sir?"

She moved to the whiteboard carrying key information on the case, including a map with Han's sightings. As she passed Powys she couldn't resist a quick check of his shoes. They were clean, polished, no paint marks.

"I went through the timings of possible sighting again on the basis he had to be back earlier using his start time from the post office. He was seen here, here."

She pointed out the locations.

"If we look at what is a reasonable route given his speed and the basis he would be back by 1 p.m. at the latest, some of these sightings associated with his return can't be correct; he would not have made it back in time. It must have been another cyclist. One or two of the more vague reports may also be questionable. The most accurate, based on the detail, are these three… and, in particular, this sighting by a coach driver who said a passenger behind him commented it was 'the young officer from the ship'.

"I think we need to consider that he did not continue on the B4545 then reverse his route; he had a GPS function on his iPhone and I suspect he was following a planned shorter route to get him back sooner. So I checked the other reports, without sightings of Yeung for a return along here," - she pointed - "the more northerly road, the old London Road. It would make a logical round trip.

"No-one saw him here, I know. But at this grass verge a bus driver reported a badly parked van with quote, "some business name on it, stupid thing half-out in the road, he had to swerve out to pass it and a car, a blue Ford." He thought he saw a bike there, but couldn't be sure.

"But if Yeung followed this route and kept to his timing I think he should have been about here, where the blue Ford was parked by that van."

She paused, done.

"So I think we should re-do the interviews with some

of these people, and perhaps try to find, if we can, the drivers of the blue Ford or the van. We should also look at the closest CCTV along the A5 for sightings of these vehicles or of Yeung."

She looked at the team assembled then sat down again.

Dafydd said, "Sayer, that's good work. Some speculation, I know, but worth checking, I think. It may lead nowhere but it has me wondering why that van didn't park properly and what did the driver, or the driver of the blue car, see that could help us if Yeung did go that route?"

Dafydd said, "Idris, you did a number of these interviews. Why don't you and Catrin..." he looked at Keith, who nodded, "re-do them and see if you can tease out more details. Glynis, can you do the check on the CCTV footage please?"

"Inspector Marshall and I are going to re-interview Trevor Gerard. Wilton and Thomas, go pick him up – and let the surveillance team know in advance, please."

Catrin noted as she addressed the team that Sergeant Idris Bowen, an older man with white hair and apparently close to retirement, was not too happy with the analysis. He was portly and his suit looked rumpled and creased. Great, she thought. I am assigned to work with an old guy I have just pissed off.

Keith watched the team as they moved to their assigned duties. Catrin's work has given some new lines of enquiry but, more importantly, put some energy back into the investigation; they had been running out of steam. And he had his own idea of what to do with Trevor Gerard.

~~

The conversation between Idris and Catrin was in Welsh and business-like as they drove to the first interview. They had already established that the key re-interview would be with a Mr. Diliwar, the bus driver who saw the van and the blue Ford on the London Road. It would have to be this evening; he was out until probably 6.00 p.m. and away during the day tomorrow.

Idris said. "Catrin, you did a good job back there, so if you think I was annoyed, it's not with you, OK? I could see your face when the assignments were given, and I understood."

He looked at her and she realised that her own expression must have been readable. After all, he was an experienced detective.

He continued, "I never went back through all the reports in the way you did. After the first round, while we were concentrating on a missing person who may have had an accident or anything, we worked only with the material thinking he was still heading away from Holyhead. So if I am annoyed it is with me and, I guess, the system. We have such a broad caseload, not just missing person enquiries.

"It's good in a sense that you and your boss are here. At least this is a priority for the brass while Scotland Yard is on the ground this week."

The atmosphere thawed. By their first interview stop Idris and Catrin were talking about Pontypridd, the town where Catrin grew up. Idris had played rugby there years ago when a police team was on a tour.

The supplementary interviews with the two drivers didn't turn up anything new. If anything, the passing of five months made it harder for them as witnesses to recall their original statement details.

They drove back to the station and ran into Glynis.

"I am now tracking down all former servicemen who are local and who served with Trevor Gerard here or in Iraq," she said, "so there may be more interviews for you two to be doing."

Then she added to Catrin, "So your boss was in the army then?"

'Was he?' thought Catrin; it would account for his smart appearance, perhaps. Other than Keith Marshall's work, his knowledge of art and that his sister has an art gallery, she realised that she knew nothing about him. She said nothing and tried to look knowledgeable.

Dafydd and Keith, it turned out, were on their way to the local branch of the Royal British Legion. They also had an interview tomorrow with a Captain Evans of the Royal Welsh regiment.

Catrin learned what happened in the interview with Trevor Gerard from others at lunch.

~~

Trevor Gerard had been annoyed to be brought in again and he made that clear. Then he caught on to Keith's 'outsider' accent and his tailored suit and he took an even more uncooperative stance.

Keith had been leading the questions and hadn't even mentioned the watch. He was asking about Trevor's service record and his life since leaving the army. Trevor was getting further into sulky responses. Dafydd had said afterwards he was wondering where this was going. Then he found out.

"Looking at your file, Mr. Gerard, you have a 'drunk and disorderly' and, reading between the lines, you had a narrow squeak with a 'drinking and driving' charge after a speed stop. But you aren't flagged to be involved in any criminal activity."

"The speeding fine was just that, nothing else."

"Perhaps we should check the record of the officer in the report. I bet he was a former soldier, same regiment perhaps?"

"Don't know," said Trevor, his face showing that he did.

"So as a former soldier, proud of your service, your regiment, you may have difficulty finding work but I don't see you wanting to get into anything criminal, such as covering up the disappearance of this ship's officer, Yeung. I can't see that, somehow."

"Right on," Trevor said.

"Unless you were covering up for someone who served with you, a mate; that is something a soldier would do, right?"

"What the hell would you know about that?" spat out Gerard.

Keith said nothing, stood up and took off his jacket, then rolled up his left shirt sleeve to the elbow. "Recognize this?" An oval scar, a bullet entry wound, Dafydd saw.

He sat down and pulled a card out of his jacket inside pocket "And this?" He made sure Trevor saw it; then he put it back. Dafydd could see that it was a military ID, not his police warrant card.

Trevor Gerard just nodded.

"Don't tell me, soldier, what I know about loyalty in the army. As much as you, I think. So forget the crap about 'someone in a pub' because it doesn't cut it with me. Who did you buy the Rolex from?"

Trevor looked up, "I can't say," he said forcefully, but with a new tone in his voice, as if he was still in the army, speaking to a superior officer. It was clear he was not going to budge on that.

Keith just nodded.

He just has, thought Dafydd. We just have to track him down. He is probably a member of his unit or regiment that drinks in the same pub.

In the car to the Legion, Dafydd asked, "Where did you serve, Keith?"

"The Cheshire Regiment, Dafydd, the bullet was from Bosnia."

Dafydd drove and waited. Keith didn't say more and Dafydd decided not to ask.

"Well, it certainly got Gerard's attention. I thought he was going to stand up and salute you."

~ ~

Early that evening, Idris Bowen and Catrin Sayers drove across Anglesey to the town of Valley, to interview the bus driver who had seen the van at the grass verge, Ravi Diliwar. Inside the small cottage his wife took over reading to the two small children as he came down the stairs. Idris told him that they were re-interviewing, hoping to get more facts.

"I didn't see the Chinese man," he said, "as I said first time."

"Tell us again about the van and the car, please, Mr. Diliwar," said Idris.

Diliwar concentrated. "I was past them in a couple of seconds, so it was not that memorable. I was heading to Holyhead and they were on my side of the road, both facing the direction of travel. The back of the van, white but it was dirty white, had a red band and some letters, like a logo or business name. It wasn't a big van but I don't recall the make. It obscured most of the car, which I only saw as I pulled wide to miss the van which was sticking out, as I said. It was small, dark blue and I thought it was something like a Ford, perhaps a Fiesta or the next size up, but not big."

He paused, "That's about it."

Catrin said, "Did you see anyone?"

"Not that I remember. There was no-one on the road side of the vehicles, I know that. I wasn't looking further on to the grass verge, so I can't say one way or the other."

"And in the first report you gave mentioned a bike."

"Yes, I thought I saw a bicycle wheel lying on the ground, on the inside as I went by. It was between the vehicles, you know, in the angle, but my sight was partially blocked by the bus."

Catrin said, "Did you see any of the frame? Was it bright yellow, perhaps?"

"No," said Diliwar, shaking his head, "What I saw was very little but it was dark." He looked into the distance, thinking. "But it wasn't black."

"Thank you, Mr. Diliwar, you have been very helpful," said Idris, standing up.

Catrin said, "One final thing, are you sure of the timing?"

He laughed. "Yes, within a minute or so. One thing bus drivers have to be aware of is our timing. Leave a bus stop a minute too early and there are complaints."

As they drove off Idris said, "Nice touch with the colours, Catrin." Han's bike had a dark wine-coloured frame.

"It's the artist in me, Idris," said Catrin.

~~

At the briefing the following morning they reviewed the updates. It was clear they all felt that some progress was being made and Dafydd made use of the energy.

"So let's summarize," he said, holding up one finger at a time in sequence.

"We have currently fourteen names of former servicemen, all from the same regiment as Trevor Gerard in the same time period and all are local. There may be more, we are still checking.

"Two. We have nothing more on the blue Ford other than it was dark blue, not light, and perhaps it is a Fiesta or similar.

"Three. Mr. Diliwar was not able to give Idris and Catrin the make and possible model of the van, but it was a dirty white and had a red band behind the logo or text; probably a business vehicle of some sort. Not bad, seeing as he was driving his bus at the time.

"Four. Most important, there may have been a bike at the scene which could match the colour of the one that Han Yeung was riding.

"So let's focus first on the van, a commercial vehicle and on the soldiers Trevor Gerard knows. To begin with, let's see if there is a correlation and, if nothing comes up, search out all possible white vans with a red band on them used for business purposes in the area."

They all knew they were now into the grind of 'find and eliminate' but the fact that they had lines to follow was an improvement.

~~

Over the next few days Catrin continued to partner with Idris. Keith Marshall worked with a young DC, Peter

Hanlon, who clearly wanted to make a good impression. At the hotel on the following evening Marshall said he sensed the young officer was thinking of spreading his wings beyond North Wales.

It was Sunday when Catrin next saw Li. DI Marshall was due to go back the following day and Worsley and Marshall were undecided whether to bring Catrin back too or leave her another week.

In part it was keeping the contact with Li that Worsley and Powys wanted to maintain and in any event, Catrin wanted to. A few times she had fleeting daydreams about actually enjoying doing postgraduate work in art history in this part of the world and having a straightforward friendship with Li, without the encumbrance of her professional duty overlaying it.

They had agreed to meet in Y Felinheli and eat at a pub there called the Halfway House. It was located near the marina where the university sailing club operated. She was to meet Li at the marina first as she would have been sailing that morning. Li had said, "I can't invite you sailing, I'm sorry, it is only for registered students and it is racing training, not pleasure sailing."

"That's fine," said Catrin, "I don't sail anyway."

On Friday she had reported her plan to Keith, wanting to tread carefully in this area. Keith just nodded. In his office Dafydd must have overheard as he came to the door and said, "That's my marina. My boat Ceinwen is there. Pity about the timing, I could have taken you and Jian Li out."

Looking hard at Keith he said, "At least Yeung could crew."

Catrin saw that her boss and Dafydd were getting along well if they could joke with each other.

Idris had dropped Catrin back at the station. They had

just returned from one more visit to see a possible van so that Catrin could pick up the pool car and head over to Y Felinheli. Keith was at their desk reading an email from DCI Worsley.

"Even though it is the weekend, Jane is in Geneva with Coltrane. It's in response to an urgent request from the Geneva Police yesterday, I gather," he said without preamble. "Something is breaking on the theft of the Komarov Sisters, so call me after you finish with Yeung. Jane will only know what the significance is after the meeting with the Swiss. You may need to come back here if it is anything useful and, if so, I suspect we will both be heading south."

21 THE RECEPTION AT
THE PALAIS DES NATIONS

Geneva, October. The large complex of buildings and parkland purpose-built in the early nineteen thirties had once been designated as the headquarters of the League of Nations. Close to the centre of the city but in its own secure area, the facility looked across to Lake Geneva and the mountains beyond.

The formal restaurant in the upper levels of the United Nations Palais des Nations was often used for receptions. From the panoramic windows along the south wall there was an excellent view of the Alps. The Jet d'Eau, the spectacular fountain in the lake, completed the picture.

It is tranquil, elegant, sophisticated, thought Sergeant Julian Wengler of the Geneva Police, taking in the familiar view. It is a pity Franz Reicher is here to spoil the atmosphere for me.

He had organized an invitation to this reception with a quick phone call once they found out Reicher would attend. Reicher was donating a valuable caricature by the Swiss artist Paul Degen, one he owned legally, in support of a UN initiative. Later in the year it would be auctioned in support of the Sub-Saharan Africa project on drought aid. In the meantime Reicher would bask in an array of new contacts, influential people with both money and interest in the acquisition of works of art.

Franz Reicher was on the Swiss Police radar as the leader of a long-standing art theft and smuggling operation, something they were sure of but so far had been unable to gather anywhere near sufficient evidence to lay charges.

That the man would make a slip-up in his remarks in somewhere as public as the United Nations was almost unthinkable; but you never know, thought Julian, optimistically. Being there, his superiors said, Sergeant Wengler would be showing Reicher that they were not letting up in their efforts. He and Reicher were old adversaries.

Gracious statements by several ambassadors and permanent representatives were made and then a photo-op with Reicher and the two other donors opened the event. Guests were served with wine and champagne as staff moved around with trays of canapés. Julian was thinking of calling it a day when he saw a quite eye-catching Chinese woman deftly gather Reicher by his left arm, talking intently to him as she led him to a quiet spot closer to the window. She must be with the Chinese delegation, he thought.

Wengler said afterwards that it was the angle that made the difference. With the shade on the window, he was positioned to see enough of the reflection of their faces. The mask of self-satisfaction dropped from Reicher to be replaced by what he could only describe as fear or anger, or both. He moved a little closer and heard only the final phrase that she spoke in in English '... within 48 hours.'

She turned away looking towards Julian and smiled charmingly at him, then she moved on to talk to the Nigerian Ambassador and his entourage. Reicher looked across at Wengler; the mask had returned but he was working his way towards the door, briefly saying his farewells to his host and pointing at his elegant wristwatch.

The following morning, Saturday, Wengler was at home when he received an urgent summons to Listgarten's office, the prosecutor assigned to build the case against Reicher and his group. "Franz Reicher is in reception with his lawyer, Katarina Weil. He insists on seeing me alone. It may be related to your report on the reception."

"It's probably a complaint of harassment."

"Perhaps, but I don't think so. He says he wants to make a statement. I will keep them waiting until you get in. You can watch it on the CCTV."

~~

About the time Franz Reicher was preparing to head to the Geneva police headquarters, Emily Yang was browsing through a high-end watch and jewellery store in downtown Geneva; not to buy anything, just examine the range for anything of interest that she could later secure in Hong Kong considerably cheaper. Playing tourist was part of the routine of killing time for her.

Emily mused that it was a strange mission that Michael Yau had given her, but at least it gave her some relief from the tedium of her role in Sydney. She longed to be back in Hong Kong, but commercial espionage was an important business line for her Triad and she had done well in her position at the Australian oil company. Her manager there thought she was taking a sudden leave of absence arising from a family emergency.

It was not the instruction to locate two valuable paintings by threatening Reicher that she found strange; it was the other part. She was to deliver messages to a number of people to turn themselves over to the authorities and discover the whereabouts of the body of Han Yeung, a sailor. In her world, people who crossed Triad interests were either dead, bought or used as trade - and bodies of dead people outside her Triad family didn't really matter.

As she crossed the bridge at the end of the lake heading to the old city her phone rang. She was to be prepared to follow up with Reicher when instructed. He had been observed with his lawyer entering the police headquarters, so clearly he had heard her message and was acting on it. Where she was going next depended on the information she got from Reicher later.

~~

Detective Chief Inspector Neville Coltrane was clearly no newcomer to Geneva from his comments on the flight to Jane Worsley.

In the months since the Art Crime Unit had been established and she had been appointed, they had sorted out a process of working with each other, knowing Taylor and Matheson would be watching them carefully. It was based on not getting cross-threaded on cases of mutual interest. There would be only one lead unit for any line of investigation but the other unit would be kept informed so no-one was blind-sided. They recognized that as team leaders they were very different personalities but each saw that the other was both strong-willed and keen to do a good job.

If Coltrane still held any resentment about the creation of the ACU, he hid it well. Jane hoped he had actually moved on but with Coltrane, one couldn't be sure.

They had talked after the discovery of the watch and the identification of a suspect vehicle in the Yeung case. If the path of the investigation now diverged from the paintings, the work on the art disappearance would be transferred back to his group.

The call from Wengler on Saturday gave Jane only the fact that Franz Reicher, the prime suspect as leader of the art theft ring, had made a statement that was very relevant to their interest. He was not being held. He and his lawyer had given an undertaking that he would be interviewed by the British police in respect to the Komarov paintings only, but it had to be within twenty-four hours or the offer was null and void.

Wengler would provide them with the first interview transcript but it was in German, so perhaps if they came out straight away? He could go through it, not just what was said but give them also Listgarten's reading of the interview. Could they come even though it would be interviewing Reicher on a Sunday?

"Oh yes," said Jane.

Coltrane's first response was, "But I was just going to Milan." He didn't say whether it was for personal or business purposes, she noted.

"Fine, Neville. I just thought I would extend the invitation but we can talk after -."

"No," he sighed, "I will be there. I will even reserve the hotel rooms if you book the flights, Jane. I know a few hotels there."

They would be expensive ones too, thought Jane, but she wasn't prepared to argue. If Jack raised an eyebrow on the expenses she would make the point she was acting 'in the spirit of co-operation'.

It was Saturday evening. The review with Wengler had been thorough and illuminating and had prepared the two British detectives well for the interview the following day, she thought. They walked down to the Rue de Dr. Alfred Vincent for dinner at a restaurant Coltrane had chosen, one that Wengler also liked.

Jane was pleasantly surprised. It turned out to be not so fancy, moderately priced and excellent food. After seeing the room rate at the hotel, she thought they would be eating in a place with a maître' d in white tie and tails, but it was good food in a nice atmosphere, with a lot of weekend bustle and plenty of conversation at other tables to drown out their own.

Neville told them that after the business discussions about a previous run-in he had with Franz Reicher over ten years ago. He had been a detective sergeant at the time. During a stake-out of an art dealer in Mayfair on a case involving a Mayan sculpture, Neville had seen Reicher coming out of the gallery with a briefcase. It was too thin to contain the item they were interested in and they had no reason to stop him. As he passed the car they were in Reicher suddenly looked and Neville knew he had been recognized.

After the trap was sprung and the Mayfair dealer was telling them all about the sculpture it became clear that a small Russian icon on their radar had also been in the gallery. It wasn't among the items found and the dealer would say nothing about its movement.

"I was convinced that Reicher had walked out with it under our noses."

By agreement, only Jane Worsley and Neville Coltrane were in the interview room with Reicher and his lawyer, Weil, on the Sunday afternoon. Wengler and Listgarten watched on CCTV.

After identification for the record Jane began. "I understand, from the terms of agreement with the Geneva Police, we are to interview you only on the subject of the Komarov paintings in the UK. So let's begin there."

She took them back over the material they had provided to Listgarten. She could not spot any inconsistencies in the responses. Franz directed his answers to Jane but otherwise was eyeing Neville.

She said, "We have the painting of the second sister, Elizaveta Komarov. It appears you know that. You say that the painting of the eldest sister is now in the UK and it was sold by a Miss Geraldine Roper and that her customer is a British immigrant, a Russian called Pyotr Yermilov. Is that correct?"

"Yes. That is so, to my belief."

"How do you know that?"

"Let us say she confirmed this directly with me. This is first-hand information. Why she did that is not on the table, so please do not ask."

His lawyer frowned at him; he was talking too much.

Worsley nodded.

"Did Roper collect the painting and deliver it herself?"

Reicher responded, "No, she would not do that, I know. This is why you must talk with her."

"Was Holyhead the delivery point? As one painting came through there it would be logical, but we want to know."

"It was not meant to be, originally. When one painting disappeared it was decided to offload the others. The value of the set had been lost."

"Why are you giving us this information?" Jane knew the answer from Wengler, but wanted it first-hand again.

"Because it may be linked in some way to the disappearance of a Chinese person; how, I do not know, but you may want to pursue the link."

"Why?" said Worsley. "People disappear all the time."

For the first time in the interview Reicher looked ill at ease. His lawyer said, "If the British police do not want to investigate information about a disappearance that is your call. Fine, it's your choice."

She smiled. Reicher did not. Worsley was watching him carefully, waiting for his answer.

Reicher said, "Because I believe the man to be dead. You have an enquiry into a murder or a manslaughter to consider."

"While in the process of another crime, smuggling stolen art", interjected Coltrane.

"Whether they are linked, I really cannot say."

Coltrane continued, "What was the sale price for the Komarov that Geri handled? I am sure we will find out in due course."

Coltrane had mentioned last night that he knew personally this new suspect, Geraldine Roper, an art expert, lecturer and critic.

Reicher looked at his lawyer, who nodded.

"I understand that £150,000 was the price finally agreed."

Worsley looked at Coltrane who was deliberately showing his disbelief. He caught her eye and took over.

"The three Komarov Sisters were last appraised a year

ago for insurance purposes at just under two million US dollars. At least, that is the last appraisal I know about. We know that the Volgograd Museum wasn't going to sell; in fact they are still owned by the Komarov family so they couldn't sell anyway. And we know they would bring in much more than the appraisal price in the right auction. You are telling me that Katarina was pissed away for £150,000. That's criminal, Franz."

Worsley hid her smile at the irony of Coltrane's tirade. Reicher was looking miserable.

His lawyer bristled, "Is there a question there? I really can't see it and...."

"The question is, why so low a price?" said Coltrane softly.

Reicher looked at Coltrane. "As a set, yes, I think close to a million, perhaps a million and a quarter if sold illegally; not the appraisal price you quoted. Broken up the set is worth much less individually. And, tied to a death and a police investigation... Mr. Coltrane, you know this so why do you ask?"

Neville ignored the question.

"So where is the third painting?"

"I don't know exactly but not in the UK, I know that so...."

"It is outside the agreed scope!" interjected forcefully his lawyer. "Do you have any more questions?"

"Yes," said Coltrane.

"Well," she beamed, "we don't have much more time."

"I was going to say, Mr. Reicher, the packing of the painting was a magnificent job, excellent, such a nice technique. But probably at the limit of canvas flexibility for the diameter of the tubing I think. Would you care to have the person publish the technique in a peer-reviewed journal?"

Reicher just laughed. "I don't think I want to discuss this with you, Mr. Coltrane." Jane could see, though, it was a subject that interested him.

His lawyer stood up, angry at the insolence of the question. "This interview is over." She led her client to the door and out.

A minute or two later Wengler came in. "I was watching his eyes when you threw in the tube limitations, Neville. You are right after all. Whoever is doing this can handle a broader array of canvases. A lot more paintings may be being shipped this way. We will have to review more missing works, I think, that may have gone through the cruise ship route.

"I hate to think of the times that Customs have examined carpets in shipping containers for any hidden works rolled in them but not the tubes they are rolled around."

"Worth coming for by itself, Julian," smiled Coltrane.

Sergeant Wengler looked at Worsley. "I think Jane is of the opinion that the name of Geraldine Roper being linked to the disappearance and probably to the death of Mr. Yeung was what was worth coming for, am I right?"

Jane nodded. She liked Wengler. It was clear now that the Yeung case was going to stay with the ACU, no matter what.

"On that score," said Neville, "I should probably advise you that Geri and I are on the same board of directors, the New Discoveries Art Foundation."

Jane said, "You didn't mention it last night!"

"It's immaterial, really. I am just thinking I will, at some point, need to ask Sir Philip to suggest to her that she resign quietly."

The look Wengler gave Worsley seemed to indicate, 'I

am glad he is yours, not mine' but what he said was, "Let me give you a ride to the airport. We can talk on the way."

~~

Jane Worsley had emailed on her mobile at Geneva airport for a conference call with Keith, Catrin and Dafydd. She went to the airport police facility in Heathrow on arrival to make it. After landing she checked her emails again and, based on the news from Bangor, realised that this case was opening up on two fronts.

"The Yeung case has just had a significant breakthrough at the Geneva end although neither Coltrane nor I can think of why at present. But you have news too, I see. I will summarize mine and then let's discuss this suspect you mention."

She gave an accurate précis of the interview and discussions.

She finished with "So Dafydd, Keith?"

Dafydd said. "Sayer spotted around midday a van meeting the description of one of the two vehicles we were looking for… so this one is down to her."

Catrin blushed visibly.

Dafydd continued, "Unfortunately, I doubt that the interview with the suspect will be in the next few days. He is now undergoing psychiatric evaluation. Keith had better summarize the situation as he talked to the psychiatrist in charge."

22 THE UNIVERSITY SAILING CLUB

Y Felineli or Port Dinowic, given its former English name, is a pretty village on the shoreline of the Menai Strait between Bangor and Caernarfon. It took Catrin no more than ten minutes to cover the five miles along the A5 road before her satnav indicated the access road down to the marina.

Li was waiting by the club house as she arrived, talking with two other members of the sailing club. Li introduced her as 'my friend Catrin' and they said their goodbyes.

"They were just making sure I had a ride back," she said.

They decided to leave the car there and walk up to the pub to get something to eat. Li was full of her sailing experience. Catrin could see how she had been settling into life in the Bangor Community and said so.

"Yes, between my classmates, the floor at Gwynant, this club and my friends in the Chinese Society I know a lot more people now. It all keeps me busy - and that makes it easier, waiting for news about Han."

As they reached the top of the road up from the

harbour, waiting to cross over the main road to the pub, Catrin saw a white van with a flash of red on the side pass by and she instinctively memorized the plate number.

"Give me a moment, Li."

Out of habit she first pulled out her notebook and recorded the details she had seen then she called Idris. "Idris, I'm in Y Felinheli. A white painter's van, red stripe on side panels and rear door, just passed heading towards Bangor. Here are the details…."

"I will look into it Catrin, thanks," he said. He was at the station.

It must have been the hundredth van they had looked into so far based on the search and CCTV footage from Anglesey, she thought, and moved it to the back of her mind.

An hour later she and Li were finishing their meal and conversation when Idris called back. "Good work, Catrin, it was a hit. The driver is from the same regiment, same unit as Trevor Gerard. His name is Stephen Harrison and he is now in custody, sort of. But I tell you, this one is weird."

What do you mean?"

She tried to keep her voice even but saw that Li was already watching carefully, picking up her voice and body language.

"No-one can get through to him. It's as if he has turned in on himself; he won't communicate or can't.

"I had Miller from traffic pull him over waving a radar gun, just to check the details and save us a visit. He was already patrolling the A5.

"Harrison was the only person in the van and he started to answer the routine questions as Miller gave the van a once over. Then he just seemed to seize up. Miller couldn't get a response and Harrison just looked at the dashboard. He started hyperventilating."

"Constable Miller called an ambulance. Harrison is now in the local hospital, Ysbyty Gwynedd, with Miller on his room door until we organize a relief. So don't rush, it will be some time, I think.

"Thompson has gone back to pick up Trevor Gerard. Dafydd wants him in custody now there is the firm link with Harrison established. Dafydd and Glynis have gone to see Harrison's mother and a forensic team is being organized for both his van and his mother's home. We are waiting on the warrant."

Li was watching Catrin absorbing the flow of information and Catrin saw she had started to tense up, expecting the worst.

Idris was still talking. "Harrison's mother lives off Beach Road and he lives with her. The reason that his name and the van didn't flash up on the first search is that the business is actually registered to his mother, as is the van. I recalled the name Harrison in the list of Gerard's contacts. When the registration flashed up, I spoke to Dafydd."

"That's it, get back but don't rush. Your boss is at the hospital now waiting to talk to Harrison, if he can."

They closed the call.

"Wow," thought Catrin, "Wow!"

She looked across at Li. "No news of Han," she said softly. "But a break perhaps, Li, we are not sure yet."

She suddenly choked up and said, "We have been working bloody hard trying to find Han or find out what happened, a lot of us. Perhaps it's a break; perhaps not."

"Does it link to Han's watch?"

Catrin gathered her composure. "It may do. We may have located a man who sold it to the person DI Powys mentioned. You know I can't give any more detail. The person is in custody."

Li said seriously, "Catrin, I am glad you said what you did just now. I need to thank you and your colleagues, I know. I was rude about all of you, including you specifically, to Chief Inspector Worsley in London. I feel badly about that. It is just so frustrating, you know, not knowing what is happening."

"DCI Worsley has heard a lot worse, Li, I am sure. Forget it, OK? It is quite understandable. Come on; let's walk back to the car through the marina before we head back. I want to see a particular sailing boat and get your opinion on it!"

"You are thinking of buying a boat?" said Li, surprised.

"No, I just wanting to see if someone's pride and joy is all it's cracked up to be."

Li laughed. "Anyone's boat is their pride and joy and knowing that you know no one in Bangor other than police officers, I will avoid any trouble. My lips are sealed. You know I can't say any more," she gently mocked.

The two women laughed and headed down to the harbour. Catrin thought it might be the last bit of relaxation for a while so she led Li on a quest for the Ceinwen in the gorgeous mid-afternoon light reflecting from the Menai Strait. They found the boat easily. It was old but well-maintained, Li observed. She explained it to Catrin.

"It's a French design, a Beneteau, a 'First 25' model I believe, and not new. You can see the age in the fibreglass, but it's lovely. It is really well cared for."

Catrin noticed three slips over a similar vessel in immaculate condition with the name 'Rusalka'. Czech, she thought, wondering if this was Professor Parry's boat. He was the only person she knew with Eastern European interests around here and he did have a boat, she recalled.

~~

The young physician from ER came out of the room, closing the door behind him. The sign said 'Examination Room 3' and below it, on white card taped to the door, 'obstetric priority use'. He saw a man in a suit talking to the uniformed PC who had come in with the patient and was still stationed outside. He took him to be the detective in charge.

"Mr. Harrison is drowsy now. I gave him a mild sedative earlier, just enough to relax him after we got some control of the hyperventilation. It seems to be some kind of anxiety attack."

He looked at the uniformed officer. "There wasn't a struggle physically during the arrest was there?"

Miller said, "He wasn't arrested, Doctor. He was sitting in his van and was simply being asked where he had been. It was like a change came over him, then the breathing problem started."

The doctor looked at Keith. "I know you want to talk to him but I have called Dr. Owen, Head of Psychiatry. I think he should see him first."

"He has some other problem, then?" asked Keith.

"I can't say, unfortunately, other than he has been here before and he is a patient of Dr. Owen. So I prefer you wait unless, frankly, someone else's life is depending on an interview this minute?"

"I can't say we know that. It is related to a missing person enquiry, so I hope it's not the case."

"Then let's wait until Owen gets here; he is on his way. If it is any clue, Owen is known to be an expert in post-traumatic stress disorder, PTSD, and there are a lot of ex-servicemen around here. So draw your own conclusion."

"I hope it is soon," said Miller. He was waiting for a replacement, his shift was nearly over.

"So do I," said the doctor, walking away, "I want my room back. Look how busy it is here."

23 PTSD

Keith had seen the older physician arrive at the floor and head straight to the examination room. After a while he came out and introduced himself as Eric Owen, head of the Psychiatry Department.

"Inspector, can I ask the nature of your enquiry, without details, of course."

"It is a murder enquiry now, we believe, but it started as a missing person case about four months ago. You can see the seriousness of the matter."

Owen just nodded, thinking. "Stephen Harrison is a patient of mine. I know that was mentioned to you. From my examination now he has had a significant setback, that's clear. If I knew the basis of it I still couldn't tell you, of course. You know that. But he has been my patient since his discharge from the Army. He was doing very well and was back at work as a decorator, I gather. At present he is calm, unresponsive and completely withdrawn, almost catatonic."

"So is it possible to talk to him, even briefly?" Keith knew the answer but, still, he had to ask.

Owen said nothing at first; he was clearly thinking what was best.

"No, at this stage, I don't think you can interview him formally and even when you do it should be with legal counsel present I would think, as a precaution. At present, I assure you, he is not talking to anyone."

Marshall looked at him and said quietly, "I've seen men affected in this way before, Doctor. So I know it will be quite unpredictable when he will be fit to be interviewed formally, but we are really struggling. We really need to know if Stephen Harrison is possibly involved, that's our priority."

Owen said, "Where did you see men like this, Inspector?"

"In Bosnia in '93, Doctor, I was a lieutenant then."

Owen looked at Keith steadily, reappraising him. "Then yes you have indeed, I think, and as you say, the timing is going to be quite unpredictable."

Keith watched him, waiting.

"Look, Inspector, I think the dose of sedative has more or less worn off now. I want to re-admit him to our mental health hospital in Llanfairfechan. I may need to sedate him further for travel there and I want to talk to his mother first. He will be in surroundings at the hospital and with staff he knows and trusts; he was there when he first came back from Iraq.

"So I am going to allow you one visit here before we move him, for one purpose only. I want to get through to Stephen if I can. Do you have a photograph of your missing person, one that is not in itself a traumatic image? I take it that would be a primary interest?"

"Yes," said Keith, "I actually have one of him, his graduation photo, on my mobile."

He showed Owen, who said, "This is that sailor who

went missing in early summer, right?"

"Yes, Third Officer Han Yeung. He went missing from the ship the *Manden Serenity*, while it was docked in Holyhead."

Owen was clearly thinking of something. "Then come in. Let's show it to him and see."

Keith followed the psychiatrist into the room. Stephen Harrison was dressed, legs covered with a blanket sitting upright in the chair at the side of the examination gurney. He was a young man, well built, dark hair with a paint splash on his left ring finger. He paid no attention to their entry.

"Stephen, it's Dr. Owen again. I have someone with me, someone who is trying to find another young man. I would like to ask if you have ever seen this person. That is all I want to know now."

He nodded to Keith. He passed the phone with Yeung's image to Owen, who gently brought it closer to his patient. At the point where it came into focus, Stephen took a deep breath and Owen said gently, 'Just relax, Stephen and tell me'. Harrison looked directly at the image and gently nodded as tears started pouring down his cheeks.

Keith was bursting with questions but tried not to show it.

"Thank you Stephen, now relax and rest," said Dr. Owen softly.

The doctor and the policeman left the room.

"Inspector, he has been in therapy for a problem brought on by his experiences as a soldier while serving in Iraq. Now something he is aware of, or has in some way experienced, has sent him back deep inside himself. He recognized me and I had hoped he would start talking, but not so far. It's a real setback not only for his recovery but for your enquiry, I appreciate."

Keith said, "I will tell Inspector Powys that we will need to wait on your word to interview this man and it may be some time."

"That is good of you. I know the pressure is on and it can cause some frictions. He looks fine but it is not a physical injury as you well know. As you can see I think there is a link between your victim and Stephen but I don't know what. Remember, if he had some innocent encounter and he happened to remember him, the reaction you saw could be the same."

Marshall said, "Dr. Owen, I know that recovery is partly based on the receptivity of the individual to work with his or her physician. Was Harrison, can I ask, working on his recovery, taking all the right medications or whatever?"

"I would say yes, at least until recently and then I can't say. His appointments with me were now down to quarterly. My last consultation with him was, well ... his last appointment was missed three months ago and immediately after that I was away for some time myself. He was re-scheduled to see me a week ago and then he postponed again. When I got the call it is part of the reason why I came straight over."

Marshall thought, so that is what Owen was working through earlier – the failure of Harrison to keep his appointments with the timeline of Yeung's disappearance.

"Would you say he was a violent man?" he asked.

Owen pursed his lips. "That's a difficult question. He was a soldier, as were you, I understand. I would say his recovery leads me to believe he could handle situations and not lose control, let's put it that way. But only if he maintained both his medication and avoided stress of the sort which brought him here in the first place."

Owen clearly needed to leave. "Look, once he is settled into the Mental Health Unit and I can see some light in this, I will inform you or – who should I call?"

Keith passed him his card, writing on the back Dafydd's direct line number, "or Inspector Powys," he said.

He thanked Owen and went out to call Dafydd. At the entrance he remembered that he had been dropped off and Miller's replacement was now on duty. He hadn't got a ride so he called Catrin to collect him.

~ ~

After the debriefing by both Worsley and Marshall they called it a night. As they finished Catrin mentioned to Dafydd that she had seen his boat. "It looks very nice, sir, Li says it is well-cared for."

"That it is, Catrin," said Dafydd, "the Ceinwen needs a lot of TLC."

"There is a similar boat further along the row in the marina called the 'Rusalka' we saw also."

"Yes," said Dafydd, "That's your friend Parry's boat. A Beneteau First also but the 30 foot model, ours is the twenty-five foot. His was built much more recently, not sure when. I thought he really liked it but it is up for sale now. It has been on the market for a few months, I think. He must be asking too much."

Catrin and Keith were going to eat back at the hotel. Their mobiles pinged concurrently in the car. 'Team meeting by phone 7.30 a.m. tomorrow, I will call hotel.' DCI Worsley had more to discuss, it seemed.

The following morning they took the call together on the speaker phone in Keith's room. Worsley was to the point.

"This is not about the process of the investigation at this point; we can cover that at the morning briefing with Dafydd's team. It's about the direction it's going on two counts.

"First, Neville Coltrane and I were talking. He makes the point that while we have to act fast on the arrest of Geraldine Roper it has to be good and has to stick. The Swiss and Art and Antiques want to break open a lot more from Reicher and the route to do this starts with her. If she feels that she has no way out she may trade some information on Reicher for dropping her in it and so the cards start to fall.

"If not, Coltrane is concerned that Reicher will buy her off and she will take any minor sentence if there is a big windfall. I agree with him and have decided that we need to let A&A in on the investigation, not simply keep them informed."

"What does that mean, ma'am, in practice?" asked Catrin.

"First, we need to find a solid communication trail between Roper and Reicher. No-one has achieved this with Reicher so far. If we link them with evidence, then we have a lot stronger case. Second, their people will participate in the arrest and interviews."

Catrin nodded, she understood that. Keith kept his face neutral.

"So after this morning, unless something comes up there as surprising for us as yesterday's discoveries, you two are on your way back here. We will work with A&A on this aspect. The other thing is the Chinese link." said Worsley.

"Catrin and I were talking about that last night, Jane, over dinner." said Keith. "A Chinese man has allegedly been killed in Wales and a Chinese woman in Geneva stirs the pot with someone who then tells us about a link."

"Exactly. So I have to ask, Catrin, is Jian Li Yeung involved in this somehow, do you think? Is that part of the reason she came here?"

Catrin said, "Ma'am, my intuition says 'no' but I have to also admit I might be becoming less objective. She treats me like a friend and, frankly, I enjoy that. Under other circumstances I would not be holding back on developing such a friendship, if you understand?"

"I do. And I also recognize that we have put you in this little dilemma, but I still want an answer."

Catrin thought a moment. "I still feel that she is not behind this, but I know that she is keeping her relatives informed of any developments, that is, other than the news that her brother was gay. She told me she cannot tell her parents that. But are people in Hong Kong interfering in this now? Possibly, but I can't say."

"The file says that Mr. Yeung Senior is a tailor, he has a high-end shop."

"Yes," said Catrin, "between dealing with his son's loss, maintaining his business and helping his wife come to terms with everything he is pretty busy, I understand. That's the impression I get from my conversations with Li."

"Not the sort of family to be involved in forcing an art smuggling ring to confess, I think," said Worsley. "Let's file it for now. Anyway, we'll talk again in an hour when you are at the station; I will call in during the morning briefing. I think Keith will assist with the interview of Trevor Gerard then I want you both to head back."

~~

Dafydd and Keith did the second interview with Gerard, with a duty solicitor sitting in.

Dafydd began, "Trevor, we are waiting to interview your friend Stephen Harrison; he is your friend, right?"

Trevor nodded. Keith pointed at the table microphone and he said, "Yes, he is."

"No major charges have been laid against him or you, yet. But we have reason to believe he was involved in the disappearance of the man whose watch you purchased. And we are going through his vehicle and home with a fine tooth comb."

"I wasn't involved in anything," said Trevor.

"You just bought the watch from him, yes?"

"Yes, I did."

Keith asked, "How has he been in the last few months?"

"How do you mean?"

Keith said, "He is your friend so you would know, right? He had some sort of breakdown yesterday. His psychiatrist said it is a big setback on his recovery. I want to know what caused that. And I would like to know what caused his original condition while in Iraq, while we are at it. If you cooperate this time and nothing else comes up, we will accept that you bought a watch from a friend in good faith. Get my drift?"

Trevor said, "Is he bad?"

"I saw him last night, Trevor, and I have seen soldiers like that before and I think personally he is in bad shape, but it is really for his doctor to decide."

Trevor took a deep breath. "Steve has been different in the last while, more like he was before the Iraq thing, confident, assertive. I thought he was actually overdoing his meds.

"He had been doing really well with Dr. Owen, gaining confidence, but not like he has been for the last while. For a time the only place we, two other mates from the same unit and me, could take him was fishing or somewhere else quiet like that. It has been like that for months.

"About Iraq, well, he was nearly killed, we both were in one incident, but it wasn't that, although it all builds up."

He looked at Marshall, "You know, I think."

"It was something that happened later, that's when he snapped."

~ ~

The unit in which Lance-Corporal Stephen Harrison and Private Trevor Gerard served had been on street patrol on a relationship-building exercise in a village that was deemed a high priority item. Trevor didn't know why, it was just the day's orders.

In the square they were providing a perimeter guard while several officers talked through an interpreter with the local elders. All was quiet. Three women in traditional robes and hijabs approached Lance-Corporal Harrison, Trevor observed. One woman was smiling and started to talk in halting English with Steve. She was young and quite good looking. 'Aye, aye,' thought Trevor, 'she is chatting Steve up, that's not good news.'

Standing orders were to be polite but distant. This is a society where looking too long at a young woman will have her husband at you with a knife. He saw that Steve was playing it just right, not ignoring her totally but concentrating on his assigned role.

Then two of the women were at his gun while the third hit him with a stone she had hidden in her robe. Not that hard, she wasn't that strong, really, but as he ran over Trevor saw his lance-corporal had just about lost the gun. Steve wasn't fighting back. Trevor thought, if he loses the strap he will lose the gun and then there would be all hell to pay.

Several other soldiers were now noticing the bustle and Trevor's run as he went full force into the women, hitting the one holding the gunstock hard with his shoulder and pushing the rifle back into Steve's hand. He then turned, raising his own weapon. Other soldiers were doing the same, covering their assigned positions.

The sergeant was calling for an orderly withdrawal to the personnel carriers as the officers, alerted, retreated also. As they withdrew he could see the three women standing there, the one he hit holding her shoulder and screaming and local men milling around them, some clearly supportive but most others displaying anger that their discussions had been interrupted by this stupidity.

~~

"No shots were fired," said Trevor. "No-one was killed or wounded. It was a minor incident, other than Steve changed that day. No-one pulled his chain about it, so it wasn't bullying or anything like that. It was all inside. He felt he had failed and we just kept telling him it was no big deal, it was done.

"I told him, 'It reminds us all to be more careful,' I said, but he seemed to brood on it."

Two weeks later, Trevor Gerard said, while on patrol a local man standing close to Lance-Corporal Harrison raised his fist in anger about something; the frustration of occupation as he saw it, perhaps, or the price the vendor was charging for figs. Trevor didn't know.

"But it wasn't an attack on Steve, I know that. It wasn't directed at him. Steve hit him really hard with the butt of his rifle and he went down."

The square turned violent. After withdrawal, Harrison was arrested and charged with an unwarranted assault on a civilian; but it didn't matter. Trevor said he didn't speak or recognize anyone right until the time he was sent back to Wales. He had visited Steve in the medical unit and it was like his friend was a stranger, in another world.

"If he is anything like last time, sir," he said to Keith, "it could be a long time."

Dafydd looked at Keith and they nodded in agreement with each other.

Dafydd said, "Trevor, we are going to go through this again slowly, getting some dates on when you saw these changes over the last months, when you got the watch and so on. We want the lot, hear me. And when you have your statement signed, then you can go. You won't hear any more about the watch if this is the whole story. If it isn't, or if I hear you have talked to anyone at all about this interview, you will be back in here in as much trouble as I can find charges for."

Trevor's head was nodding.

~~

Keith was driving as they headed back to London. They had been talking about the case for a while then he mentioned to Catrin more about next steps in her development; training courses that might be suitable, aspects of other cases he was working on that would involve her. He was still concerned that she had started with them awkwardly, by being dropped into a difficult situation with the woman Jian Li Yeung.

After a lull, she said, "Sir, can I ask a personal question?"

Keith smiled. "Yes, if I can choose not to answer without offending you."

"Idris, Sergeant Bowen, said that in your first interview with Trevor Gerard you showed him a bullet scar. Were you shot in the line of duty?"

"Yes, in the arm. Not a bad wound, compared with others you hear about. The bullet had lost a lot of energy by the time it hit me. There is still some residual damage in the arm.

"But I wasn't a policeman when it happened, Catrin, it was when I was a soldier, a lieutenant in the Cheshire Regiment, back in the early nineties."

He glanced at her. "You are trying to think what was happening then, right?"

She nodded, still serious. "Yes, I was in school."

"British soldiers wore blue berets. We were part of the supposed peace-keeping force in Bosnia."

"Ah," she said, "So you were shot there."

"And worse, in a sense," he said.

Catrin said, "I didn't mean to intrude, honestly, it is just that one of the things new police officers talk about is this issue of guns, getting shot, shooting someone. You know. It was part of my interest in seeking firearms training, to remove the mystery of it all, if I am to be honest with myself."

Keith said, "I was in training myself, I know. Bosnia for my lot was not like Iraq or Afghanistan. It was more like Rwanda. There was the sense of frustration at our inability to stop bloodshed and sectarian killings. Being trained as soldiers but acting as policemen in almost impossible circumstances, a society of hatred.

"And then the horror of it all emerging, massacres like Srebrenica. The damage was psychological to a lot of men. If anything, the bullet was a blessing for me."

She looked at him sharply, "How so?"

"I was brought back to the UK to a military hospital where they did some fancier repairs on my arm. And despite what you hear to the contrary, the army does first class psychological assessment. I was showing signs of depression after leaving my unit. I thought it was because I was a young officer feeling the sense of loss of my role, my team. I felt a strong sense of responsibility for them. But once the shrinks started on me a whole lot I had bottled up from the Bosnian experience came out, the anger, the stress.

"So that's what led to art, funnily enough. It was part of my therapy. I had always been interested in the subject and enjoyed paintings but I had never painted before myself - and didn't again after I left the service. While I realize that I have the ability to do so I don't have the motivation; not like you, for example. You really produce interesting work, you know."

"Well, thank you," said Catrin, "I must admit, as busy as I am with this stuff I can't see myself ever not doing something artistic, one way or another. It constantly changes for me, the different ideas for a new work."

"So my turn," said Keith. "How does an artist from Wales end up a policewoman in the Met?"

"You have a better basis for knowing this than I have about you," she laughed. "You at least see my personnel file. So you know I was born in Pontypridd."

"Near Aberfan," said Keith, "The word about hitting Taylor with the Dorothie Field painting did get around.

But go on."

"Normal sort of upbringing, really, other than my mum had a drinking problem which caused issues, you can imagine. She got sober in my mid-teens and, apart from one relapse a few years ago, has been fine. Dad stuck through it all and so later on it has been a good family life. But earlier, well, it was awful at times. I was good at school and artistic but I had also joined the Brownies, then the Guides and so on. There was something; structure, reliability, I'm not sure what, but it stuck and made me comfortable with organisations and teams.

"There were a couple of times when the police were around at the house because of my mother. I still recall a talk I had with one female constable; she was helping me deal with my anger and frustration. I guess that was an 'Ah-ha' moment. I wanted to be like her, not the person she was talking to, me.

"When I went to university at Aberystwyth I knew that, like music students, talent in art doesn't translate to employment easily unless luck kicks in. There are a lot of good musicians and artists now working in office jobs they don't really enjoy, I think. I set out with two goals; to pursue my art and join the police."

Catrin paused. "I had a boyfriend at Aberystwyth. It was a very intense relationship for a period. I thought we were going to get married, actually, until he realised I was serious on becoming a copper. Hurt a lot, but it was the right thing for us to finish.

"He is down in Cornwall somewhere, teaching I heard. I think he is happy there; I know I wouldn't be. I set my sights on London and the Met. That's it, sir."

He nodded. "And now you get to chase Russian

paintings as a police officer, the two pursuits have come together for you."

"In a sense, yes. I liked the Garin paintings but the truth is I don't think about them at all. It is the mystery of Han Yeung's disappearance that keeps creeping into mind."

"Good," said Marshall. "This is the ACU not A&A. That is what you are supposed to think about."

The discussion of David Jameson, her near-fiancé in Aberystwyth, made her think of her nagging concern about being twenty-four and having a lack of success in establishing a serious relationship with another man. After the break-up with David she had her finals, then the training for the Police Service. Whether it was the break-up or the new challenges, she didn't date for well over a year and then it was another cadet. But he fell seriously for another female officer in training, so that was off. Since then she had met a couple of men but nothing lasting had developed with either.

She realised time was passing. Somehow between her police work and her art her life was full. Other than hoping that someone 'right' would cross her path she was not sure what to do.

Keith interrupted her thoughts. "I'll drop you off and then take the pool car home; I can return it in the morning."

She saw they were coming up to the M1/M25 interchange. They were almost back in London.

~~

The call number showing on Franz Reicher's mobile

phone was a Geneva number but when he answered it the connection seemed to indicate a call from a much longer distance.

"Herr Reicher, I take it you recognize my voice?"

"Yes," he said. It was the Chinese woman. "I complied with your... request."

"We know. However we now want to locate the third young lady and would very much appreciate your guidance. And I assure you that the matter for us closes there."

The paintings Katarina Komarov and Elizaveta Komarov were now in police custody in the UK or would soon be there, he knew. Franz sighed. Giving up Geri and her links were not too painful; giving up Dieter was potentially far more problematic as they had worked together closely from the outset.

She didn't press him. She knew he would be thinking it through.

"I suggest you talk with Herr Dieter Haussmann. He is now a member of staff of Sheikh Qasim ibn Masar in Dubai. He is the Director of Service on his royal yacht. I take it this concludes our business."

"I believe so, Herr Reicher, and if not, I will certainly let you know. Goodbye."

24 DUBAI

When he moved to Dubai in May, Dieter Haussmann made a resolution. He would not, he told himself, repeat his mistakes at the Manden line, particularly no relationships, casual or short-term, with women he was involved with professionally. If he hadn't given that woman on the *Serenity* a sense she could walk into his office whenever, she would not have poked around in there to help out Yeung by taking the tube. And he had to learn to control his outbursts, he knew.

He had been hard on her in his anger at the loss of the painting. The captain had been made aware of both the relationship and her reprimand by him so that was that; he was out.

With his excellent résumé, a five-star reference that the Manden line provided despite the incident and with Franz's contacts setting it up, he had walked straight into a management position for Sheikh Qasim ibn Masar. The luxury motor yacht was no cruise liner, but it could go anywhere and had sixteen guest suites on board. The standard of hotel management had to be five-star. And he benefited from a lot of free time ashore.

He missed the bigger travel aspects of the cruise line but the work was similar and it had some major plusses, not the least the salary and no shortage of competent staff. The owner and his guests demanded excellent service but they also knew how to behave. The biggest problem for any cruise line hotel manager was not the staff but the guests; too many were demanding and rude.

Franz had sent only one final message which had ended, 'Stay out of the circuit for a while, Dieter; no contact with anyone until everything is settled'. The mobile and satellite phones Dieter had supplied were deactivated later the same day.

~~

Now his long-time partner had clearly sold him down the river. Dieter was angry, hurt and frightened all at the same time.

He was in his one bedroom apartment in the Dubai Marina complex with two people who were making it clear they ran things. He had been hopeful for the afternoon, having picked up this stunning Chinese woman who had told him she worked for the Royal Caribbean line. That was a lie, despite the cruise ship ID tag she had flashed in the store for the discount.

He had found her at one of his favourite spots where cruise ship staff shopped or relaxed away from their ships. She told him that she was with the spa staff on board and often didn't get shore time in port, but had all day today.

The haunt was a regular trip for him, sometimes giving him a girl on limited funds who wanted a good time while free in Dubai for a few hours. He had commented on the cruise ship tags and smiled his way in. This one had been quite easy.

He had taken her for lunch in the open air restaurant along the Marina only two minutes' walk away from his apartment block. Afterwards, he had invited her there and had opened the door to allow her to enter first, ever the gentleman, to find himself pushed hard in the back by the Asian man just happening to pass the other way along the corridor. Everything she had told him at lunch had sounded fine, but it was obviously fabricated. Now he was sitting on his bed, with the man standing near him, saying nothing. She had the floor and she looked nothing like a salon specialist.

"This gentleman has very interesting tattoos. Do you understand the significance?"

Dieter looked at her and nodded. Triad or something like that, he knew.

His one attempt at resistance, trying to push her out saying this was all a mistake, had resulted in her grabbing his arm and inducing so much pain in his elbow he had screamed out. The man hadn't even tried to intervene. And he, Dieter assumed, was the muscle.

"I understand he does not particularly like European painting but our employers do, apparently. So, first we want the Maxim Garin painting. Is it close by? Please do not take too long to answer."

Dieter said, "No, the one I had is with a client in Wales, not here."

He saw she was disturbed by this news.

"Herr Reicher told us you would have it. And if you are misleading me..."

"As Franz Reicher has told you about me, let me tell you a little about him. This operation he set up is compartmentalized, you understand? Franz is the only one with the complete organisational picture; the rest of us know only the contacts we need to know.

"Franz has people that obtain the items, prepare them for shipping and look after the sales. My part, until recently, was to organize the transfer and delivery, either myself or with others within the Manden Line, on the *Serenity* or with people on other ships. It's a supply chain process; I know the receiving agent in each country, the person who collects the work from the ship and reframes it to the customer's specification then delivers it, that's all.

"In the UK as in most other countries, the sales and identification of buyers are conducted by people known to Franz. I don't know who they are. In the UK I had one contact person, a woman.

"When the Holyhead thing went down and the painting went missing I phoned Franz. After he calmed down we realised there were limited options available to us. First, if the tube could be retrieved from Han Yeung easily, if he still had it, we could proceed. Given he was planning to mail something in it - my assistant told me that - we did not think that option was likely, but you never know.

"We agreed I should ask the receiving agent who was coming to the quay to collect another item from me to check that out. If it could be stolen from Yeung easily, or even with a bit of roughing up so he could say it was a minor theft by locals, that was fine. But I was to emphasize with her that it couldn't look as if we were trying to retrieve that tube specifically; the important thing was to maintain the secrecy of the process we use to transfer the art. We wanted no attention from the police. That was worth much more than any individual painting."

Dieter could see he had her attention.

"I met the receiving agent, transferred the item she

was supposed to have anyway and briefed her on the Yeung fiasco. Then I told her of our intent regarding Han Yeung, if she could find him. She made a call for someone to help her. I told her I would go back on board but would meet her if she had any news. I would also look out for Han's return, just in case he still had the tube and had encountered difficulties posting it, for whatever reason."

"It was four hours later when she called and told me what happened. I called Franz and he had already talked with the buyer in the USA to see if a sale was still possible for the paintings of the oldest and youngest sisters. It wasn't; the buyer wanted all three or none. Franz decided that New York deal had gone now, it was too messy.

"He had also talked to his UK sales agent. I don't know who that is, as I have said, but the receiving agent does, of course. Franz's seller had a home for one painting so I was to give the Katarina Komarov to her before departure.

"Franz assumed I would keep the third on board. I didn't want that, given that Han had taken one of them and it had been sent to someone. Now Yeung wasn't coming back to the ship. If the painting and Han's disappearance were linked during the period we were sailing to New York then I could see the police waiting for our arrival – and I could be in deep trouble, particularly with one painting still in my possession.

He paused. "Can I have some water?"

The woman nodded and the man behind him went to get him a glass of water. Dieter continued talking, watching them both.

"Franz had said that was highly unlikely. Who would connect the tube with his disappearance? That's the way he left it with me.

214

"When I talked to the receiving agent shortly before sailing, she said she could find a home for the remaining painting with someone locally if I wanted, but the buyer could not pay immediately. By then I was in a panic and told her to take it, I would sort it out with Franz, and so she took both the tubes with her. It is somewhere in Wales."

The Chinese woman said immediately, "So why did Reicher mislead us, saying you had it?"

Dieter looked at her. "I didn't tell him because the morning after we left Holyhead we were in port in Dublin. Franz had sent a message to the local person we use there and I met him at the quay. No further contact from my end; Franz would get in touch later.

"On the way to New York I received an email that flagged I was to check a voicemail message using my satellite phone. It said that the Swiss Police were interested in me due to the argument I had with my assistant over the loss of the tube. Somehow he already knew about that.

"My assistant had filed a formal complaint and I had been reprimanded by the Captain. He had passed it on to higher management and I knew it would have repercussions with the Manden line on arrival. Franz's message said the visibility of the incident now linked me possibly to Yeung's disappearance.

"By then we knew about the missing person enquiry in Wales and I was scared. I was told in the message to apply for this job here, it had been fixed, and that I should get out of America and Europe and to make no further contact with Reicher or anyone in the network. I was out in the cold, he said, for as long as the Han Yeung investigation was active.

"So I said, 'screw it', I will leave it to the UK people to

sort it all out with Franz. I guess he was never told and he thought I still have the other painting here, on ice. But the last time I saw the tube, it was in the UK, on Anglesey."

Emily looked at him, feeling he was telling the truth.

"And her name and number, this contact of yours?"

Dieter gave her Lyn William's information, and then added. "I made her give me the name of her prospective customer for the third painting also, as she was not paying for it then."

He told her who it was.

Emily Yang had been watching him carefully, assessing his words and his facial expressions; *gweilos*, Europeans, were so easily readable. To try to get more out of him would involve a serious change of plans and timing. It would also be against her specific instructions, as he would be in no condition to surrender to the authorities afterwards.

When she opened her purse and pulled out the small bag with the syringe and vial his eyes widened.

"This is an illegal narcotic in Dubai, methylphenidate." Emily said.

"Please, don't ...."

"Dieter, just listen. The dose in this vial is sufficient to have you convicted of possession and use; it will stay in your system long enough and the syringe will be here when the police get here, with your fingerprints on it. You know the penalty for illegal drug use here in Dubai. Refuse to do what we ask and I will inject enough to have you euphoric and passed out on the bed, lost in your erotic dreams about me.

"Before the police come, that is. Then you will have at least a four-year low, understand?"

Dieter knew well the mandatory penalties for use of drugs in the state. He nodded.

"And your sex life will become a little different, I think. Your only alternative is to book a flight to Frankfurt. Lufthansa flies there every evening. You will turn yourself in regarding your role in the smuggling of the paintings and the death of your shipmate, Han Yeung."

Dieter looked at her as if she was mad.

"I had nothing to do with the death of Han Yeung."

His voice rose in protest.

"Other than to phone a colleague from your art smuggling network and have him stopped," Emily said.

"But I didn't kill him!" he protested again.

"I think the German authorities will charge you with some accessory role. But a term in a German or British prison on an art theft may be a little easier than one here on drugs, no? Now fire up your laptop and find the airline web site."

Dieter did it almost mechanically. He even booked himself First Class. It might be the most pleasurable few hours he would have for a while.

She watched him carefully as he filled in the details. "And, of course, this meeting never took place. You had a crisis of conscience, or whatever. Remember that a voluntary confession will reduce the sentence. My colleague will stay with you and drive you to the airport in time for your flight. And you will have no discussion with Reicher, Williams or others."

He suddenly realised that, other than his still-painful elbow, she had touched nothing in the room. She put the bag with the drug and syringe back in her purse saying, "You made your choice, Dieter, now stick with it. My colleague has no need of these if you don't, I assure you.

"And if you were incomplete on the location of this woman or her customer someone will be back to see you. Even in gaol."

He watched her walk to the door, open it with a handkerchief that she must have pulled from her bag and then walk out. He looked at his watch. Thirty minutes ago he was thinking she would give him a fun afternoon; now she had just ruined his life.

He couldn't understand it. The painting was worth a bit, but not an operation like the one he had just witnessed. She was Chinese, Han was Chinese. It had to be something to do with that. But his role in that matter had been trivial, really.

He realised that he had no idea why this was happening other than Franz Reicher had betrayed him. Had the Chinese got to him too? Probably, he thought.

Emily exited the building and walked out through the adjoining shopping mall to the marina. In a trash bin she emptied the contents of the bag delivered to her on arrival. The Ziploc bag went back in her purse. A syringe and a vial containing water tinted slightly with food dye went into the trash. Given the complication regarding the painting, she was not pleased with the afternoon but would report it all back to Mr. Yau. She went back into the mall and entered the small store where it had been organized that she would leave the tube and had a quiet word with the owner. He showed her into a back room where her suitcase had been stored.

It was a four hour time difference to Hong Kong but she knew intuitively that Mr. Yau would be sending her to the UK next. Emily knew that she would need some warmer clothes and thought she would try to change planes in Paris. But first she should talk to Mr. Yau.

~ ~

Later that evening in the Lufthansa First Class lounge Dieter had no idea whether he was being monitored or not. Changing his flight would have consequences here perhaps, if it was spotted. And if he went to anywhere other than Germany, he could be screwed too. This Triad, or whatever organisation it was, would have adequate time to meet him at the arrivals hall of his destination if they were widespread and organized. He had no illusions what would happen then.

But he didn't want to spend part of his life in either an Emirates or a German gaol.

He took out his mobile phone and called the number for Lyn Williams he had used during the Holyhead panic; the receiving agent, who was now known to the Triad. She answered after one ring and he told her briefly his situation.

She said she was already in trouble; the police were looking for her, this Chinese issue had already impacted her. She just had been warned that morning and had left Bangor in a hurry.

"You say it was a Chinese woman. Well, there is a Chinese woman, a student here, the sister of the sailor. I think she has been pressing the issue with the police. It could be linked."

Dieter asked some questions about this sister. Clearly it was not the same person he had encountered but, he thought, it all could be linked. The idea formed in his mind.

"We have both been turned over by Reicher or others in his network," he added. "How would you like to try to get out of this? No guarantees, but I have an idea."

Five minutes later he left the lounge for the boarding gate, stopping at two ATMs to max out his cash reserves from both his credit and debit cards.

On board his flight after they reached cruising altitude people started to move around. Dieter beckoned to the in-charge attendant for First Class. He explained that he would have an additional ticket waiting in Frankfurt due to a late change of plans; his colleague was organizing it. Could a concierge sort it out and escort him over to the departure gate? He had received a bit of a shock and would appreciate the assistance.

The in-charge was extremely helpful. It would be no trouble, of course, for a First Class passenger – did he know which flight he would be taking? The captain could communicate it to the airport and they would organize the details.

Dieter said, "I am not sure - but the next Lufthansa flight into Manchester, I think, after our arrival. The ticket will be in my name."

25 LONDON

Catrin had been assigned to interview Geraldine Roper with Neville Coltrane. Worsley had decided it was time to give Catrin the opportunity to show her paces in an interview and she and Neville had talked about the advantage of using a junior officer to disconcert Roper, at least in the initial stages of the interview.

Roper and her lawyer Chris de Loos sat next to each other across the table in the interview room at New Scotland Yard saying nothing, assuming they were being watched.

Worsley, Sayer and Coltrane were watching them through the one-way mirror. Coltrane said to Catrin, "Geri and I are on the board of the same Foundation and know each other socially. She is extremely manipulative, which can be useful in fund-raising for the Arts. She is a real expert on the French Baroque and will try to use her airs and graces to her advantage and lord it over you, given half a chance. Mr. de Loos is sharp, top grade, also.

"So you are to lead the questioning. That will unsettle her; she will think you are there to sharpen my pencils or something; it's the way she treats students and any support staff she comes across anywhere. I will stare at her looking disappointed and we will see how it goes. She will be embarrassed that this is all unfolding with me there. How does that sound?"

"Fine, sir."

Neville's pep talk hadn't exactly helped Catrin's nerves, Worsley thought. But he thought she could do it, clearly; Roper's link to Reicher was too important for him to screw up now.

Coltrane continued, "Good, but if it goes off-plan, I will kick straight in and take over. Don't be put off by that."

"Yes, sir," Catrin said, trying to believe it would go well, but her heart was in her mouth.

They entered the room and Geraldine Roper said, "Neville, what is all this about?"

Coltrane just said, "Chief Inspector Neville Coltrane and Detective Constable Catrin Sayer are entering the room at -", he looked at the wall clock, "11.07. Also present are – please state your names for the record."

As he sat down and Geri gave him her full attention, smiling, he said brightly, "DC Sayer has some questions, Geri."

"Miss Roper, you know a Franz Reicher of Geneva, I believe," Catrin began.

Statements are statements, de Roos had warned Geri. Don't treat them as questions. It is not a conversation, it's a fencing match.

Seeing she was not going to get a response, Catrin said, "Let me re-phrase. Do you know a Franz Reicher, a resident of Geneva?"

"Franz," smiled Geri, "Yes, I know Franz. We see

each other from time-to-time at galleries and at the occasional opera or concert. Nice man, but don't know him enough to say he is a close friend."

"When was the last time you saw him, do you recall?" said Catrin.

Geri shot straight back, "Ambronay, last September, so about a year ago." She looked at Catrin and began indulgently, "Ambronay is a village in in eastern France, near the Swiss border."

"Yes, in the Rhône-Alpes, with a baroque music festival at that time of year," said Catrin, showing she knew what Roper was talking about. "And when was the last time you talked to him, please?"

"Not sure, actually," mused Roper, starting to look bored.

"In the last week, perhaps, Miss Roper?" said Catrin, helpfully.

"No, not in a long while ..."

Catrin stared at her hard and waited. Geri stared back.

Catrin said, "Three days ago Franz Reicher made a statement to the Geneva Police giving, he said, a complete account of the illegal transport and distribution of three paintings by Maxim Garin known as the Komarov Sisters. They had been stolen from a gallery in Russia. In his statement..."

She paused, appearing to look down at her notes.

"In it your name, the alleged role you played in the recent sale of one of these stolen paintings and its current location were provided. As were the dates and times of several telephone calls he had with you over the past four months, including one last week. As was the telephone number he called, which we know is not your usual mobile phone number so -."

She passed over a sheet of paper.

"We have a search warrant for any and all premises, vehicles or storage units you may use. Of course, if we come across other items of interest in them, as well as the phone you used to talk with him, we will act accordingly."

Roper was suddenly looking defiant.

"And, Miss Roper, the warrant covers both the lockers you use at the gym facility close to your apartment."

Geri suddenly recalled the face. Yesterday at the gym she had been replacing Franz's mobile phone in the locker. She had charged it up as usual during her workout as if it was her everyday phone. This woman had been sitting in work-out attire in the locker room apparently lost in texting someone.

Her face had changed as the significance of the revelation unfolded. "That is where I saw you!"

Her lawyer put his hand on her arm.

Mr. de Loos said, "We need to see this report alleging involvement of my client and …"

Catrin cut in sharply. "Other than the warrant, you won't be seeing anything until charges are laid.

"We are going to give you and your client a few minutes to talk. I would advise you, Miss Roper, to consider any way you can help us with our enquiries before we come back. A voluntary statement may be to your benefit before charges are laid. Do you understand?"

Catrin looked at the clock and didn't wait for a response.

"Interview suspended at 11.17."

She and Coltrane stood up. Neville was looking even more sorrowful as they left the room.

In the observation area outside they watched the lawyer and client huddle. Coltrane said, "Sayer, I think you handled that very well."

Worsley nodded to her in agreement.

"Thank you, sir." Inside she was feeling overwhelming relief that it hadn't gone belly up with a tirade from Geraldine Roper or her lawyer. She had seen her on the occasional chat show on television, heard her on radio arts broadcasts over the years and knew that this woman could dominate any discussion.

Geri sat thinking. Damn it, they will get the phone. Her contact with Franz Reicher always began with a friendly email or text that contained a date and in some form or other, four numbers. By the date and time given in the number sequence provided she would retrieve the bag from the gym locker containing the phone.

The locker had been owned by her friend but never used; Geri had just taken over the payment for it and kept it in her friend's name; she thought it was foolproof.

"I need a painting, Russian, about £100,000, Franz." She had said to Reicher after telling him about her new customer, Pyotr. "Can you get one in the next three months, hopefully?"

He had said he would look into it. Then he came back much sooner than expected pressing her to sell two - but Pyotr only had money for one, dammit.

Her fee was fifteen percent of the sales price, paid into the off-shore bank account she always referred to as 'family wealth'. In fact, her mother lived modestly in Pittsburgh and had an entirely different concept of family wealth than Geri; one needed to knock off a few zeroes from the numbers.

"Christoff, what do I do?"

Christoff de Loos looked at his client. "Geri, they appear to have the location of this painting she mentioned and the buyer. He or she will probably implicate you. If the police can show also any details of phone transactions with this man Reicher who has claimed your involvement, they will have plenty of evidence to charge you and possibly secure a conviction.

"The issue will be around what is the charge? I take it this in not a 'one-off' transaction… no, I see that. Then you need to deal. You have to minimize the charges and particularly, we need to keep you away from any organized crime aspect. It will help sentencing options greatly, if it comes to that. If I am to find a way to do that for you, you need to make a deal, I suggest."

Geri nodded. "Well, perhaps we can talk with Neville about other information I might have on paintings. Can it get me out of this jam that way, do you think?"

The lawyer shook his head. "No I don't think so. Neville is sitting in on this but that DC is part of Superintendent Jack Taylor's area, Serious Crime Command, part of his new Art Crime Unit. Art isn't the primary issue, I suspect. They are after some other crime here, I think."

Geri thought. "Thank you, Christoff; that is very helpful. I think there may be something."

They talked for several more minutes, with de Loos nodding at the end and, without looking, he waved at the mirror. Coltrane and Sayer went back in.

"My client will admit to selling a Garin painting to a Pyotr Yermilov."

Catrin said, "We will want a lot more than that, I think."

Christoff de Roos ignored her, looking at Coltrane.

"She also has information that may assist a current missing person enquiry. Are we open to a discussion of the charges?"

Coltrane said, "Not my call. But I will talk with Chief

Inspector Worsley and we would need to talk to the Prosecutions Service but... you know the ropes."

The lawyer nodded. "I will hold you to that. Geri?"

When she spoke it was clear she had lost all the self-confidence shown previously. "The woman who delivered the painting for me was Welsh, like you." She looked at Catrin. "Her name is Lyn Williams."

Catrin nodded, "Go on."

"It was just after that ship's officer disappeared, the one in Wales. I know that the painting arrived on a cruise ship but I was worried that this was more than just hot art, you know? I had a customer for one Russian painting lined up but nothing to supply him with. Then this offer of the Garin was quite out of the blue, not... the normal process. Yermilov leapt at it.

"Williams was updating me on the preparation of the Yermilov sale. She said another painting by Garin was for sale; that Franz had agreed. I said I knew that from Franz but I wasn't interested. The business had never been so loose before and I thought something must have gone wrong. And Yermilov didn't have the money, anyway, for another painting. I asked her if the news of the ship's officer going missing related to all this and how? Williams said it was, but that it wasn't a problem anymore; her brother had taken care of it."

"What did she mean by that?"

"She gave no detail or further information but from her tone of voice I took it to be he had killed the man. That's all I have. I don't even know the name of Williams's brother."

Coltrane looked at de Roos. "She'll testify to this?"

"Yes. We agreed on that," he confirmed.

Coltrane said, "If this helps in securing a conviction related to the disappearance of Han Yeung, the young man in question, I think it may well help your case, Geri. For my part, I suggest you prepare a complete list of paintings that you handled for Reicher because once we have finished here today any new implication of your involvement in this smuggling operation will bring fresh and separate charges. I think Mr. de Roos would want the benefit of your co-operation to be considered during sentencing and I hope he has explained this to you already."

Worsley was smiling to herself in the observation area. Coltrane sounded so helpful, as if he was there to be Geraldine Roper's best friend in this awful mess she was in, not a policeman wanting ammunition to pass back to Julian Wengler.

They all sat down to the laborious task of finalising a statement that Geraldine Roper would sign voluntarily before charges were laid.

~~

Pyotr Yermilov had been all smiles when he opened the door of his High Barnet home. Keith and a former colleague in A&A, Gordon Smith, now also a DI, were on the doorstep. Two uniforms and a SOCO technician were content to stand back and watch the opening play.

Ten minutes later Yermilov's shoulders were drooping, his wife was looking scared and Keith was eyeing the north wall of his dining room. It had started as soon as Keith showed the warrant. Russian defiance tends to involve a lot of shouting, thought Keith Marshall.

"We will find the painting, Mr. Yermilov, believe me, and if I need to have the officers move this bookcase with crowbars, I will. It will all help the prosecuting barrister convince the judge you were uncooperative, you see." His voice was even, matter of fact.

Yermilov swore in Russian and then said, "It just slides, that's all."

He slipped off his left house shoe, pressed with his toe on the polished trim at the base of the bookcase and then with one hand he slid the whole unit easily on its hidden rollers along the wall. A narrow doorway appeared. He reached in and switched the light on and then he moved back.

Keith nodded to the uniformed officers to watch him, then he and Smith moved into the hidden room, noticing the air-conditioning and humidifier control panel. Inside were three paintings beautifully mounted, hung and lit with a space for a fourth. The only furniture in the room was a chair, presumably to be moved in front of any painting Yermilov wanted to enjoy.

DI Smith said, "It looks like there is more we will be talking about than the Garin, Mr. Yermilov. You will accompany us to the station. I will be charging you on the suspicion of buying and receiving stolen goods. You had better call your solicitor now to meet us there, it will save time, I think."

His wife gave a cry and slumped down in an armchair. Her face showed anger and misery as she glared at her husband and the door to the secret room; two wealthy retired people who should be enjoying life and now this – Pyotr and his stupid obsession with paintings. It was all over her face.

They had, of course, relieved Geri Roper and Pyotr Yermilov of their phones with their other belongings and ensured that, other than their respective solicitors, they had no outside communications.

The SOCO was still working through the Yermilov

home and Mrs. Ludmilla Yermilov, talking incessantly, complaining about her husband, suddenly asked to go and visit her sister. She didn't drive and her husband was under arrest. A uniformed officer was told quickly to take her by police car to her sister's place several miles away; the SOCO wanted her out of the way.

After a mutual sympathy session with her sister, Carol, on her situation and Carol's solid agreement that Pyotr had been damn foolish, she suddenly thought to make a telephone call. She had remembered the mobile number of that Welsh woman that Pyotr thought he had so carefully hidden. Her husband, who wouldn't know what 'call log' on a phone meant if it was to save his life, had been in discussion last week with his friend Geri about planning yet another painting to fill the last damn space in his 'gallery', as he called it.

She told that young woman exactly what trouble she and that Geri had caused. Then Ludmilla had taken great pleasure in telling her that she would make sure that the police would prosecute both of them, too, even if her husband resisted their interrogation techniques; she would make sure of it. Then she slammed the phone down.

"It was very satisfying, I can tell you, Carol. 'They should go to prison, not my Pyotr,' I said. I think she got the message."

Carol's husband Charles nodded his agreement, bringing his sister-in-law yet another consoling gin and tonic.

"I would have been damn rude, Ludi, I really would. You were too polite," he said, treating himself to a fresh large whisky and soda.

Charles was wondering how long Ludmilla would be staying with them; from past experience she was rather too talkative for his liking.

~ ~

It was early evening. Worsley, Marshall and Sayer were finally able to find time to get on the phone to Dafydd Powys and bring him up to speed.

Catrin said, "I have just finished checking records. Lyn Williams was born in 1978, her mother being a Susan Williams, no father identified. I haven't got all the background yet but she was fostered by a Frank and Teresa Harrison in Bangor in 1981 for several years, following which she returned to her mother. Later she was back again to the Harrisons. She did not legally change her name but called herself Harrison during her childhood and early teens, it seems.

"She reverted to her original surname after her reconciliation with her birth mother at age thirteen. However, as she spent much of her childhood with the Harrison family she would think of Stephen Harrison as a younger brother or foster brother, I believe."

Worsley said, "So we have just been told by a second person that Han Yeung is a victim of a homicide. We have a suspect linked to his disappearance in secure psychiatric care, a man who may have killed him. We now know that this woman, Williams, with a family connection to him, is linked to the disappearance of the painting and that she and her foster brother in custody were in contact with Yeung. It all ties in."

She paused. "Dafydd, we are coming up. Can you bring in Lyn Williams now and call my mobile when she is taken in?"

They closed the call.

She said to her team, "Go home and pack some

things. I am authorising a helicopter for early tomorrow morning. You will get an email with pickup details.

"We are going back to Bangor to get this unravelled."

26 THE CHINESE LINK

Dafydd was in the car outside Lyn William's house when he called Worsley. She had said to call her when the arrest had been made.

"Not sure how, ma'am, but Lyn Williams wasn't just out or away, she has gone. It looks like a rapid departure. There is an open bottle of milk on the table, a pasta dish half-cooked on the stove but switched off. A neighbour says she saw her getting into her car around midday and Williams had a suitcase and backpack with her. There is an alert out for her and her car; it's a small blue Ford, so it probably was the one that was seen by the van.

"She also has a bedroom set up for art work, including, it looks to us, the capability to make frames for paintings."

"Thank you Dafydd, clearly somehow she was tipped off. But we will still come up tomorrow. We need to try to get to the bottom of this Chinese activity that is stirring all this up, if we can."

~~

"I called," she said.

The young Pakistani man who opened the door of the dirty van didn't say anything, just nodded, his mind on the radio blaring out. He had no uniform and was unshaven. The van had a hubcap missing from the rear passenger-side wheel and a scrape on the side.

She had been standing there for ten minutes watching the vehicles from nearby hotels and rental lots drop and collect people. Clean smart vehicles, attentive smiling staff, exactly what she did not need.

This was perfect.

Lyn Williams had driven directly to Manchester Airport and parked her little Ford in the darkest part of the airport lot, partly blocked from sight by a Transit van. When she switched off the engine she closed her eyes, resting for a minute or two. She was worn out.

Lyn had been on tenterhooks anyway for days after Stephen had been taken in, hospitalized. She had called his mother, Susan, when she heard. She treated it as a coincidence to hear her former foster-mother's bad news about Stephen's relapse. Susan was worried that the police had suspicions that he could have been involved in something bad; she herself was sure it was a relapse from the Iraq thing.

"He's been doing so well, a bit quiet until recently but back at work. It's a real worry, Lyn."

Lyn and Susan had stayed in touch but infrequently; an occasional call or a visit to see her foster-mother a couple of times a year. Lyn offered her sympathies and hoped Stephen got well again soon.

His mother had no idea of her contact with Steve.

Now she had the additional shock of the call from the Russian's wife, pompous bitch that she was. She had to get out. She had only half-formulated her plan when Dieter Haussmann also called her.

Lyn walked into the terminal pulling her luggage with her hoodie up, peering over a pair of cheap reading glasses she had bought in a chemist's shop on the drive to the airport. She headed straight to the Arrivals area looking at the array of rental car booths. Then she saw the sign on the post saying "Discount Car rental – off airport location – we collect and return – why pay more?" There was a phone beneath it.

She picked it up and was told to wait outside.

She was the only passenger and the van took her to the rental lot on an industrial road nearby. It was no Hertz or Avis location; that was clear. The man in the trailer that served as an office went through everything mechanically. She was watching him carefully, as she had weighed the risk on the best way to get a replacement vehicle.

She was sure her own car would be flagged by now and by parking it at the airport she hoped it would lead to the conclusion that she was already out of the country when it was found. If an alert flagged her here in this car lot through her photograph though, she was stranded. She had no way out. If she had rented at the airport, she knew she would have had a variety of routes out including her own car perhaps as a last resort, but she would also have been under constant CCTV exposure.

So she had chosen this crappy rental lot and hoped it would work. She was out of options.

Lyn thought the credit card and alternate driver's license Franz had made her acquire when she started this work would not have been compromised yet, but she couldn't be sure of that either. When she started this work she had no idea she could get a second license until he took her through the steps. At the time she wondered why bother, but now was she was hoping it would be her ticket to freedom; at least, the first ticket she needed.

Mr. Discount Care Rental, the young driver's father she thought, looked bored throughout the whole process and gave her a Toyota Auris, one of his better vehicles, he said. Looking at the odometer, it was probably a Hertz sell-off.

Within twenty minutes she was in the 'mobile phone waiting area' at Manchester airport. Dieter Haussmann would call her when he was cleared through customs and immigration, he had said; but if he did not or she got a call with three rings and then a hang up, she was on her own.

If he made it they would be off, initially to the one place the police would least expect her to be now; Bangor. And then she would leave for good.

~~

The helicopter ride for Catrin had been exhilarating, starting in the dark and watching the sun rise as they flew above cloud. Keith nodded off and Worsley was talking with the co-pilot a bit, her aviation interest evident as she pointed at the panel, asking questions. Half-way there it crossed Catrin's mind that probably Keith Marshall had spent enough time in helicopters in the army to be able to sleep in them easily. She was tired herself, she knew, but it was all new and exciting.

They landed at the helipad at Colwyn Bay Police Headquarters. As they arrived Catrin suddenly realised that they had pretty much a full working day ahead. They may have crossed the country but they were arriving at the same time as everyone else starting day shift.

In a more spacious and equipped conference room than the one at Bangor Police Station the two teams met and reviewed their progress. Superintendent Morgan had made it clear to Dafydd Powys that he wanted the senior management team to be briefed separately later. Worsley and Dafydd would do that this morning.

Keith and Catrin were going to visit Lyn William's home and see the studio she had set up.

The forensic results on Harrison's van were also in. No blood or body fluids were found but a paint mark on a tool box was consistent with the colour of the bicycle from the *Manden Serenity*. The manufacturer was supplying the paint analysis from that model and the sample from the tool box was being analysed.

Catrin was also given the job of talking to Li again and told exactly what she could reveal. Depending on the responses, they may bring her in for a formal interview which, Worsley said, Keith would lead. Catrin would not be present during the questioning.

"It will be all business with her. I don't like art smuggling but I don't like either the coercion tactics going on here; someone is going to get hurt," Worsley said.

Catrin contacted Li by phone, to find her day was fully occupied with course commitments, so they arranged to meet for quick lunch in the Teras Lounge in the Main Arts Building of the university. It was the earliest opportunity without hauling her out of lectures or tipping her off that she was being interviewed.

Idris took Keith and Catrin to the Williams residence, a small terraced house, now with police tape across the entrance gate and some neighbours talking in clusters in the street.

Inside they found two SOCOs going through the house. "Upstairs, at the back, when you are gloved and into coveralls, please," said one of them.

Catrin and Keith looked through the work area. Lyn had a well-finished work bench and work area set up, all the equipment to make stretchers for mounting the canvas and a wide array of frames plus high end tools to cut and finish them.

"She has had training in this, she is no amateur," said Keith. He was looking at a part-made frame.

Idris said, "We don't understand, though, the need for this."

Catrin looked at the large roll of canvas. It was very good quality.

"Idris, she may have used this canvas to re-line the older works, that is, glue the original to the stronger new canvas prior to framing it. If she knew how to do that properly for valuable old paintings, as DI Marshall said, she is no amateur."

Keith was looking at the array of paints and brushes. "She probably did some touch-up work too, a real conservator service for the customer."

Idris said, "We found out from neighbours that she works as a substitute art teacher in high schools, part-time. She covers for absences of regular teachers in arts and crafts throughout North Gwynedd. She studied here in Bangor.

"We are looking for her car, of course, a dark blue Fiesta ST, just as Diliwar said. She was often away overnight, the neighbour across the road says. The husband thought it was the nature of her work; the wife thought she had a man somewhere. She says we will find her no problem, just look for the sparkle."

Catrin and Keith looked at him. "Apparently she loves jewellery, nice stuff, not cheap. Always wears it, a lot of it. The neighbours thought she was paid too much for her job."

"Which was no more than a nice cover for her real income," said Keith. "She was probably busy visiting cruise ports or airports elsewhere as the paintings came in. Holyhead must have been a bonus for her, being so close."

"Until she found out about the Komarov problem, that is." said Idris.

Catrin had been examining a bin. "Look sir, the number of roll ends in here. They are dusty, so they have been here some time. I would say these two are a match and are similar to the tube we found at Zhou's – perhaps they are from the painting of the oldest Komarov sister for Yermilov. But these two seem to be of a smaller diameter."

Keith smiled. "Perhaps I was right after all; she had another painting to collect in Holyhead. That's why she was there to begin with."

~~

When she met Li, it was obvious that her friend was expecting some news rather than just a chat. Catrin could see the anxiety on her face. She quickly told her that they no further information on Han.

"You know what I thought," said Li.

Catrin nodded.

"Li, we have in custody, actually in psychiatric care, a man who may be involved in Han's abduction. What his role was we do not know yet, but we believe him to be involved. We also are searching for his foster sister, a woman called Lyn Williams. I can tell you that because the media will be briefed very soon that we want to talk to her. We are sure she is trying to evade arrest and believe she was involved in moving the stolen art from the *Serenity*."

"Again, it is a step forward but no answer for you or your family. Given the time that has passed it is not looking good, I am afraid. There is nothing to suggest Han was involved with this criminal group so we are now convinced he has fallen victim to them in some way."

Li nodded but said nothing.

"The reason we have had this break is that the criminal group that stole and transported the paintings is starting to come apart and, in doing so, turning over information. You knew already from our lunch in Y Felineli that we had a break in finding the man in custody."

"That was his van you saw?"

"Yes, it turned out to be so and he was apprehended. But the link to his foster sister and to the second painting came from evidence provided from abroad. The person who provided it, we feel, had no reason to. In doing so he has exposed himself to further scrutiny and in the past he has been a very cautious man, hard to pin anything on."

She was watching Li closely.

"The reason he came forward was to give information specifically about the Komarov paintings and to link them to Han's disappearance. This came directly after a meeting he had with a Chinese woman. She brought some pressure to bear; what that was we don't know, but it made him speak to the police in his country. In fact we are sure he was intimidated or threatened.

"So, I have to ask you, are you aware of this? Or are you aware of any efforts by people back in Hong Kong to pursue such a line of investigation? We have checked already that this is not an action by any Hong Kong police authority."

Li looked surprised then hurt. She realised that this was a police interview, not just a meeting with her friend.

"Catrin, this is all news to me. My family wouldn't, couldn't do such things."

"Can I ask then who else you have told about developments?"

Li paused. When she spoke again Catrin could hear the lawyer's careful phrasing in her voice.

"I have discussed this matter only with my parents and my uncle. With my mother I talk only of things positive; she is not well, still grieving for Han and for my absence. I have not mentioned that Han was having a relationship with Cho, or that he was gay. I have not spoken to anyone else about it.

"As I said, I asked my friend Jenny to send Han's computer files over, but did not tell her anything about why I wanted them. That is all."

"Do you think your father or uncle could have asked others to become involved?"

"I don't know how. My father is a tailor, as you know, and a devout man. He is up to his eyes managing things both at home and in his business. My uncle is a busy man who works in the shipping industry, a senior executive, but he is quite elderly now."

Catrin nodded. "I had to ask."

A silence lay between them for a moment. Catrin couldn't think of anything else to ask regarding the case, so said, "Enough of that. I am sorry we do not have better news for you. How is the course work and sailing going?"

Li's response was a little cool. "The course is very busy

as I said earlier this morning, but I am holding my own. The sailing, well, I have stopped it, at least for now. There are less sailing days as the season closes anyway. They are nice people and it is good sailing on the Strait but, frankly, it also reminds me too much of Han. He taught me and we sailed together quite a lot before he went off to work for Manden.

"And I am sorry, Catrin, but I am not hungry any more. I will get back to my studies, I think. Please excuse me."

As Li walked away Catrin thought how hard it was to do this. Li had no idea that she had been saved from the more rigorous exercise of a formal interview at the police station with her boss. Nor would she tell her.

Li's thoughts were elsewhere. She had deliberately neglected to clarify for Catrin that the term 'uncle' as a form of address in Chinese society went far beyond direct family relatives; it was a term used with older males who were close to the family, as the term 'Auntie' applied to older women. She had lots of 'uncles' and 'aunties' at the Methodist Church as she was growing up and, even now, would refer to them in that manner when she met them. But this was the first time she had referred to Mr. Lin as an 'uncle'.

Li was not sure what he would think of the use of this familiar term of address, but she felt it was appropriate under the circumstances. She now had a suspicion about what was going on and, from her legal training, felt the last thing she should do is ask Mr. Lin about it.

~~

That evening Catrin had just come back to her room in the hotel after working out in the fitness room. The day had bothered her. Her personal phone rang and it was Jean calling.

"Hi, I am just about to shower, I have been working out," panted Catrin.

"Going well?" asked Jean. Over the years the friends had settled into an easy conversation mode where boundaries on confidentiality of police business were clear and Catrin knew, if she slipped up and blurted something, it was safe with Jean.

"We are making progress, been a busy day, but the truth is I am out of sorts," said Catrin.

"Take a shower and call back on Skype later," said Jean, "We can chat."

Later they caught up. Catrin felt better for seeing her friend, hearing about life back home.

"You know this case, this Chinese girl?" She had told Jean she had become friendly with the person she had first gone to Bangor to check out.

"Well, I had to interview her today on something difficult. I did it to make it easier for her by hearing it from me, but it just annoyed her."

"You should have left it to Grandpa," was Jean's instant response.

Grandpa was the name they used for Idris. Catrin had told her how much she enjoyed working with this old Welsh detective in his rumpled suits.

"You know, you are probably right," she laughed.

"Anyway," said Jean, "you need a new web site. For the pottery."

"We have a web site, well, the Cwmbran Kiln has a web site and we are all on it."

"Liz wants a specific artist web page for us, with you as the primary element. She needs it for a compendium of artists she features for her gallery; it's part of a network with other galleries."

"Well it should be us equally, Jean, but I haven't got time now, obviously," said Catrin.

Jean said, "Leave it to me to map out, I have Liz's template. Catrin, you are as wrong about the balance on the web site as you were in doing the interview with the Chinese woman. You have a real talent and I like working with you, but it is you that should get the recognition for the art."

They argued it a bit and Catrin knew Jean was being logical. When they finished and she went down to the bar to meet Keith as planned, she felt a great deal better.

27 THE INVITATION

While driving along the North Wales Expressway Dieter explained to Lyn his proposal in detail; he had already given her a synopsis.

"It may seem strange what I am going to say, but I have spent a great deal of my time working with Asian staff from many countries on cruise ships. If this Triad or whatever it is had wanted us dead for our respective roles, we would be so by now. Wednesday afternoon I could easily have been killed."

Lyn drove and listened. Her plan was different but she wasn't going to tell this man that.

Dieter said. "I am not wanted yet, but it won't be too long before the Chinese know I have not given myself up in Germany, as they instructed. I need to phone Yeung's sister and we need a place to do the meeting, one with good mobile phone coverage, as I suspect we will end up calling Asia direct."

Dieter had explained that for Geri to turn Lyn in, Geri must be in a similar situation to himself. Franz Reicher had been forced to turn them both over to the Chinese he concluded, but why?

"It has to be about Han, sure, but something more, I think. They didn't threaten to kill me; they just wanted me to choose a gaol term. Triads don't deal that way. And I had no real role in Han's death, let's face it; all I did was alert you to Han taking the tube."

"That's not a good way to win my help, apportioning blame, you know," she said, a little grimly.

"I'm not doing that, I am trying to explain. I think they want to know where Han is and what happened. But it is also about good and bad luck; superstition. They don't want the paintings for themselves. Hell, they probably put more money into this exercise than any profit from the sale of the paintings even if they had taken them and found a buyer."

He could see that Lyn wasn't following.

Dieter said, "Ask any Chinese person how they sweep the floor. How would you sweep a floor?"

"Easiest and fastest way to do it, I suppose."

"A Chinese woman will always sweep from the front door to the middle of the house. The dust pan will always be emptied through the back door. It's to do with maintaining good fortune. They will do it whether they are Taoist, Buddhist or Christian; it is just the way Chinese are. Same with the use of numbers, how many stairs there should be in a staircase, a whole bunch of things we wouldn't give a second thought about."

"Someone is planning to restore the paintings to their owners for good luck, I think, as part of the process of finding Han, whether consciously or … just because they are Chinese. So I think we need to talk to them, whoever they are, ask them to be open to other ways of making some payback, amend, call it what you will."

"And if that doesn't work?"

"For me, I will then decide which prison system I want to serve time in, German or British perhaps, certainly not Emirati, and how to minimize the sentence. Fighting the Chinese on this is not viable, I think, particularly if they are Triad. The woman in Dubai implied that with her comment about the tattoos. If it was worth a head-on fight, Franz would not have folded so easily; he would have brought someone in to deal with them. But if you fight a Triad member, you fight them all; they don't stop."

He looked at her. "You will have to decide for yourself, Lyn."

She changed the subject. "To talk with them, we have to talk to this sister and, whether she is involved in this or not, we have to get her to make the right contact. So you will have to call her. I have someone who can provide a place we can use. He has been keeping an eye on Jian Li Yeung since her arrival."

"Who is it?" asked Dieter.

"My customer, the one I told you about," she said.

Lyn thought, you look at giving up as a last resort if you want, Dieter, but I want no part of that eventuality.

They had just passed through Conway; not far now.

~~

At the hotel at breakfast Keith said, "I am heading up to see Dr. Owen later to find out how Stephen Harrison is doing and whether we can question him soon. I could call, but I may get more in person. It will depend on when Owen will see us. I would like you to come along."

It was late morning at the police station when Keith came to see Catrin. "Let's go, we have some time with Owen now."

After the drive over to the hospital they waited for about fifteen minutes before Owen could see them.

"It will have to be quick," he said, without preamble.

"Dr. Owen, we are now pretty sure that Stephen Harrison's foster sister is involved in a criminal activity, art smuggling. It may be linked to her brother's condition. There is a strong chance that he was also involved with her somehow in the disappearance of the Chinese officer off the cruise ship at Holyhead.

Owen said, "Do you think she may have drawn Stephen Harrison into this somehow?"

"We don't know yet, but, if so, it may relate to his condition. Is it possible to interview him yet?"

"Not until I have seen him again, no. He is out at Llanfairfechan and I will see him this afternoon. I'll let you know. He is making some progress, Inspector, so it is a possibility.

"So this could be the cause," Owen mused, "Now we have to find out about the event, perhaps... and deal with it."

"Thank you, Doctor," said Keith, remembering Catrin hadn't met the psychiatrist. "My apologies, this is Detective Constable Sayer who works with me."

Owen said hello and when he heard Catrin's accent he started talking to her in Welsh. Then he said, "When you do interview Stephen, Inspector, bring Miss Sayer along; he will respond in Welsh at times, even if he is being spoken to in English."

~~

Li received the call on her room phone at Gwynant. "Miss Yeung, My name is Dieter Haussmann. You don't know me but I served on the *Serenity* with your brother. I am just visiting a friend who lives locally. You know, catching up; when he mentioned that he had read about you coming to Bangor to study. It's a bit impulsive, I know, but I thought I would search you out and call and say how sorry I am and how hard it must be for you.

"We were all upset about it on board, Han was very much liked."

Li was surprised. "Thank you Mr. Haussmann. That is very kind of you."

"I take it there is no more news?"

"No. We continue to wait. It has been, well you know if you were there, a long time now."

Dieter continued, "Well, I don't want to bother you further. As I said, it was a spur of the moment thing. I am in Caernarfon at present, just heading to Bangor with my friend. I don't suppose that it would you possible to meet and have coffee? I could tell you more about Han and what he did on board, for example. I head back to Manchester later so it's a bit tight. But if it's not convenient, I understand. And please call me Dieter."

Li felt it might be a good idea. "I think I would like that, but I have a class soon. Could we meet early afternoon, perhaps?

"My friend and I will be not too far from the university then, so that would work well." He gave the address.

Li said, "It is actually very close, only a few minutes' walk for me."

"Fine, well, if it works for you, I will see you there then."

"I look forward to it. And please call me Li."

Li was feeling good about the opportunity to talk with someone about Han particularly after the negative conversation with Catrin yesterday.

As she walked over to meet Dieter Haussmann after the lecture it suddenly dawned on her that perhaps Catrin chose to ask the questions rather than have another police officer do it; she had missed that possibility entirely. Given their interest in whatever Mr. Lin had initiated - or perhaps Mr. Yau, she thought - she could have been brought in for formal questioning; she was the only logical link. And Catrin had tried to deal with it delicately.

She called Catrin's mobile and got to her voicemail.

"Catrin, it's Li. I am sorry about leaving so abruptly yesterday. I apologise, I was wrong and rude again. So can we meet later?

"I am just on Craig Y Don Road, going meet with one of Han's colleagues from the *Serenity*, a Mr. Haussmann, who called out of the blue. He is visiting a friend here and wants to tell me more about Han as a ship's officer and colleague. If anything comes out of the discussions that I think you or Chief Inspector Worsley need to know, I will tell you later. Bye for now."

28 THE CONFESSION

They were sitting in the lounge in the house in Craig Y Don Road after introductions. Li had seen the professor around the university but did not know him. Dieter had seemed personable at the door and the lady with him was quiet, eyeing her a lot. She was wearing too much jewellery, Li thought; not very tasteful, either.

"Li," began Dieter, "This is not what it seems. Sorry, but there was no other way. I was on the *Serenity* at the time your brother disappeared, as I said. I have to tell you, I am sorry to say, that he is dead. You probably thought that was the case by now but in case you hold any secret hope, you need to know the truth. And the truth of how he died."

Li's shock was evident on her face.

"Both myself and Lyn are in trouble now. Lyn is being sought by police and her brother is in custody. We are all involved in an art theft, in different ways.

"Two days ago I was in Dubai, facing the choice of either a drug injection followed by a lengthy gaol term there or the option of turning myself in to German

251

authorities for my role in an art smuggling operation. The choice was given to me by a Chinese woman, a member of a Triad. My partner in Switzerland was also threatened, I believe. Everything is linked to the same woman or group, one you are part of, obviously. This is why we needed to see you.

"Part of what is required from us is that the three paintings, the Komarov Sisters, are returned. Two are now in police hands and the third is here, in this house. Parry?"

Tom Parry opened a cupboard and pulled out a tube, placing it on the coffee table separating them. He seemed loath to let it go. He had only received it from the boot of Lyn's car a couple of hours ago.

"The other thing they want, we think, is the detail of Han's fate and for the guilty party to go to gaol. So we want to meet these conditions but talk to the person in charge at your end and reach some accommodation for ourselves, if we can."

He stopped, waiting for an answer.

"I know nothing about this," said Li.

"Then I think someone you know does, here or back in Hong Kong, someone with money, influence and the ability to bring in Triad people to Geneva and Dubai; people who can threaten violence and bring down our organization so quickly."

Li thought. She said, "My brother, what happened to my brother?"

"Connect us to the right person and we will tell both of you, right now."

Li paused then said, "I will use my mobile phone; I will put it on speaker phone." She wasn't sure how this would pan out. "I first call an 800 number and then they will call back. You can watch me dial."

"Just speak in English, not Chinese, please," said the woman, standing close to her.

Li's phone rang through to the 800 number "Uncle, this is Jian Li. Please call back urgently. I need your help very badly right now, sorry. Thank you."

Li pressed the 'end' button and sat still. They watched her, saying nothing. She wondered if Catrin would return her call and, if so, what she should do if Catrin voice came on the phone before that of Enlai Lin.

It was only five minutes later that her phone rang, even though it was nearly 11 p.m. in Hong Kong. She accepted the call and put it straight on speaker.

"Jian Li?" She heard Mr. Lin's voice, anxious.

"Yes, Uncle, it is me. Please do not identify yourself at this time. I am with three people who were involved with Han's disappearance. I am alone with them."

Dieter spoke. "She is in no danger; let me assure you of that. And we don't want to know who you are. I am Dieter Haussmann. I think it was one of your operatives in Dubai with me two days ago, giving me a choice of prisons either in Dubai or Germany and wanting from me the last painting."

"We want to find a solution not involving prison if we can. To discuss that, you first need to hear how Han Yeung died and understand. It was linked to the art work, as you surmised, but it was not intended at all. That's the truth."

Enlai Lin had got up from bed when Mrs. Cheong called urgently expressing concern about Li's call and its message. "She is under great stress, Mr. Lin, I can tell."

He had called Li using his house phone. His wife had put on her dressing gown and was looking at him intently.

He pointed to his mobile phone by the bed, asking for it. He had no idea what to make of this call other than Li was in trouble and activities by Michael Yau had led to this.

"Please continue, Mr. Haussmann."

He needed time to think.

"Let's begin on the day the ship was in Holyhead," Dieter said.

~~

Han Yeung had not slept well for a number of nights after the last discussion with Cho. He knew Cho was right; it wouldn't work for any long-term relationship. The geographic and job issues were reasons, but ultimately he could not face his parents about his homosexuality; he was caught both ways.

He was passing through the Serenity's art gallery when he saw one of the staff there. They had talked from time to time and he said, suddenly, "Any good deals for me?"

He had an impulse to close out with Cho by sending him a work of art, something to remind him. He knew it was a passion of his.

She asked him what he was interested in and he talked vaguely. Something he could mail tomorrow, he said, from Holyhead for a friend who liked surrealism, he thought it was called.

She liked him. He was a friendly officer but knew nothing about art; that was clear.

"Look, I have this Magritte print, nothing expensive. It was part of a promotion effort – a giveaway prize in art quizzes on earlier cruises. Providing I have something reasonable for the books, it is yours – and it is quite nice."

"Thank you Marion. That would be wonderful."

She added, "To mail it in Holyhead you may want to talk to Annabel in hotel services for something to use, I know they have packing materials there and she is very helpful."

Han signed the purchase to his onboard account and thanked her.

As suggested, Annabel in the hotel manager's office was more than helpful. She had a quick look round her outer office, then went into her bosses' office and found a packing tube that was just a little bit too big. It was sturdy too, but he didn't mind the extra postage cost, he knew it was the right thing to do to seal the closure with Cho.

The following morning, the weather was fine. He had seen on the internet map that there was a post office in Holyhead not too far from the harbour. Apart from one turn he missed by a church when he quickly re-traced his path, he found it without problem and sent off the package. A short ride for some exercise now, he thought, and then back to the ship. He had watched carefully during the entrance to the harbour. He wanted his own performance on exit to be flawless.

While riding back towards Holyhead along the old London Road he saw a woman standing by her little blue car, arms waving, "Can you help?" she called.

He stopped, not sure what to do other than offer her his iPhone to call a mechanic. He was having difficulty with her accent; excited, local. Then the van came up and drew to a halt at a slight angle in front of them. Good, he thought, a local person who knows what to do and can actually help her.

The young man, a decorator by the looks of him, came up looking at her.

She suddenly said, "Where is the tube that you brought off the ship? Where did you send it?"

"Who are you?" he said, "Now look -".

He raised his arms as he spoke to her; mentally rejecting what he realised was a set-up. Then he felt the blow on the side of his head and his head turn; then it was blackness.

~~

"So my foster brother, Stephen Harrison, killed Han," Lyn said. "He was a soldier. He thought Han was going to use some martial art thing. He reacted and his punch caught the side of Han's safety helmet, his head went round and… that was it. His neck was broken."

Li could see it. Han was always gesticulating. The family said, 'tie his hands, he will be struck dumb'. But they both had trapped Han and killed him.

"Stephen Harrison has had a mental breakdown. He had a similar breakdown in Iraq as a soldier. He will go to a psychiatric ward in a special prison for a long time, I expect, when this comes out, so the person who killed Han will be put away, as you want," Lyn continued.

Mr. Lin was already spotting inconsistencies between Haussmann's story as related by Michael Yau to him and the events described by this woman. If Han did not have the package, why did the woman even stop him and ask about it? Perhaps she was thinking of chasing it down with the recipient, but then Han would have known something was wrong. He did not understand the logic.

"So what happened then with Han Yeung?" said Mr. Lin.

Lyn Williams looked straight at Li as she responded. "Steve and I put him and his bike in the back of the van.

I think we both panicked and I knew I had to decide what to do, but couldn't think. I phoned him -." She nodded at Parry. "He suggested that burial at sea might be best, to hide all traces. We used his sailboat. We took it out the following morning, as we needed to take the body and bicycle on board that night in the dark. Steve brought some quarry stones and already had plastic sheeting. We wrapped and weighted his body before placing him in the water. He sank straight away."

"Do you know exactly where he was 'buried'?" asked Enlai Lin, his difficulty very clear in saying 'buried'. Mrs. Lin was looking anxious, seeing her husband's face.

"I know the exact coordinates, but what that means now, I can't say," she said, "the Menai Strait are tidal and have very complex current systems."

Li was somewhat amazed at the coolness of this woman.

There was silence.

Dieter said, "So where do we go from here? Everything is out now, so what next? How can we resolve this without us going to gaol? I know you have the means to put us there or worse but if we can find another solution, we want to talk about it."

Enlai Lin thought about what to say.

"Mr. Haussmann, I appreciate your candour in organizing this call and making the information known. I would say that your role in this appears to be comparatively minor. I did not involve myself directly in any of the actions which caused you to seek me out.

"But my response is that you should let Jian Li Yeung go now and turn yourselves over to the police and tell them the same story, as you were told to do. I am at a loss, though, because I can't understand why others there with more to lose would agree to this discussion in the first place. But my answer would be the same."

Li saw Williams nod slightly towards Parry, positioned to her side.

"You are very perceptive," said Tom Parry, speaking for the first time. Li looked round. Professor Parry was holding a small gun, pointed at her.

"The answer would be - for the opportunity to talk to you," he continued.

Dieter Haussmann said softly but clearly, "Sir, there is now a gun being pointed at Jian Li. I am not sure why, but I want no part in this."

"We weren't offering you any," said Lyn, "Sit next to her, close."

"Whoever you are," she addressed the phone, "You have resources to mount an operation in Switzerland and Dubai and who knows where else. Dieter has explained to me that this is about fortune, good or bad, appeasing spirits and about finding Han Yeung and returning the paintings. I am not sure I go along with this 'fortune' theory, but it doesn't matter.

"We have things you want, the safety of this girl, one assumes, seeing as you are going to so much trouble about her brother; a painting you want and a location for her brother's body. We are on the run and need money. And neither of us will be turning ourselves in. Haussmann's idea is ludicrous.

"At worst, you could have both Han and Jian Li, the sister and brother, dead and perhaps you will find neither of them. Whatever happens to us, and I have no qualms you could get to us eventually, what would that accomplish for you? Revenge, when you could have avoided this. If you hadn't interfered ..."

Her voice had been rising in frustration and anger as

she spoke.

"So what do you want exactly," asked Enlai Lin, softly.

"Two million US dollars total, one million in each of two accounts. I will give you the details. Not a lot, I expect by your standards."

"It is after 11 p.m. here in Hong Kong."

"Then I suggest you call someone, somewhere that is in business hours. If this line breaks and you don't re-open it within thirty seconds, the whole opportunity is lost, I assure you."

Mr. Lin said, "I can do it but it will still take time. I will leave this line open but must go to another phone and call someone. Please keep Jian Li safe."

Then he added, "I have no assurance for Jian Li's safety, even if I do, do I?"

Lyn Williams said, "No, other than our word they won't be harmed. She and Haussmann will be tied, gagged but not otherwise harmed and we will leave them somewhere. That is our undertaking. And you will get a call to this 800 number or another number you give me, once we are safely away from the UK, letting you know where they are."

"I will be back," said Mr. Lin.

29 WHERE ANGELS FEAR TO TREAD

They had decided to have some lunch in the hospital food court and discuss next steps after the meeting with Dr. Owen. Catrin was picking up voicemails as Keith drove them back to the station from the hospital.

"Sir, there is a voicemail from Li. She is meeting someone from the *Serenity* crew at a place on Craig Y Don Road; a man called Haussmann. He has just made contact with her and it sounds like she was walking over to meet him."

She checked the timestamp. "It was left about three-quarters of an hour ago. We were in with Dr. Owen and I put the phone on mute, but I missed the vibration somehow."

Keith's response was, "The call from someone from the ship sounds too coincidental for me, with this lot unfolding. Haussmann was the name of the man who went to Dubai, the man we suspect had the Garin paintings on board. Did she say where?"

"No, she didn't." She was thinking hard as she returned the call to Li. Her line was engaged.

"Look, this may sound crazy, but the only house I have been to on Craig Y Don Road is Parry's place. I went over once in the week I was here. He is an enthusiast of Russian paintings. And I have had the feeling when we talked he wanted me to tell him more about the case, but I didn't say anything. I know he is a consultant to the police on art but..."

Keith's expression didn't convey she was crazy at all. "Give me directions. If it turns out to be nothing we will deal with Parry's complaint later."

They parked a few yards away from Parry's house and walked up the short path to the front door. Catrin pressed the bell.

After a few moments they heard footsteps and Tom Parry opened the door, "Catrin, Keith..."

Catrin said "Professor Parry, we are looking for Jian Li Yeung. She called me from this road. We wondered if you have seen her."

"Yeung, no, I can't say I have." He stood there, not inviting them in.

Keith said, "Parry, do you mind if we look around?"

Marshall stepped forward. He had no intention of receiving a refusal.

The sound of the shot and Li's voice screaming 'Catrin' seemed to overlap.

~~

They had been five long minutes into the silence on Li's mobile phone waiting for the person at the other end to come back when the doorbell rang. Parry moved over to Williams and passed her the gun.

"I will see who it is, get rid of them and be back."

261

In the lounge they heard the front door open. Li took a breath as she heard Catrin's voice. Dieter Haussmann, saw Williams's arm extend as Li screamed, so he threw himself from his chair, his hand trying to reach the gun as it fired.

Li grabbed the tube with the painting. It was heavier than it looked, she realised, as she swung it and hit full force on the side of Lyn Williams' head. Then she moved forward to hit her again.

Keith Marshall had grabbed Parry's arm, spun him round and said, "What's going on in there?" as Catrin bolted inside. Marshall's "Catrin, stop!" was the second time her name had been yelled out in as many seconds.

Catrin ran through to the lounge, following the source of the commotion, to be greeted by the sight of three people. A woman she recognized from her photograph now being circulated as Lyn Williams was sitting on the floor with her arms out behind her, her elbows stopping her from ending up on her back. Li, in tears, was standing over her with a tube, dented on one side, lashing out again. The third person, a man she did not recognize, was sitting on the sofa holding one hand in the other, in shock. Blood was spurting between his fingers.

Catrin saw that Williams was holding a small gun in her right hand and that her arm was starting to come up. She ran forward, jamming her foot on Williams' wrist, full weight pushing it to the floor as the woman screamed and her fingers opened. Catrin reached down to retrieve the firearm. As she moved back she saw Li about to hit her again.

Catrin said, "Li, don't."

The tube stopped in its descent and Li threw it away.

Keith Marshall came in and Catrin passed him the gun.

"Handcuff her," he said, pointing at Williams. "Then bring in Parry."

He held the weapon with his finger and thumb.

"It's a Baby Browning. Who does this gun belong to?"

Li said, "He had it, the professor, then he gave it to her."

Keith had never seen one before, even during his army service, but he knew what it was well enough; a 'baby' Browning pistol of World War II vintage, a French manufacture automatic pistol. He had not been armed himself but knew from experience the danger that Catrin had just put herself in. He put the safety catch back on before putting the gun carefully on a bureau as he pulled out his mobile phone and called Dafydd.

Catrin had Lyn Williams on her front, arms behind her back, handcuffed.

"She killed Han," said Li, "She just told us, her and her brother." She sat back down in her armchair.

"How did you know to come here?" she asked Catrin who was already out of the room into the hall.

Li put her head in her hands. Haussmann was coming out of his shock and loudly asking for help with his hand as Williams started crying. In the commotion no-one noticed Jian Li Yeung speak in Chinese, head forward, close to the phone on the table, "Police here, everything OK now, don't pay, will call later." She reached over, picked up her phone from the coffee table and put it in her pocket.

One third of the way around the world Mrs. Lin ran from the bedroom to inform her husband of these developments. He was energetically talking on his mobile phone to a bank, she realised.

Catrin found Parry handcuffed with his hands behind

his back, sitting on the stairs at the bottom of the hallway, his front door still open. He looked dazed. She pulled him up and led him into the study. "Oh, no," he said, "Oh no!"

She looked. He was staring at the dented tube, "My painting."

The sound of sirens in the distance was coming closer. Keith retrieved a towel from the kitchen, folded it and pressed it on to the man's hand hard enough to make him yelp.

"I am Dieter Haussmann," he said to Keith.

Keith had seen that the left middle finger was mainly severed but the blood was pouring from the palm, where the metatarsal below the finger had been replaced by a hole. He continued to press hard and keep his eye on the two individuals handcuffed.

Catrin had pushed Parry on to a chair and gone straight over to Li and put her arm around her. She was saying something softly in her ear and Li was nodding between her sobs.

~~

The ambulances and police cars with the injured, the prisoners and Jian Li Yeung had left the scene when the four police officers, Worsley, Powys, Marshall and Sayer stood in a huddle outside. The SOCOs had shooed them out as they took over.

"I don't see how Williams would have found a way out of this," said Worsley. "The impression I get is that this German wasn't on board with her kidnap attempt."

Dafydd said, "She improvised right from the time Han Yeung got on his bike, I think. She was still doing so. Who knows who else would have been injured or killed?"

They would be doing interviews and taking statements later but fragments of what had happened had already come out. Dieter had seen Li open her mouth to scream and the Browning come up in Lyn's hand. He pushed it away and the shot had gone through his hand into the wall.

Dieter had said as the ambulance staff dealt with his hand, "I am prepared to make a statement and cooperate fully."

Then he looked at Li and said, "I am sorry, I hadn't wanted it to be this way."

Strangely enough, Catrin thought, Li's face seemed to indicate she accepted his apology but she said nothing.

Worsley said, "There may be talk of a review of our actions; a firearm was discharged and a person shot." She looked at Keith and Catrin, then at Dafydd. "I think it had better be your call, Dafydd. Can you fix it, quash it if you can, fast, with Superintendent Morgan?"

He nodded, clearly agreeing, "I will get right on it."

Worsley said, "Now, let's get sorted for the follow up with this lot. We still have a lot to do."

Catrin went in the car with Keith; Dafydd took Jane Worsley.

"Why did DCI Worsley suggest the procedural review should be quashed so fast, sir?"

"She's happy with the outcome, the arrests. But she wants to keep as much as possible of what went on just now out of Taylor's radar. Catrin, you just charged into an incident scene after a weapon had been discharged. I called you, but it was too late. You know it goes against your training and I understand why, but you could have been killed.

"I know she wants to keep you but Jane is concerned, no doubt, that Taylor may want to transfer you out of the

ACU if he hears about it. I haven't talked to her yet, but that's my read."

30 THE BABY BROWNING

Li had first been taken to the Gwynnedd Hospital to check for shock and after-effects, but once she stopped crying she seemed to be back to normal. She had insisted on speaking to a man who had called her on her mobile while she was waiting there, a Mr. Lin. It was family, her uncle, she said.

Idris and a uniform female PC had then taken her back to Gwynant and she was being looked after by friends. They had been informed of the basic facts by the PC who was still accompanying her and who would be with her until DCI Worsley arrived, she said. Li asked after Catrin but the female officer said that DC Sayer was busy. She wanted to see her, Li insisted, but the officer just said nothing.

Then DCI Worsley came along to check on her and asked if she would be up to making a statement; they would take her back to Gwynant afterwards but it was best done at the police station.

Dieter Haussmann was in a secure room at the same

hospital after surgery on his hand. He still had to be interviewed. Ivan Leigh-Jones, a local solicitor, turned up there during surgery after calling the police station to advise them that he had been retained as Haussmann's legal adviser. He then spoke to Dafydd Powys, whom he knew well, insisting that his client must be completely free of the effects of anesthesia before being interviewed.

Lyn William's was also there. Her counsel had similarly insisted that she not be interviewed until the doctors had assured them that she was free of concussion. Keith had been joined by Idris and they were there waiting outside the examination room. The female PC assigned to guard her stood in the room, the lawyer glaring at her. Everyone was waiting for the doctors to decide. Idris wanted to get her to the cells.

When the lawyer came to the doorway and made some remark about the possibility of a civil lawsuit against Jian Li Yeung and the police force in the event of any brain damage incurred by her client, Idris said something in Welsh that seemed to offend her a little, Keith thought. Then Lyn William's voice could be heard from the bed.

"I won't make any statement without first speaking to Jian Li Yeung," she said suddenly. Her lawyer's eyes showed that statement was not on her game plan at all.

"Your client appears remarkably clear-headed at present," said Keith.

~~

Worsley had kept Catrin at her side throughout the remainder of the day, other than insisting that she stayed away from Jian Li Yeung until her statement had been taken and her own report written. At Gwynant she had instructed her to stay in the car and when Worsley came out with Jian Li, she made Catrin ride back with the PC in the second police car while she rode with Yeung and the driver.

"And no, you won't be in that interview, Catrin," she told her, "Dafydd and I will do that."

Catrin was about to head to her desk to prepare her own report when Worsley said, "First I want you to sit in on the briefing to Superintendent Taylor in twenty minutes and then before you write anything I also want you to observe the interview with Parry. Dafydd and I will do that one too. You will collect him from the cells with a PC, bring him in and sit by the door. If we get to discuss his plans being ruined, it will be helpful when I tell him it was your bright idea to go to his home; increase his anger. Then he may tell us more than his lawyer wants."

"Thank you, ma'am – I think."

The call with Taylor, Catrin thought, was a clear example of why Jane Worsley had her job. She may not know too much about art; she managed a police team well and was a good decision-maker, but in the politics at senior management levels she excelled. Catrin didn't realise until it was past that Jane had conveyed but not stated that Catrin had line of sight of the lounge and had made it a priority to retrieve the weapon from the spread-eagled Williams before it could be trained on anyone. She and Keith Marshall had then restrained the parties and assisted the wounded.

Catrin just recalled the bedlam of it all.

At the conclusion, after talking about next steps, Taylor said, "Well, DC Sayer, it sounds like you and DI Marshall behaved commendably. You showed good intuition on going to Parry's and then prompt action to contain a nasty situation; so well done. Jane, give Keith my regards also."

"Thank you, sir," said Catrin.

She looked at Worsley after the call closed. "And thank you, ma'am."

Worsley just looked at her and said, "Write very carefully later on, Catrin."

She stood up.

"First, Professor Parry; bring him along to Interview Room 2, if you please. His lawyer will be nicely steamed up, I think, given the wait."

The first round of questioning was to concentrate on the gun, Dafydd, Jane and Keith had agreed.

A 'baby' Browning of French manufacture made before World War Two, illegally owned, had been used to shoot a man. It was the most serious charge they would make at present. Discussion of the painting would follow. And then the rest, particularly the leakage that may have occurred in ACU on this case and others involving A&A in which Parry had been a consultant over the years.

Neville Coltrane has become so inarticulate when Jane had called him to give him a 'heads up' that she almost felt some sympathy for him. He said he would come on up to Bangor once the scope of Parry's activity had been established.

Parry and his counsel were sitting opposite Worsley and Dafydd.

"Why did you do it?" asked Jane. "You are a person of standing, responsibility, reputation. Why?"

She was reading from the silence of his legal counsel now and comments made during the preliminaries that

Parry would say something. She had to find the limits.

"The painting, I guess. I became obsessed with owning the Svetlana Komarov. It was an unexpected opportunity."

His face reflected it. Catrin was watching from the side; she wondered if he was mentally sound.

"It all sounds good, the life of an academic, I know," he continued. "The house I live in is actually owned by my sister. Other than my boat and some paintings I have nothing, really. I am tired of teaching students and of the interminable bureaucracy of universities. All I want really is the art I like. Sounds stupid, but the Svetlana was a must for me."

Worsley said, "We are checking through the other paintings in the house now."

"You will find," he said sharply, "that they are all above board. Most are mine, I have the purchase receipts. Two are university loan items, properly documented."

"We will make sure the university paintings are returned," said Dafydd.

"Thank you," said Parry, apparently oblivious to the inference. It would be some considerable time before he would be enjoying any paintings again, Dafydd thought.

"So before these paintings, the sisters, you were not...."

"I was certainly not involved in any criminal activity, no. What do you take me for?"

I am not sure, thought Worsley, but if it proves to be true, Neville will be a little happier. But I am beginning to see why his lawyer is letting him talk.

"And the gun is illegal and old. Can you explain how it came into your possession?"

"It's mine. Unregistered, of course, but belonged to my father and his uncle before him. So I inherited it through them."

"And how did your great-uncle get it, may I ask," said Dafydd, his disbelief evident in his tone.

"The government gave it to him."

He paused. "My great-uncle, Arthur Parry, was in the Special Operations Executive in World War II, in Europe. I have the papers and his other memorabilia in my home and you can check government records."

Of course," he added earnestly, "the ammunition is not that old."

"You loaded and brought this weapon to the meeting today in your home. Is that correct?" said Worsley.

He nodded, "Yes, but I never shot anyone."

Catrin watched the process from the side. We have one suspect in a mental health hospital in Llanfairfechan with PTSD and another here who may be a candidate for the same facility, she thought. It was going to be a long process. The main thing is to get them charged, she knew.

"So, the painting," said DCI Worsley.

"Is it alright?" asked Parry.

"I mean, please describe how you came to acquire the Garin painting of Svetlana Komarov, and how you know Lyn Williams, who we know received it in Holyhead."

He sighed. "When the Han Yeung thing happened, she called me. She was a former student of mine. In fact, we had a brief fling some years ago but had lost touch, although I knew she taught art at the school level somewhere around here.

"She said she had the painting but would not at first say how. I was thunderstruck. I had seen all three during a visit to the museum in Volgograd. She offered it to me for £150,000, can you believe it? I didn't have that sort of cash available, I said."

"There was no thought of phoning DCI Coltrane and

turning her in?"

"A fleeting one but… as I said, I just suddenly had to have it. Lyn and I agreed that if I helped her by letting her use my boat to dispose of Yeung, and then sold it to make up a cash sum the painting would be mine; she would hold it for me. But the boat hasn't sold yet".

"Did you accompany her, to get rid of the body?"

"No, she is a good sailor but her brother went with her, not me. But she motored, I know, and I don't think it was too far, but can't really say."

He looked across at Catrin. She kept her face blank.

He said, "Then, ironically, Neville called me to help you."

Worsley asked, "When did you become involved with the plan to take Jian Li Yeung hostage?"

"Yesterday; it came out of the blue. Lyn Williams phoned me. If I helped her with the plan she had thought up, she and I both would be more than compensated from elsewhere. No matter how it went, I would have the painting today and a lot more. I was in a panic about being exposed but she said it would be no problem. There would be no loose ends and she would be out of the country within a day. She asked me if I had a gun; I said yes."

Dafydd said, "I don't understand it though, Professor Parry. The plan called for each of you to receive a million dollars. You would suddenly up and leave, disappear, become a fugitive. And you decided that in a moment's notice; really?"

"Yes," said Parry.

Catrin could see he was lying and knew her superiors would see it too. Parry's lawyer was getting very attentive.

Worsley said, "So you are aware that there was a possibility of this 'plan', for want of a better word, resulting in Miss Yeung and possibly Mr. Haussmann being killed if payment was not made? Or perhaps even if it was made, I think. Two more bodies in the Menai and life would be back to normal for you."

His lawyer saw the trap.

"That's speculation, Chief Inspector Worsley, so don't answer that, Professor Parry."

He doesn't have to, thought Catrin; it is in his eyes, the cold bastard. Parry was hoping Li and Dieter would disappear in the same way as Han did. She wondered if Williams had intended to bind and gag Haussmann and her friend as Li had told them in her statement. She shuddered at the thought of Li being disposed of in the same manner as her brother.

He hadn't considered, she suddenly thought, what would happen if a different Chinese woman then came looking for him. She needed to look back to Li's statement and see if Parry's identity had been revealed at all to her uncle, the person she called in desperation, she said.

~~

It was the following day, Saturday. Dafydd, Jane, Keith and Catrin were sitting in Dafydd's office.

Dafydd Powys had just got off the phone with Lyn Williams' lawyer. He brought them up to speed then added, "We can't allow this, I think."

Yesterday they had taken Williams from the hospital to the police station. She had been interviewed, during which she had answered no questions, said nothing other than once, to repeat her demand to speak with Jian Li Yeung.

The lawyer had reiterated William's request, stating it

as a precondition for answering any further questions while being interviewed.

"I know Williams is not co-operating," Dafydd continued. "Her counsel will have a field day in court if this goes wrong. I think she wants some agreement from Li that she saw that the gun was discharged accidentally, perhaps because Dieter grabbed it, or she wants something else in return for the location of Han Yeung's body."

Keith Marshall said, "Dafydd, she is far guiltier than Stephen Harrison, I think. She placed her foster brother she knew to be mentally fragile in the line of fire in a confrontational situation. She will be arguing that Yeung's death rests with Harrison; that she was only trying to help by disposing of the body with him."

Catrin added, "She may not even admit to being on the Rusalka that day. She could easily contest forensic evidence by saying that she was on it separately with Parry earlier, as they were lovers. We know what Jian Li told us about Han's death is not evidence; only her evidence on the kidnap and the firearm's offence would be admitted in court. We need the body and William's admission to some involvement in the death on record, don't we?"

They had been around the pros and cons of giving into Williams's request twice now, once before the latest call from the lawyer.

Jane Worsley had sat very quiet during the latter part of the discussion. She suddenly sat upright and said, "I am going to grant the request, not this weekend or Monday, but on Tuesday. Let her stew a bit. I will sit in with Yeung.

"In the meantime today we will charge Williams and Parry with the firearm offences and Parry with the possession of the Komarov painting; it was in his home.

Once we have forensics linking Williams to the painting and the other painting in our possession to the room in her home, we will charge her with her involvement in that theft also.

"Dafydd, please call Lyn Williams counsel back and tell her that the meeting is going to happen, but by our rules. Jian Li Yeung can have 15 minutes, no more. And Dafydd, I will take full responsibility for this if it comes unstuck.

"From what we know, Han Yeung was killed on May 14th. We don't know where his body is and neither we, nor Yeung nor her family have closure. It is about time she had some say. The location of Han Yeung's body may come out in due course during our questioning or it may not. But if Williams wants a meeting, Yeung has the right to ask, and ask first.

"Catrin, you and I will talk to Jian Li. No harangues or diatribes from her will be acceptable, and that is a precondition. But she can be in front of Lyn Williams and pose the question and Williams doesn't get to say her piece until that is on the table.

"I am going to be very interested in the response."

Her tone made it clear that the discussion was over. Catrin suddenly felt an overwhelming desire to hug her boss for standing up for Li's interests but simply said, "Yes ma'am."

Li listened carefully to Jane Worsley.

"I will do it, Chief Inspector, but to be honest, I have no great hope of an answer. You should have seen her in Parry's house. Talking about Han's death and dumping my brother in the water, she was as cool as a cucumber."

Worsley nodded. "It will be hard, I know. But, Jian Li, anything which gets her talking gives us leverage for further questioning and with it, an opportunity to break her resistance down so we find out more.

"At the very worst, it gives the prosecution counsel the opportunity to bring it up in court; that you tried and still she would not tell you. Remember, whatever she asks or is trying to get from you, you don't have to say anything either. And I will limit it to fifteen minutes maximum, I promise you."

Li nodded. "Will Catrin be there?" She looked at her friend.

"Only you and I will be in the interview room but Catrin will take you to Colwyn Bay and watch it; you and she can spend time afterwards and I promise you, and I have many years of doing these interviews, I will not let anything happen that will give Lyn Williams some advantage in court."

Li's face indicated she was decided. "Thank you, it is an opportunity, as you say, and I must do the best to find Han, for my parents as well as my own peace of mind."

It was clear that Williams would want something from the meeting, probably in return for the location of Han's body, Catrin told her later, after Worsley's departure. What it was she didn't know, but they suspected that the woman was trying to put as much blame on her foster brother as possible; it was something to do with that, perhaps.

Or she still wants the money she asked for, thought Li, through the route that had been presented before the police arrived and will make that clear somehow.

Li felt a huge desire to beat this woman at her own game. The interview might be the only time to do that. She was tired of being informed piecemeal by the police and knew from her training she would be no more than an observer in the court process, if it came to trial while she was still studying here. In the British system, this was highly unlikely, she thought.

She thought back to seeing the woman in Craig Y Don Road; how she acted, what she looked like, what she wore, trying to understand her better. That gave her the idea.

It was worth bothering Mr. Lin with one more call, she concluded. He had sounded so relieved when she called back and she knew it wasn't about the money; he would have paid that without a second thought. She had asked him only to make sure that her father was not told of this incident.

She was also very careful in her discussion with Mr. Lin not to mention Catrin's question about the Chinese link. He in turn gave no insight into the issue which had been driving Dieter to make the call. But she was also sure now that Michael Yau knew of the events which had sent Haussmann flying into Manchester to meet with Lyn Williams.

When she spoke to Mr. Lin regarding her proposal he was very accommodating. It would be no problem and he would fix it immediately, given the urgency.

Enlai Li got some tea and sat down to make a call to Michael Yau.

~~

It was later the same day. Li had decided to spend some time studying, to take her mind off the events of the last few days and the meeting to come. She had taken her books and iPad to the Old Library in the Main Arts Building and spent several hours working. She had seen it from the outside when she had a familiarisation tour but had come here to work the first time with Andrea Teller. The older student said that the place had almost a cathedral quality and was very conducive to study.

She was leaving the building later when a Chinese woman she hadn't seen before in a smart suit came past her and said hello in Cantonese. She responded and the woman stopped. She introduced herself as Professor Iris Huang.

They talked about where they were from. Professor Huang was also from Hong Kong originally, she said, but now taught at ANU, the Australian National University. Li thought she was extremely well-dressed for a professor but just said that she hadn't seen her at the Chinese Society meetings; did she attend?

Professor Huang smiled regretfully. "I am only visiting for a few days. In fact, I will be leaving shortly for Bristol University, for a symposium there."

She was looking at Li's face quite intently.

They said their goodbyes and Emily Yang turned away, fixing in her mind the face of Jian Li Yeung. By now she had a good idea what this was all about, if not the details and the client.

Her plans to approach Parry had been cancelled. She had arrived in Bangor via Manchester and a rental car also, expecting to reconnoitre Parry's faculty building and home address for a suitable opportunity to approach him for the painting. It was her local contact on arrival who told her that police cars and ambulances had been seen a few hours ago in Craig Y Don Road at the Parry address. At the time they were still trying to find out what had happened. In fact, the information to Yang came from Mr. Yau, ironically. He heard it from his client.

The new developments had worked out very well for

her. She now had a very pleasurable task in Manchester on Sunday afternoon then a flight via Istanbul to Hong Kong. Mr. Yau had said she could spend the remainder of her time there before returning to her role in Sydney. He had made it clear she would also be receiving a large bonus for her efforts on this assignment.

31 ABERYSTWYTH

The idea occurred to Catrin the same evening. She phoned DCI Worsley and obtained her agreement easily enough. Worsley also fixed it with DI Powys for her to have a pool vehicle for Sunday. Then she phoned Li.

"Li, tomorrow we are going to Snowdonia and a little further perhaps, just you and me as friends; if you want to, that is, if you have time. I have the use of a car for the day."

Li paused before responding. "Just as friends; it would be wonderful."

She thought a Sunday sightseeing drive away from it all and finally to see Snowdonia up close would make a great change.

Catrin picked her up early and took side roads up to the Llanberis Pass through into the heart of Snowdonia. The weather was not too bad but it was cloudy, misty at times and seemed to Li to be threatening to close in at higher elevations.

Li said, "I sail with someone who is also a climber, a

mountaineer; he says you really need to know your stuff to be up here in winter. I can see why."

"On those slopes, Li, you need to know what you are doing any time of the year."

When they stopped at different places for photographs Catrin was glad of her coat, the wind was sharp.

Their discussion on the outbound trip was mainly about the scenery, the history and a silly game with road signs that evolved. Li would try to pronounce the Welsh name; Catrin would say it slowly in sections and Li would keep trying. Results were very variable and hilarious at times for both of them.

When they picked up the A487 after Blaenau Ffestiniog, Catrin said," We are going to Aberystwyth before we turn back and I have a surprise."

Li suddenly looked serious. "What now?"

"We are going to have lunch with my parents at a place we always went to when I was a student there. I want them to meet you. They are driving up from Pontypridd about now."

Li looked at her. "I am not very well dressed for this."

Catrin smiled. "It won't matter; it's my mum and dad."

Li had been nervous about the lunch plan until they settled in the restaurant on the Aberystwyth sea front. Catrin's parents were already there. Within a few minutes Li had taken to them. There was no formality; they were straight out with their condolences about the loss of her brother and she could see their genuine concern for how she was doing.

Half-way through the meal Catrin's father had Li in stitches with his comments about Catrin as an undergraduate student at Aberystwyth. Her friend's denials and responses just made it even funnier. She had seen a lot of Catrin's serious side; this was so completely different.

"And the things she wore then, you would just not believe," he went on.

Li saw Catrin and her mum exchange smiles, roll their eyes and knew she was in for some more exaggeration and family banter. It felt good.

When it came time to finish lunch it was clear that her parents knew they were going sightseeing, just the two of them, a quick tour of the university before heading back. It had all been arranged by Catrin, she could tell. Her parents hugged Catrin in turn and then, as Li held out her hand to shake theirs and thank them, they did the same with her.

"It's lovely to have met you, Li," Catrin's father said. Yes, she thought, that is what it was, lovely.

Later Catrin took the coastal road back through Porthmadog and Caernarfon. During a quiet spell Li pulled a small card out of her purse.

"While you were in the loo your mum gave me this; she said she was sorry she had no card for me, being short notice and a Sunday, but it was something she found comforting and wanted me to have it. I think it is quite old."

Catrin glanced over, recognizing it.

"I have known that all my life," she said. "It is old and is very special to her."

Li was reading the verses.

Catrin said, "Do you know it?"

Li shook her head, absorbed.

"It is a poem called 'Death is Nothing At All' by a man called Henry Scott-Holland. He was a clergyman at

St. Paul's Cathedral in the nineteenth century. The card belonged to my grandmother and was passed on. It has always been a favorite of hers."

Li said, "Your mother knows about St. Paul's and Cho?"

"No Li. I would never discuss police work with my parents. It's a coincidence. All they know is we met because I was investigating a case and your brother was a victim, that's all. And, I told them, of course, that you are my friend."

Tears were forming in Li's eyes. "This should belong to you, really; it was your grandmother."

"No, she wants you to have it, and so do I."

Catrin reached over and squeezed Li's hand.

"Look," she said, "We are coming into Llanllyfni. So say it …"

"Your mother is a very nice person, Catrin Sayer, and so are you. That's what I should say."

32 THE EARRINGS

Catrin was assigned to collect Li the following Tuesday and drive her to the North Wales Police Headquarters at Colwyn Bay for the interview with Lyn Williams. As Catrin drove up, Li was waiting outside Gwynant in her winter coat, holding a Bangor University Rugby Club travel mug with tea. Catrin could see that she was wearing a formal dark suit and dress shoes also. She hadn't seen Li dressed like this before and thought she was responding to the formality of the event. She looked more like a business woman now than a student.

On the drive over Li was pretty quiet and Catrin reassured her that Jane Worsley was very well prepared and would look out for her in the interview. They had been through the many possibilities of Williams' tactics as a team.

"Just remember, all you have to do is ask. You don't have to answer anything."

On the journey Li had made one call from her mobile, apparently getting an update on something.

Catrin knew that Jane and Keith were already in the

police headquarters building; they had an early morning call with Jack Taylor on some other case.

When they arrived, Li said, "It's a big building, much bigger than the one in Bangor."

"It's the headquarters for the North Wales Police, Li. Everything to do with Han's case will now be handled from here; interviews, preparation for the trial and so on."

Li's eyes were searching the car park and entrance area. "I am waiting for someone who is going to meet me here, Catrin. I can't go in yet."

Catrin said, "It's only you and DCI Worsley allowed during the interview, Li."

"Oh, I know," said Li, not explaining further.

As they spoke a motorcycle came into sight on the drive and Li waved. It rode up to them and the rider switched the engine off, dismounted and unlocked a pannier. Inside he took out a small metal case and a mobile reader, the sort a courier uses and asked to see Li's passport, which she already had in her hand.

They spoke briefly and he unlocked the small case after having her sign the screen. Then he passed over a pouch. Li put it in her purse and confirmed with him he would be in the waiting area later.

He nodded. "I will park my bike properly and wait inside, in the public waiting area. I guess I just made it on time."

Li turned to Catrin, smiling at the puzzled look on her face. "We can go in now," she said.

As they cleared security a constable came to meet them and took them along to the interview room area.

Li said, "Catrin, just a minute. Can you hold the box while I put these in, please, I am a bit nervous."

She had taken a jewel box from the pouch and had

opened it.

Catrin saw the Mappin & Webb logo on the velvet box and then its contents, a pair of hoop earrings in white gold with a series of large, identically cut diamonds, tapering in size towards the outer edge. They were stunning. She had not seen jewellery like it before.

"Li they are... they must have cost a fortune."

The constable, who had been watching all this said, "Thank God my wife isn't here, she would squeal over those."

Li was all business though. "Can you help please, I don't want to drop them and there is no mirror."

Catrin held the box while Li put the earrings in carefully.

"Do they look right?" she asked.

"They look a million dollars, and so do you, Li."

"We can go now," said Li.

DCI Worsley shook hands with Jian Li and paused. Clearly she was struck by the change in appearance but only said, "Li, you will need to leave your bag and that mug outside with Catrin. Are you still OK with this?"

Li nodded.

Jane said, "Shall we go in?"

Catrin moved into the observation room, where Dafydd and Keith were already waiting.

Jane Worsley had just finished the identification of the persons present.

Myra Hargreaves, Lyn Williams' solicitor who had so incensed Idris some days earlier said, "Chief Inspector Worsley, my client has asked for this meeting but let me make it clear to Miss Yeung that we are treating this as a formal interview, on record."

"Duly noted," said Worsley. "Miss Yeung?"

There was a pause. Li looked first at the lawyer.

"Miss Hargreaves, I am studying for a degree in law. I understand rules of evidence. My purpose in coming here today was simply to ask for the whereabouts of the body of my brother, nothing else."

She didn't pause for a response, just turned to face Williams head on.

"Miss Williams, our family is Chinese and our culture is very different to yours, as are our religions, our justice system and our process of respecting the dead. We have been waiting from the time of Han's disappearance first in the hope he was alive and then in the hope of providing him with both a Christian funeral - my family is Christian - but we also have family members who are from other religious beliefs. They too want to pay their respects in their own way also.

"Please know we will never give up on this matter and, as you have found out already I think, Chinese people can be very committed. I assure you it is in your best personal interest, independent of your defense strategy for other charges, to provide this information to us. We must know where Han is and we need to know it right now."

She turned her head to Worsley and said, "Thank you."

She started to rise and Worsley touched her arm, motioning her to sit.

"Thank you, Miss Yeung," she said, staring impassively at Lyn Williams.

Catrin was watching Lyn Williams. Her eyes constantly returned to the earrings as Li's head moved gently as she talked. Presumably the diamonds were catching the light nicely.

Then they sat there in silence.

Catrin knew Worsley was waiting for Williams to make her negotiation statement or for her lawyer to call for time alone with her client. Hargreaves in turn was digesting Li's statement and glancing at Williams.

Keith suddenly said, "Clever. We know Lyn Williams likes jewellery; look how many pieces she was wearing when we arrested her and how she fussed when her belongings and clothes were taken away for forensic examination. She is sitting there entranced by these earrings and wondering how this supposed Chinese student could own a pair like them. Li must have seen how much jewellery she was wearing too at Craig Y Don Road.

"And the message she gave her was, 'I am not here to help you with any plea bargain and we will never give up on getting Han's location from you, independent of the legal process'. Look, Hargreaves is trying to decide if she can object to it as some sort of coercion. It's on her face."

Dafydd said, "But she worded it very carefully, that's why Myra is hesitating. If she objects now, without basis, Jane will be all over her; she was the one pushing for this. She has to wait on her client."

Catrin thought, Jane will sit out the full fifteen minutes in silence, if she has to.

Suddenly Lyn Williams spoke, looking at Li. "Do you have a pen?"

"No," said Li. "My bag is outside."

"I have the coordinates from the GPS memorized. I am also prepared to go with a police team to the exact spot that I believe Yeung's body was placed in the Strait. That is as much as I can do and is all I am prepared to say at this point."

Worsley passed over a piece of paper and a pen. "The coordinates, please."

Lyn Williams wrote them down and passed both the paper and pen back, then sat back in her seat staring at Li looking more puzzled than angry.

Li stood up.

Worsley stood also. "Interview suspended at 10.40 a.m. Miss Yeung and DCI Worsley are now leaving the room."

She eyed Hargreaves. "I will be back," she added.

The lawyer knew this was going to be a long day.

As they came out Catrin left the observation room to join them. Worsley was thanking Li and asking if she was alright. "Catrin, can you take Li for a coffee or tea and then see she gets back to Bangor. Li, that was excellent, thank you so much for doing this.

"We will be getting a dive boat organised now. I assure you we will be doing all we can to find Han but it is not a lake or pond, this is the Menai Strait. But keep praying."

She headed back into the interview room and Dafydd Powys followed her. Williams had started talking; now they needed her to continue doing so.

Keith Marshall said, "Li, well done. That was very fine work and congratulations on getting the coordinates." He shook her hand.

Li nodded to him and asked Catrin to hold the jewel box again while she took the earrings out. "I just need to give them back to the courier."

She walked out to the man in the Waiting Area dressed in motorcycle gear. He spoke to her and pulled out a mobile reader, pressed some buttons and then asked her to sign the screen. The box was placed in the small security case that Catrin noticed was now chained to his wrist. Then he was out the door.

"What are they worth, do you know?" asked Catrin.

"A great deal, in more ways than one," said Li. "They are on their way back to Manchester. A family friend arranged them for me. But I do not know what they cost, just what they did."

"Coffee?" said Catrin, smiling impishly, "There is a cafeteria, restaurant and coffee shop here."

Li said, "Let's go to the coffee pub where we first went in Bangor, could we?

"Sure," said Catrin.

~~

Later, in the café in Upper Bangor they went back to the subject of the interview. Li had been a little subdued on the short drive, which Catrin ascribed to the aftermath of the interview and the tension and nervousness that Li must have felt.

Catrin said, "She couldn't take her eyes of the earrings."

Li stifled a yawn. "That was the idea. She had to see that there is world she is not part of which has the power and wealth to find out the truth about Han."

"And are you part of that power and wealth, Li?"

"Catrin, I am a law student with a dad who is a tailor and one of my newest friends is a policewoman."

In fact, Li's thoughts had been on how much more to tell Catrin and when to tell her. She suddenly said, "Catrin, let's go for a walk. I am sleepy and need some air. And I have a story to tell you."

33 GLANRAFON HILL

Li led Catrin back along College Road. The Main Arts Building of Bangor University was looming in front on their left.

"I don't know exactly what happened to cause the names of people involved to be revealed, but I think I know why it happened," she began as they started their walk together. "As my friend, not as a police officer, I will tell you a story, a true story. You can then see if the pieces fit together because you and your colleagues have more of the puzzle than I do, I think."

Catrin Sayer said nothing, she just looked briefly at Li then her eyes went back to the Arts Building. When they passed by it they would start their descent along Penrallt Road and Glanrafon Hill towards the town centre.

"I am from Hong Kong as you know, but my family is originally from mainland China, from a place called Tongzi, about one hundred miles south of what is now the city of Chongqing. My grandparents with my father, he was a baby then, left there suddenly in 1949. My grandmother An Li used to say that granddad bravely but

292

foolishly got into a fight with a soldier. That was the reason. Granddad always said it was the American Lutheran bishop that uprooted our family.

"We became Hong Kong Chinese then."

Li led her friend though her family story; how her father had become a fireman before a tailor, how he had met Mr. Lin, the shipping magnate, and Mr. Yau, the Triad boss, and the development of the strange bond between the three men.

To the world about them they could have easily been lost in a discussion of a lecture or seminar. If someone passing had picked up snippets, it would obviously have concerned a course in Asian studies or modern history. The Chinese woman was the more animated student, doing the talking. The blonde one just listened and occasionally nodded.

~~

The two women were near the bottom of Glanrafon Hill, walking slowly now as Li wound up her family story.

"So you see, there is strong *guanxi* between these men." Li said. "I mean, they do not live in the same circles, do not even share the same values, but... they would help each other; they have something linking them, they understand that."

"When I said I was coming to Bangor after Han's disappearance I had a call on my mobile phone from Mr. Lin. He told me that whatever I needed while I was over here looking for my brother, I was just to call and ask. In the end, the only things I asked for was whether he could press people in the British Embassy to get the police to do more; I had no idea about the effort you were putting in at the time. Just a few days ago, I asked him for the rental or loan of expensive earrings. They had to be stunning, I said."

Catrin was processing the information. "So you are not linked…."

Li said, "Catrin, I am not linked to anything. I have already said that. I gave Lyn Williams the advice that any good prosecution lawyer would give. She assumed differently and I did not correct her; that is all. She obviously likes jewellery so the earrings were meant to intimidate her, for good cause. And if you think that my father's friends, let me call them that, were interested in the art, you are wrong. They simply wanted to find Han, I think, to bring closure for my father and my family. They too had lost sons.

"When I told Mr. Lin what happened and how this all related to the paintings of the Komarov Sisters he said, 'It is hard to find anything good in this sad news'. I agreed with him. But now I recall you telling me that the paintings of the sisters will be reunited and returned to Russia, to the people who love and should own them."

Her face was neutral, enigmatic. "She was a flyer, you said, in World War II, the woman in one of the paintings?"

"Yes, the youngest sister, Svetlana, she was a navigator of a bomber. She was a brave woman."

Li looked lost in thought. "Perhaps a little good came out of it after all, yes?"

Catrin put the pieces of Li's story with the facts they had gathered through the police enquiries, seeing how they came together; how two old men in Hong Kong had set out to find the body of Han Yeung and remove all doubt about him being involved in this art theft. Given the world of the Triad, they had achieved that objective but, in doing so, had unwittingly placed his sister in danger.

She was sure Worsley would be placed in a dilemma if she ever told her the story, but Catrin had no plans to do so.

Jian Li looked at Catrin. "So now I have told you, what happens now... will there be repercussions?"

Catrin could see the anxiety on Li's face.

She was not going to break Jian Li's trust a second time. She said, "Li, it does put it all together for me, but you told me a story as a friend, so it goes no further. It has no bearing on the charges that will be laid here and it is probably wise that we don't mention it to others."

Then she smiled, "And what happens now is that we go to the Glan for lunch." The Old Glan pub was one she liked. When they had started walking it crossed Catrin's mind that it was a long time since her breakfast.

"So will you complete your course?" Catrin asked as they crossed the main road.

"Yes, I plan to. Then go back home to finish my final year and after, who knows? I still like the idea of maritime law. But I like this place. I will enjoy the rest of my year here now, I think. There is a Chinese society and we meet regularly. I met an engineering student there who has taken an interest in me, so we will see what comes out of that; I quite like him but haven't agreed to a date yet. After all, life has been a little weird of late!"

She paused, thinking.

"My parents will come over and we will have a cremation service here for Han when the body is released, if it is found. Will you come?"

"If I can, Li, I will. But I don't know what I will be involved in back in London. I am just starting with the

Art Crime Unit so I don't know what my commitments might be and when I can get time off."

Li turned to Catrin before they went into the pub. "Catrin, I am very conscious of the issue that you are a police officer and cannot accept gifts related to cases you work on. But I would like to give you something. Even if we see each other more here or in London, I would like at some time to show you my home, my island, my world, and for you to meet my parents also.

"If you book and pay yourself for a discount flight - as cheap as you can find - on Cathay Pacific anytime to Hong Kong, you will find yourself upgraded on board to First Class. That is already arranged; that is my gift."

She started laughing, looking at Catrin's face, "Not money, not jade, not terracotta warriors..."

Catrin looked at her. "Thank you. If I do, I will have to clear it, you understand... but I would love to, honestly. I have been to Paris once but that is nothing like travelling so far as Hong Kong." She raised her eyebrow and half-smiled, "We have *guanxi*, right?"

"You will stay with me and my family," continued Li, "and travelling on Cathay Pacific in First Class is... worth the ride itself, I assure you."

She suddenly realized what Catrin had said about *guanxi* and took both of Catrin's hands in hers. She looked intense, serious. "Catrin Sayer, yes we have *guanxi*. We certainly do."

Then she smiled again. "And I will feed you excellent Chinese food with beef you will rave over. Then I will tell you it is dog not beef, or sea slug not oyster, just to see your face change. But you will enjoy it. We will enjoy it."

Catrin smiled. "Let's go inside and see if we can find some good Welsh lamb for now."

34 THE 'CEINWEN'

Menai Strait, November. Among the police diving team members there was the perennial discussion of whether funding for each search would run out before they achieved success or failure by their own yardstick. Despite the precise location of the body being dropped overboard, the considered opinion was that they may find the bike but not the body.

Over the years these divers had become as knowledgeable about human decomposition in aquatic environments as any forensic pathologist; after all, they were the ones to first encounter the victim, if they were found. Comments such as 'wrapped in plastic, not just thin stuff, industrial grade', 'gets buoyant after a while with the gases', 'these tidal waters and the flow through the Strait, it could be half-way back to Hong Kong by now' were murmured as they made their preparations.

The location turned out to be one of the deeper pools that formed the complex sea bed of the Strait, formed and reformed by powerful tidal flows around Anglesey. They thought that the location was not a random selection; Parry knew these waters well and probably had advised Williams of the spot. It was not too far from his home port but it had limited visibility from the roads on the mainland and the island. He may not have gone out on the boat to dispose of Yeung, but they didn't think he was as detached from it as he had stated.

The first day of the search became a washout after two hours, the weather proving uncooperative. But they were then promised two days of fair weather. It was no real surprise to find the bike early on the third day, only about 40 metres from their starting point. But it was described as good luck later the same day when a flap of plastic was seen and the body found in small gully in the same area, wedged in at some point by tidal flow.

'Chalk one up to Donnie' they said. Donald Halford had been their first team leader, forever the optimist, now long dead.

Catrin went with Dafydd for the post-mortem debriefing with the forensic pathologist. Worsley had said on the phone it was not an order, it was part of the job of the team, but this would not be an easy one. Catrin had seen dead bodies before, including one found after two days in warm weather in a car park, but not one that had been under water - and for five months, at that.

She chose to go. Somehow the clinical atmosphere and detachment of the pathologist helped but she flinched when she saw the state of Han Yeung's remains, having until that time only seen pictures of him alive and smiling. The probable cause of death - the pathologist went to some length to say it could not be conclusive, given the state of decomposition - was a cervical fracture. This would be consistent with the blow described by Lyn Williams, he said.

The hardest part for Catrin was the skull. A clear imprint of the cycle helmet could be seen on the bone. The pathologist explained that the skin lifted off when the helmet was finally removed and the plasticizers and dyes from the lining had already migrated into the bone surface, leaving the patterned imprint.

They went on directly to meet with Li in Gwynant, to confirm formally that the body found was Han. The dental records had matched, as did the fragments of clothes. A DNA confirmation against the saliva sample Li had provided was in the works but it was purely confirmatory at this stage.

"Can I...should I see him?" said Li, her eyes filling with tears.

"We won't stop you doing so but recommend not to; Han's body has undergone significant decomposition and it is not needed at all for positive identification purposes," said Dafydd softly.

Li looked at Catrin who said, "Best remember him as he was, Li."

Li realised that Catrin must have seen Han at the autopsy. She suddenly let out a howl of grief and Catrin put her arms around her. Dafydd moved to a position where he could see Catrin's face, trying to hold back tears herself and nodded to her to stay, then he left the room.

Later, as the two women came out together he was having coffee with Andrea and a woman Catrin did not know in the kitchen area. Catrin said she would call later as the two women sat down with Li.

As they left Dafydd said, "She's a student counsellor for the university; the Vice-Chancellor's office sent for her when I called."

~~

Catrin had then been in Bangor and Colwyn Bay an extra week working with Dafydd Powys' team. She knew Worsley was coming back up by train that morning; she and Dafydd had a meeting with senior officers and Crown Prosecutors that afternoon.

Dafydd drove Catrin back to the Bangor Police station where Worsley was in the process of finishing up a call. The two senior officers spoke briefly and Jane came over to Catrin. "Now, Detective Constable Sayer, we are going to lunch at a place called the Boatyard."

"Thank you, ma'am. But I can't say I am that hungry, to be honest."

"I am; and I think you will be. Besides, I want a stiff drink before Dafydd takes me to Colwyn Bay for more politics - and you are driving me to the pub."

Catrin did brighten up over lunch and was hungry, as Jane had predicted. Worsley specifically steered the conversation away from the case. She asked questions about Catrin's art and her personal life and in return shared some of her own. Afterwards Catrin realised how little she had known about Jane Worsley compared with her growing knowledge of Keith Marshall.

Worsley had come into the police service with a degree in political science and an MBA from the University of London, one of the 'fast-track' recruits arriving in a wave when the Met was under pressure to deal with its 'Policeman Plod' image. She had weathered more chauvinism and 'old boys' network-ism' than Catrin, it seemed, and had given back as good as she got. Catrin's tale of Sergeant Hallam posing nude had her shrieking with laughter.

She was single. Her love life, she said, could best be described as 'not good at long term relationships... or short term ones, for that matter'. She was a private pilot, one-tenth owner of a small Cessna at an airfield in Surrey, and she confessed to an unfortunate weakness for both private and commercial pilots who always seemed to fly away.

Worsley had last been in the Met's Diplomatic Protection Branch and had made the heinous mistake of arresting someone she thought deserved it, to find it sent shivers through Westminster, with career repercussions. Jack Taylor had pulled her into the new Art Crime Unit.

"He never asked me about art, though. He just said, 'We'll get you some good people who know about art and stuff.' I haven't had a case with 'stuff' yet."

"Stuff," laughed Catrin, "he didn't ask me about 'stuff' in my interview."

By the time they had finished lunch, Catrin was in tears of laughter. She realised that between Worsley and Marshall, she had good mentors in the ACU. She had made the right call in applying for this job, after all. Jean and Melanie had done the right thing to stop her panicking before the interview.

~~

The following morning Dafydd and Idris went over to Llanfairfechan, to the Bryn y Neuadd Mental Health Hospital, to charge formally Stephen Harrison now that the autopsy result had been confirmed. Dr. Owen and a lawyer were with him. Harrison was to be transferred immediately to an appropriate prison facility with medical care.

The weather forecast was good for a day at the beginning of November; some sunshine and cloud, light winds, cold but not freezing. In the afternoon Dafydd collected Catrin and Li and drove them to Y Felinheli where his wife Marjorie had been preparing the Ceinwen; they were sailing, or motoring if needed, over to the spot where the divers had been. Catrin had borrowed a warm windproof jacket from the station. Dafydd had offered to do the trip for Li in Gwynant yesterday.

Catrin, Marjorie and Li had brought flowers and Li had a small scroll in Chinese.

They had a fair wind for the sail out and Li was kept busy by Dafydd helping with the boat while Catrin got to know Marjorie a little, hiding from the wind in the cabin. At the site they leaned over the side, placing the flowers gently in the water. Dafydd and Marjorie shared the reading of a prayer they had decided to bring. Li stood with her eyes closed and then read in Cantonese the script she had written, giving a translation afterwards in English.

She then placed it gently on the water. It was still floating visibly as they turned back and Dafydd started the motor rather than tack home. Marjorie appeared in a while with mugs of tea and coffee. Li never cried, just held tight to Catrin's hand for a minute or so after the turn-round.

They were half-way back when Li said, 'Do we have time to sail?"

Dafydd said, "Only if you take the tiller."

Li came back and they cut the engine and set sail again. Dafydd said nothing and watched as she set course into the wind.

"Han taught me well," she said.

They sat back as she concentrated on wind and water. At the point where she decided they needed to come about she swung the tiller and called it out. As the mainsail swung Dafydd dealt with the jib sheets. So they took the time to beat their way back, until they came towards the approach to Y Felinheli.

Li said, "We need to motor now, Dafydd, right?"

He started the engine as Marjorie and Li dealt with dropping and stowing sail. Li expected Dafydd to take her into the quite confined entrance to the marina but he just stood back and said, "Li; take her in."

She slowly guided the Ceinwen into the marina as Dafydd pointed out where to turn for the slip. He and Marjorie handled the fenders as they docked and he jumped down to secure the vessel. Li cut the engine.

Just before they arrived, a car with Gwyn Roberts and Andrea pulled in, to Li's surprise. She was expecting to help close up the boat and carry things to Marjorie's station wagon but Dafydd said, "It's Catrin's last evening; go enjoy. We will deal with this."

Li and Catrin hugged them both in turn and went over to the car. "Who fixed this then?" said Li.

"Dafydd and Catrin," said Gwyn Roberts. "We are off to Caernarfon to a pub for a meal and a bit of singing there; it's that sort of place we are going to. Big Gwyn is already there. He is probably telling the locals they need a bit of choral training from us."

"They will drown you out or punch you out if you repeat that remark there," said Catrin.

Li looked at her friends and knew this was all staged for her benefit. So she just said, 'thank you' and got in the car.

EPILOGUE: CHINA

St. Stephens College Chapel, Hong Kong, January. Reverend David Cavendish turned back into St. Stephen's Chapel after shaking hands and saying farewells to regular members of the congregation for the morning service. David had spoken briefly to the visitor before the service, a Chinese man in a dark suit, a little more formally dressed than most of the attendees these days. He had addressed him first in Cantonese.

"I'm English", he had said, "My Cantonese sounds a little different, with this accent."

If David had closed his eyes he would have thought he was in the vicinity of Bow Bells; the accent was East London.

As David re-entered the chapel the man was still there, looking at the stained glass windows with the images of the camp prisoners in World War II. The priest had seen several parishioners talking to the young man about the windows after the service. They had then taken him into the annex for coffee and more socialising. He had obviously come back to see the windows again.

Two of the windows were a memorial; they had images depicting the period in World War Two when prisoners-of-war were kept on the college grounds in an internment camp. The history of the college included worse events; during the invasion of Hong Kong it served as a hospital. In the violence of war it became a killing ground of nurses, patients and doctors.

He walked up to the visitor and spoke to him again, "So you are visiting from London, I gather?"

That was all David had established in the brief introduction given the preparations for the service.

"It was a beautiful service, thank you. Yes, I came for a memorial service at the Methodist International Church in Kowloon on Friday."

"I saw that you were being briefed on the history of the chapel," said David, smiling at him.

Cho said, "Yes, they were very kind, but I had heard much of the story from a member of the clergy at St. Paul's Cathedral. I work there; I am one of the administration staff in the gift shop. As I was visiting Hong Kong the chapel was on my list of things to see."

"It's a long way to come for a memorial service, but I am glad you could worship with us today," said David.

Cho Zhou smiled. "Thank you. The service was for Han Yeung, a close friend of mine. He was a sailor, an officer on a cruise ship, but sadly he was murdered in Wales. I didn't make it to the service before the cremation there, unfortunately, but his sister arranged with a wealthy family friend for me to have an airline ticket so I could attend the memorial on Friday. It was very kind."

David nodded, he knew of the incident involving the young sailor and also of the memorial service at the Methodist church. It had a large turn-out, he had heard.

By now he had some inkling why the man had made such a long journey.

"Well, look," David said, "you would be very welcome at the service tonight at St. John's Cathedral; it's a great group of people. And if you have a couple of days here and have any time to kill please come to visit me and my wife? Her brother spent some time as a curate in Stepney and loved St. Paul's. It was some time ago, of course, but she also loves the place and it would be a great chance for her to catch up. Would you be open to that?"

He walked back towards the door with the young man.

~~

Chongqing, China. Around the time Cho Zhou was visiting Hong Kong, Dieter Haussmann was not that far away, in mainland China. He had recovered some use of his finger and the scar tissue had healed nicely. The small support brace he continued to wear when not undertaking his 'strengthening' exercises attracted the attention of passengers. It had given him several variants on a story in which he had an unstated heroic role and, with an exotic backdrop of scenery like the Three Gorges Dam, anything was believable. Dieter had almost convinced himself that sometime one of these wealthy women cruising with a friend or mother would drag him back to Texas or wherever, to a life of luxury.

The lawyer who had turned up at the hospital in Bangor, Mr. Leigh-Jones, had been adamant that he say nothing, even though Dieter wanted to get it off his chest. Two days later, Inspector Powys and Sergeant Bowen had come to see him.

Powys said, "Mr. Haussmann, we know that you have been involved up to your eyes in a smuggling racket. We also know that your visit here was to associate with a person who has now been charged with various other crimes related to the events in Craig Y Don Road. She will be charged with more soon, I guarantee."

"No charges will be laid against you in regard to that incident at this time. Whether other authorities charge you in due course in relation to the art smuggling is for them to decide, but at present, you are free to go when discharged from the hospital. We would, however, like a statement of events that occurred at Professor Parry's residence."

"My client would be delighted to co-operate now, Inspector Powys," said Ivan Leigh-Jones.

After the two detectives left the room Leigh-Jones explained. "You are a German national. You are allegedly involved in crimes committed elsewhere mainly, although they could have charged you for the paintings delivered into Holyhead. But you also saved the life of a Chinese national visiting Wales and were injured in the process. You are too complicated and expensive a case, at least at present. That was the Prosecutions Service's view."

He opened his briefcase. "Now I am to give you this," he said, handing him an envelope.

"My invoice, no doubt," said Dieter as he opened it awkwardly.

Inside was a letter formally inviting him to apply for the position of the Senior Restaurant Manager on the Yangtze Lotus, a river cruise ship. He knew it was one of several vessels owned by a cruise company with headquarters in Shanghai, China. A separate note was included that provided contact arrangements for an interview. They were a small but quite high-end and successful cruise line.

"There is Chinese lettering in handwriting at the bottom of this note." said Dieter.

"Yes. The person who couriered it explained that. It is Chinese for 'Second Chance'. My job was to stop you talking yourself into prison in Wales or anywhere else. And my fees have already been paid."

Dieter thought about it. Back to Dubai or off to cruise ship work again, this time in Asia? He would have to decide.

The Yangtze Lotus ran regularly between Shanghai and Chongqing along the most spectacular stretches of this mighty river, generally taking on a full complement of passengers at each end. Compared with his experience on the Manden line and his knowledge of other cruise lines, the passenger mix was more international in nature, not dominated by American cruisers.

Dieter was starting to enjoy the life on the river, despite his start-up being in the winter months. Several European staff had told him that the mild winter was actually preferable to the summer heat and humidity and he felt he could happily spend his time here for a while. So far he had received no contact from Franz Reicher and had no idea how things had developed after he left the UK.

His duties as restaurant manager had him working three nights in a row followed by two nights off, in rotation with assistants. On these days he supervised the lunches held in the main dining room. It was not too onerous at all. It would be four months before he would receive his first vacation leave.

So he was surprised one evening on a duty night just before arrival into the turn-round point, Chongqing, to see his deputy manager in white jacket and black tie come over to him; he was supposed to be off-duty.

"Sir, you are to join the lady at Table 23. I am to take over this evening."

Dieter's mind wandered away into his dream world for a second but as he approached the table he went cold. The silhouette of the beautiful woman seated there was the same as the one he saw leaving his apartment in Dubai. He walked up and faced her wondering what this was about.

"Good evening," she said and indicated with her hand that he should be seated. "Please order, I think you know the menu for tonight."

"I have not seen you on board this trip," Dieter said, "yet you are here now."

The waiter came over and took their meal orders before she responded. He fussed about, serving not only his manager but the beautiful guest who accompanied him. When she did speak, she ignored his implied question.

"Mr. Haussmann, we have been deciding what to do with you. It has taken some time."

"Do with me?"

"Given the inconsistency in the story of how Han Yeung died and who was responsible, the decision has taken some time. Your story given to me in Dubai made it clear that you and Franz Reicher did not want Yeung stopped unless it was possible to retrieve the tube with the painting easily. It was important to ensure the theft would not be associated with a special interest in the tube itself. It had to appear incidental. Am I correct?"

Dieter was looking concerned. "Yes, that is right."

Emily Yang continued, "So why did Lyn Williams and her brother stop Han Yeung when he no longer had the painting? That was what we were puzzling over."

Dieter said, "I don't know. I put it down to ineptitude, inability to see one step in front of another by that woman but I have no idea and, as I said in Dubai, I had nothing to do with Han's death. If you want to know more, you will have to ask her."

Emily nodded, "We did, just a few days ago."

Dieter stared at her. He had heard before leaving Wales that Lyn Williams was in Styal Prison in Cheshire awaiting trial. This woman appeared to get everywhere and Dieter wondered whether she or another Triad member had talked to or interrogated Williams in a manner similar to his experience in Dubai.

She continued, looking him in the face directly, "Just as you threw a tantrum with your assistant Annabel about the loss of the tube, you neglected to mention a similar tantrum with Williams the first time you met that day. She said you went volcanic. That now you were stuck with two paintings from a set of three; you had two weeks at sea before you could offload them and had no idea what would happen to the tube Yeung mailed.

"If the tube was discovered to contain a valuable painting before you arrived in New York, you ranted, Han would be contacted, he would say where he got the tube and the whole thing would collapse on top of you. In fact, you gave her the impression you wanted to be rid of the paintings long before Franz Reicher had even had a discussion with the original client."

She was quite matter of fact about it, Dieter saw. She sipped from her wine as the first course was served.

When they were alone again Emily said, "You really got through to her; it fired her up, put an admittedly crazy idea in her mind when she went looking for Han. If she could get both paintings off you and track down the recipient of the one Han had received, even if he had mailed it, she would have a set for resale that was worth far more than the payments from Geraldine Roper would ever amount to.

"That's why she stopped Han Yeung. She was going to get the name of the recipient come what may and actually had no real concerns about what to do once she had spoken to him.

"Of course, her brother's reaction not only killed Han, it killed her plan. The rest you know."

Dieter was thinking back, nodding, and seeing it at last.

He said, "But the tube was then in the postal system. If Han came back and reported the loss and the interest in it, how would she have got it later?"

Emily nodded. "She thought the police would file the story from a foreigner who was then off and away from the UK and it would go no further. Who would bother following up on a weird story about a man being accosted or roughed up to find out about a cheap print sent by mail?"

She looked at him.

"So do you still say you had nothing to do with Han's death?"

He thought for a moment. "No, I don't say that now. I was a component in it, I see, more than simply asking Williams to try to recover the painting. I still think that she is... unhinged. But, yes, I can see how my frustration and diatribe could have given rise to her mad plan."

There was a silence as Emily finished eating her first course. Dieter hadn't touched his plate at all.

"So what happens now?" he said at last.

Emily beckoned the waiter who came rushing over and asked Dieter if the first course was not to his liking, did he want something else?

He shook his head.

Emily said, "Could you bring another chair and place-setting please, someone is joining us." She pulled out a mobile phone and dialed a number, then spoke briefly in Cantonese.

"Well," said Emily as the waiters scurried, "I don't think the disappearance of a German cruise ship officer from the Yangtze river in the middle of mainland China would be as diligently investigated by the police as that of a Chinese sailor on the coast of Wales. So I think you had better do what we ask of you."

The young man in a dark suit who came in to the restaurant and headed over to the table had timed it to perfection; his chair and the table settings were all in place as he arrived.

Emily said, "Mr. Dieter Haussmann meet Mr. Feng. He is a representative of a business in the same world as my own, so to speak. They deal in international transport of items but, frankly, have no business as yet in art. They are interested in this growing market segment.

"You, Dieter, have certain knowledge and a whole bunch of contacts around the world that can probably help them in this regard. While you enjoy shuttling between Shanghai and Chongqing, you can be of great assistance to his organisation in providing information and making phone calls."

She eyed Dieter. "In my world, you have just become an asset that has been traded. Good luck in your new role."

Dieter just sat back, bowled over by the news. "I thought the 'Second Chance' came from the man I spoke to so that I could have a new start."

Emily smiled. "It is a new start, Dieter, and 'Second Chance' is open to a lot of interpretation. I contracted the lawyer Mr. Leigh-Jones for you and I also wrote the letters he passed on. You aren't in a European gaol now, so help Mr. Feng and his colleagues and you may well become free, as you thought."

"Now, here comes our main course. Mr. Feng, I took the liberty of ordering for you. I do hope you approve."

The young Chinese man smiled at her performance. She was clearly enjoying it and his boss had told him to be very respectful of this woman; she was a particular favorite of Mr. Michael Yau.

She raised her glass to them, saying "A toast, gentlemen; to happiness and prosperity," then directing her attention at Dieter. "And may no more sailors be lost from cruise ships."

NOTES

The Metropolitan Police Service in London does have an Art and Antiques Unit within its Specialist Crime Command that was established back in 1969. However, its people and activities described herein are entirely my own creation. The 'Art Crime Unit' in the Metropolitan Police described in this novel is an invention that has no real-life counterpart.

There was, however, a World War II surplus 'Dakota' aircraft called the 'St. Paul' in the service of the Lutheran Church in China in 1949; it later disappeared under mysterious circumstances.

The events in World War II mentioned in the Epilogue regarding St. Stephen's Chapel and College did occur and the stained glass windows in the Chapel do exist.

The tragedy at the village of Aberfan in 1966 was represented in a painting by the artist Dorothie Field (1915-1994).

ABOUT THE AUTHOR

Allan Jones lives in Ontario, Canada. He was born and grew up in Merseyside, England. By profession an industrial chemist, he is now retired, but he worked for many years as a consultant on international chemical regulation. He has lived in or travelled to most of the regions featured in the Catrin Sayer novels.